"ZAKIA, WE NEED TO TALK," HER HUSBAND SAID.

Zakia was relieved Jay didn't seem to be upset with her for not cooking dinner again. That was good. Less pressure on her.

"Jessica is pregnant. She's the finance secretary at my church."

"So!"

"The baby is mine."

The revelation that he was having an affair sent Zakia into a state of shock. She was numb and couldn't speak, so Jay continued.

"You are obsessed with your church, neglecting me and your family, alienating your friends. Now, what about your marriage? Is that the kind of God you want to serve, one that makes you lose everything important in your life?"

Zakia mustered all the strength she had to spea

"Get out," she managed to say without burst into tears. It only took him minutes to pack a few things. He left her sitting on the bed, still in shock . . .

Saved Folk
in the House

Sonnie Beverly

WARNER BOOKS

NEW YORK   BOSTON

This book is a work of fiction. Names, characters, places, and incidents are the product of the author's imagination or are used fictitiously. Any resemblance to actual events, locales, or persons, living or dead, is coincidental.

Portions of this book have been previously published in novella form.

Copyright © 2006 by Sonnie Beverly
All rights reserved.

Book design and text composition by L&G McRee

Warner Books
1271 Avenue of the Americas
New York, NY 10020

Printed in the United States of America

Originally published by Warner Books with Walk Worthy Press™
First Mass Market Edition: May 2006
10 9 8 7 6 5 4 3 2 1

To my loved ones who left me way too soon:
Book, Cherry, Tiger, Angel, and Jean.

Acknowledgments

Always my survival tools: The Love of God, The Blood of Jesus, The Peace and Comfort of The Holy Spirit and The WORD of God.

My mom, Ms. Claudette G. Beverly, who is my rock-solid foundation and home base where I am always safe; my aunt Gwen, Mrs. Gwendolyn B. Mitchell, who is wisdom and elegance, grace and beauty, trust and understanding personified: I am who I am because you two gave me the best of you.

My spiritual aunt, Mrs. Katie White: you have what you say. You told me to just love, believe, and trust Him and everything will be all right. Well, guess what? Everything is better than all right.

Shaunonell (my children, who have always filled my heart with joy, pride, and hope for the brightest of futures for our family): Shaun Chappell, take it to the big screen. Shannon Chappell, take it to the stage. You twins are my fruit, extensions of me, and can do all things through Christ, Who strengthens you. You have the baton (vision), now run with it. Shannell "Yale" Chappell, you are too many things, so you let me know if you are going to sing, dance, design, write, act, major in journalism, be a foreign correspondent, or practice law. Just let me know when you and Jesus decide.

The Quivers (my godchildren): Scott and Sánta, Saván and Christian. All my children sure know how to take care of each other, and that makes my heart glad.

My church families: Faith Alive International Ministries and pastor, Dr. Steve Parson Sr.; my big boo, Mrs. Florence Taylor, you are the epitome of accountability; my pop, Elder Richard Luster, you are a model of class and grace; Brother's Keepers Ministries; my unk, Rev. Harold Luster, always wise, always GQ sharp; and especially my guardian angel, the right Rev. Ray N. Smith Sr., you are all that and a bag of chips, with your calm, cool, and clean self; his wife, who he confesses deserves the Congressional Medal of Honor, Sis. Karlyn Smith. I love and appreciate y'all so, so much. World Changers Church International and pastors, Dr. Creflo and Taffi Dollar, thank you for exposing me to the world we are called to change.

The Professionals from Walk Worthy Press and Warner Books: Denise Stinson, my mentor and publisher, who let me know that she is not my mother—I love your style. My editors: Karen Kelly, who knew that I had a lot to say and just how to help me say it, and knew what to say, and especially, what not to say. Thank you for your patience and kindness, KK; Chandra Taylor, for hooking me up even while you were going through.

My girlfriends that substitute as my checks and balances: Denise Wooldridge, thanks for taking me to paradise, while keeping me on that spiritual straight and narrow; LaFarn Burton, the hangingest role model I know, who never gives up on folk; DC Pam Dickerson, the closest thing to a real sister I have—you're my Gayle, girl; Vanessa Michelle Grey, my love for you continues to grow, even if we don't talk for months; Ascension, Inc.—The Philosopher, Charlita Wye; The Intellect, Tanisha Jackson; and the one who will always and forever keep it real, Davina Thomas. You're my inspiration and my FGs. Octavia Lee Hall-Banks, you know the deal. You are all my sheroes.

Tyler Perry and Oprah, and my partners Joyce Meyer, Kenneth and Gloria Copeland, Marilyn Hickey, and Bishop T. D. Jakes, for all you do to help a sister stay encouraged by seeing with her own eyes what God will do with the willing and obedient.

Contents

Saved Folk
in the House

PART ONE

Saved Babies' Daddies

Richmond, Virginia

I will therefore that the younger women marry, bear children, guide the house, give none occasion to the adversary to speak reproachfully.

1 TIMOTHY 5:14

Chapter One

Oh. My. God. Help me, Jesus," Zakia Wilkes said to herself as she made eye contact with one of the finest men she had ever seen. The stranger approached her as she stood on the front steps of her dormitory.

"How you doin', baby, with your pretty self?" he said in a deep, sexy voice. He slowed down long enough to acknowledge her with a smile, but he did not stop.

"Fine," she stammered in a barely audible baby voice. She dreamily watched him go through the front door of the dorm. When he was out of sight, she sighed heavily.

How am I going to stay focused here at Manna State University for the next four years and get my degree with all these men around? Zakia wondered.

She had never seen so many fine-looking men in one place at one time. There were beautiful black men in every shape, size, style, and color. Impressive black men who were Christians, Muslims, sophisticated, funny, smooth, cool, and intelligent. They were from all over the world, and they overwhelmed her with their mere presence.

Since Zakia arrived on the beautiful, huge campus with its magnificent blend of modern and nineteenth-century architecture four weeks ago, after her high school class of 1984 end-of-the-summer party, she had been awestruck. The landscape boasted lovely, colorful gardens with huge shade trees and benches where the students socialized between classes. Statues of college beneficiaries and famous African-Americans such as Frederick Douglass and Harriet Tubman dotted the campus and reminded the students of their heritage and purpose. All the men Zakia saw looked like they were ready to meet the challenge. In the beginning, when one of them paid her a compliment, she either found it difficult to speak or simply got weak in the knees. She was much more in control of herself now, but every once in a while, she'd be overcome and revert to her awestruck behavior.

Zakia was a pretty girl, sweet, innocent, smart, and intimidated by her mother. She had a reverential fear of Alexis Wilkes, which kept her out of any serious trouble and helped her to make the best decisions in most situations, but she was in Baltimore, three hours away from home and Alexis in Richmond. She needed strength to handle this newly found freedom.

After she had gotten herself together from the exchange with the fine stranger, Zakia contemplated what part of campus she was going to explore next. Just as she decided to check out the library, the fine stranger and a beautiful woman came back out of the dormitory holding hands. He looked at Zakia without smiling. Zakia smiled at the woman, who returned her greeting with a friendly grin. Zakia glanced at the man, who maintained a serious expression.

Okay. Now, how am I going to do this? Zakia thought.
*These men flirt with you, get you all hot and bothered,
then when they're with their women, they act like they
don't know you. Okay, I see. That's the game here too. I
played it in high school.*

The only difference was that during high school, Zakia
was the player, thanks to her twin brother, Zachary, and
his gang, the Execs. Besides, the guys in high school
seemed a far cry from the worldly Manna men. She determined very quickly that she'd have to learn some defense.

In high school, Zakia was Miss Popularity. Her
mother, Alexis, was a strong black woman who didn't
stand for any bad behavior from anybody, including the
father of her children. Rahlo Brown was an old-school
player who had three children by two different women.
One time when they were doing really well and Alexis
had fleeting thoughts of having a nice wholesome
together family, she allowed herself to want to marry
Rahlo when the twins were four years old. Then she
found out that Rahlo had fathered her neighbor Mavis's
baby girl. So much for a wholesome family. Alexis
depended on no one but herself, and she trained her little
ones to be as self-sufficient as she was. Rahlo, however,
was expected to provide for the twins financially.

It was no secret in the neighborhood that Rahlo was
Mavis's baby's daddy. Four-year-old Zakia was thrilled
beyond measure when she overheard her mother on the
phone fussing to her friend Jean Harris about what a dog
Rahlo was, messing with a neighbor right around the
corner and giving her children a baby sister by some
other woman and that she would never marry him and he

better take care of the twins or she would have him locked up.

I have a baby sister was all Zakia cared about. She told Zachary.

"We have a baby sister."

"Where is she?" Zachary asked.

"At Miss Mavis's house."

"Why is she at Miss Mavis's house?"

"Because Miss Mavis is her mommy."

"So how can she be our sister?"

" 'Cause Daddy is her daddy too."

"How?"

"I don't know, but Mommy told Miss Jean that we have a baby sister and Miss Mavis is her mommy. Let's go see her."

"Okay," Zachary said, following his sister into the kitchen.

"Mommy, we're going outside to play," Zakia said to her mother, who was in another zone.

"Okay," Alexis said, glancing at her twins, but not noticing the up-to-something look on their faces as she continued to vent to her friend on the phone.

Zakia and Zachary figured they would be back before their mother got off the phone. They walked to Miss Mavis's house. They knocked on the door. Miss Mavis answered.

"Hello, twins," she said in a sweet, friendly voice.

"Hello, Miss Mavis. Is our baby sister here?" Zakia asked matter-of-factly.

Surprised at the child's question and not knowing exactly how much Zakia knew or understood about the situation, she said, "Yes, would you like to see her?"

Both twins lit up like Christmas trees because it was true that they had a baby sister.

"Yes, ma'am!" they shouted in unison.

Mavis opened the door wide and stepped aside so that the twins could enter. She led them into her bedroom, where their half sister was amusing herself in her crib. Zakia fell instantly in love with the baby, a real-life doll, and wanted to pick her up and play with her.

"What's her name?" Zakia asked.

"Raquel, but we'll call her Raquie," Mavis answered.

Zachary thought the baby looked just like his daddy and was still puzzled about how Miss Mavis had his baby sister living with her.

"Is she gonna come live with us?" he asked.

"No, baby, Raquie is my daughter," Mavis explained.

"But she's my sister, right? Zakia is my sister, and she lives with me," Zachary responded in total confusion.

"Ask your mother to explain it to you, baby. You can come see her whenever you want, okay? Now, does your mother know where you are?"

"No, ma'am," Zakia said, playing with baby Raquie's feet through the crib rails.

"Well, you better go on back home before you get into trouble. You know how your mother is."

"Yes, ma'am. Can we come see her tomorrow?" Zakia asked.

"Yes, sweetie, but make sure it's all right with your mother first."

"Yes, ma'am," Zakia said.

From that moment on, when Zakia went outside to play, she visited her baby sister. Alexis eventually found out by overhearing her twins talking. When she questioned Zakia about her visits, she realized Mavis may have been a man-stealer, but she would never harm the twins. Alexis allowed the visits. Zakia loved Raquie so much. They grew to be very close.

Their old neighborhood, by Richmond's James River, was built at the turn of the century and was fondly referred to as the village, even though it was considered lower-class. Many of the houses were more than half a century old and were not very sturdy. Some of the houses were single-family dwellings with a small yard, but most of them were attached. There was a buzz of excitement about the city building a housing project to be occupied by neighbors known as the villagers.

Some of the villagers dreamed of making enough money to move to a nearby suburb of Richmond. In fact, most of the villagers who were fortunate enough to get good government jobs or steady factory work immediately bought nicer homes in other parts of the city as a sign that they had "arrived." However, some of the villagers loved the neighborhood where they grew up, and stayed on even though they could afford to leave. Some maintained homes that had been in their families for years. Others stayed because they did not have the money to move.

Everybody in the village knew one another, and many of the people were related. The number of homes with a married couple could be counted on one hand, as could the number of homes with no children. The village was the type of inner-city neighborhood that bred issues that would follow its inhabitants wherever life took them.

As the years passed, Raquie grew closer to Zakia than to the other children Mavis bore after her. Mavis, who never married, received aid for her three other children by three different baby daddies, but Rahlo took care of Raquie. Alexis also saw to it that Rahlo took care of their twins, never hesitating to remind him of the consequences if he didn't.

Rahlo would take Zakia and Raquie for rides, for ice cream, school shopping, and all kinds of fun events. They loved their bachelor daddy and often had sleepovers at his apartment. He would get up and cook breakfast, and they would eat and watch cartoons together. He enjoyed having them. As the three of them sat around eating and playing, he would tickle them. They would laugh and try to get away or lie all over him, relaxing on the floor, watching TV, just having a wonderful time.

Zachary would sometimes ride with his daddy and sisters, but he'd rather hang out with his friends Micah Robinson and Eli White, who regarded Zachary as their leader. They had a club, the Execs, short for Executives, and never got into any real trouble. The club was mostly for organizing business ventures to make money. They went door-to-door trying to sell things such as bouquets they made from stealing flowers from the neighbors' gardens when they couldn't get Zakia to bake cookies for them to sell. They'd use the money for candy or the movies and later, as they grew up, concerts. As they got older, they began to venture out to other neighborhoods, going door-to-door to raise funds for what they said was camping equipment for their Boy Scout troop. None of them had ever been near a Boy Scout, but the scam netted them a fifty-dollar profit.

Eventually, they made most of their money hustling on the basketball court. They were all good athletes, and each of them made it onto the Booker T High School basketball team.

Zakia was a cheerleader and didn't have a lot of time to spend with Raquie as she grew older. Boys took up a lot of her time, but Raquie didn't mind. She adored her sister and was very proud of her. She told everybody who would listen, "My sister is a cheerleader and gets straight As."

Zakia was an excellent student because Alexis demanded good grades from both her children. She was proud when Zakia graduated from high school and earned a full scholarship to Manna State University. She also insisted that Zachary study so that he, too, could get into college. He tried, but his entrepreneurial spirit and short attention span interfered with his studying. Frustrated, Alexis began focusing less on Zachary and more on Zakia. She was determined that her daughter would never have to depend on a man to take care of her. She would be able to get whatever she wanted for herself. College was not optional for Zakia.

Being a brainiac rubbed off on Raquie, and she, too, excelled under her sister's influence.

Chapter Two

In high school, Zakia had been focused, to say the least. She had felt her mother's wrath when she brought home a B in conduct despite the fact that she had earned As in everything else.

"If you can get As in your studies, surely you can behave yourself, and you will," Alexis had said. "No phone for a week, and you can't go out with those boys this weekend either."

The phone was the worst thing Alexis could have taken from Zakia. She was on it with one boy or another every night. Zachary didn't like talking on the phone, and Alexis was glued to the TV in the evenings, so Zakia owned the phone. Her mother sure knew how to hit her where it hurt. Zakia also loved hanging out with the Execs. She was an honorary member, since it was a boys' club and girls were for getting with, not doing business with. But they treated her just like one of the boys, not taking it easy on her, ever.

When they snuck into a football game by jumping a

barbed-wire fence behind the stadium brush, Zakia was the only one who landed on her feet without a scratch. Micah ripped his pants, while Eli sprained his ankle and walked with a limp for a week. Zachary's leg was bleeding from a gash he obtained by not completely clearing the barbed wire when he jumped. The Execs carried him into the men's room to doctor his wound. Zakia rolled on the ground laughing hysterically once she was sure he was all right. Some girls from school walked up on Zakia, who was still laughing to herself. Nikki Harris, Sheba Spencer, Eboni Black, and Pam Pierce were cheerleaders with Zakia.

"What's so funny, girl?" asked Pam, who was in love with Micah.

"Girl, those scrubs said I had to jump the fence if I wanted to hang with them tonight, and I said, 'Bring it on.' They all got hurt and I didn't. Now they're in the bathroom fixing Zach up because he hurt his leg, but he'll be all right."

"Oh my! Are you sure he's okay?" a concerned Sheba asked.

Zakia nodded, still laughing.

"You be hanging with those brothers," Sheba said in amazement.

Sheba had a serious crush on Zachary, who messed around with her, but never officially.

"He's suffered worse and survived. And they be trying to hang with me, ha ha!" Zakia said, still tickled.

"I know that's right, girl," Nikki said to her fellow cheerleading captain. Nikki and Zakia had led the cheering squad together for three years and had seen their friendship grow.

"Did Micah get hurt?" Pam asked.

"Naw, he just ripped his pants," Zakia said.

"Whew, I didn't want to have to go up in the men's bathroom to take care of my man," Pam responded. "Who else is in there?"

"All of the Execs," Zakia said.

"With their fine selves," said Eboni, who dreamed about having three babies with Eli, all of whose names would begin with the letter E.

"Zakia, when are you going to ask your twin about making us official, girl? He knows he's my man, he needs to just go on and admit it to the world," Sheba said.

"Never, girl. I stay out of the Execs' business, and they stay out of mine. You need to handle that."

"Fine. Consider it handled," Sheba said.

When the guys came out of the bathroom, the girls ran over to them oohing and aahing, asking if they were all right and if they could make them feel better. Zakia thought it was hilarious—pitiful but hilarious—and she fell back into another fit of laughter.

Zakia was part tomboy, part princess. She had a beautiful, delicate exterior and a tough-as-nails interior. She could make you feel like you could fly and then thoroughly beat you down every which way if you crossed her.

When Zakia was in princess mode, she hung with her fellow cheerleaders, who were the Execs' girlfriends. When she was in tomboy mode, she liked hanging with the Execs. And hang she could. She often worked out with them. She had a die-hard competitive spirit with which women just couldn't compete. She had to win, and when she lost, she just got more competitive. Even in the dating game, she had the advantage because she was privy to the Execs' conversations about their flock of female admirers. They knew she could keep her mouth shut—after all, she was almost one of them—so they didn't monitor their words and said exactly how they felt about girls, what they did to girls, and what girls did to and for them. If she asked, they would explain things to her that she didn't understand. They schooled her to be able to handle herself when she went off to college. She listened and learned.

A lot of the guys at Booker T High School wanted to be Zakia's boyfriend but were concerned about the Execs. She knew everybody but wasn't interested in dating anyone at Booker T, until a new tall, dark, and handsome star basketball player transferred in from Dunbar High School. Xavier Slade was admired by more than half of the females at Booker T. It was love at first sight for Zakia. After a game where Booker T had just embarrassed the competition, she waited patiently for Xavier to receive all of his congratulations for scoring thirty points before she walked up to him. She looked him deep in the eyes, then whispered in his ear, "Great game, Mr. Slade," as she ever so softly and sweetly kissed him on his cheek. She turned and walked off, then glanced back at him, knowing he was watching her walk away in her short little cheerleader uniform. She smiled, winked at him, turned, and subtly swung her hips as she walked out the gym door. He was putty in her hands from that point on. It was only a matter of time before he was her official boyfriend.

Xavier was the point guard and the star of the basketball team, so it was written in the stars that he and

Zakia would be the most popular couple in high school; however, they were popular as individuals first. Zakia's other suitors didn't stop calling her just because she had an official boyfriend, and she didn't stop talking to them, although everybody knew Xavier was her man.

The Execs had taught her well. She just had to manage her social schedule. When she spent time with other guys, she made sure it was a group setting—at a party, burger joint, or game—with plenty of her girlfriends around to cover for her in case Xavier's spies were on the lookout. The only private time she spent with anybody besides Xavier before they broke up was on the phone. She thought she was well prepared for whatever college had in store.

Ruby Glass was Zakia's college roommate. She was from a wealthy Long Island, New York, family. Her father was an attorney, and her mother was a social worker. Ruby fascinated Zakia with her footloose and fancy-free attitude. Ruby wasn't concerned about making good grades and, unlike Zakia, was even less concerned about what her parents thought. Ruby didn't have to worry about maintaining her grades to keep a scholarship. She didn't have one. Her parents paid her tuition. Her main reason for coming to college was to meet men and party for as long as it lasted. She was Daddy's little girl. He would take care of her.

Ruby had come to the right place. She was always trying to get Zakia to loosen up and take a hit of marijuana or a drink of beer. She thought her roommate was too uptight and wanted to help Zakia alleviate her stress about books and men.

Although it was more difficult to maintain an A average in college, Zakia was more concerned about the bold forwardness of the men, particularly a star basketball player named Malik Jackson. He openly had a girlfriend, yet he begged Zakia to be his girlfriend and promised to dump his sorority sweetheart the minute she said yes. Even though she was attracted to Malik, Zakia wanted no part of him, knowing that he would dump her just as quick for the next cute, young coed that came along.

"Why doesn't Malik just back off, Ruby?" she asked her roommate one day after taking the long way back to their dorm room in order to avoid Malik.

"Because they always want what they can't have," Ruby answered. "Now, I wouldn't mind going over to the town house and getting with that fine roommate of his, Melvin, but he won't give me the time of day. He must be gay, ignoring all of this," she said, pushing up her breasts and admiring her profile in the mirror.

Zakia laughed at her roommate, thinking surely Ruby was going to flunk out of college if she didn't get her priorities in order. Zakia always encouraged her roommate to study, but Ruby shrugged her off, instead encouraging Zakia to party. Neither one of them succeeded in swaying the other. They were the odd couple and got along well together, respected, cared for, and trusted each other, and had each other's back.

"I'm going home this weekend," Zakia told Ruby. "I can't wait. I need—you hear me, *need*—some home cooking, girl. I miss my boys too. I can't wait to see them. I hope Micah and Eli have time to hang with me because I need some schooling. I'd better call them and make sure they don't have any plans. Mom said all my brother does is work."

Zakia went down the hall to the pay phone and called Eli collect, and he excitedly accepted the charges.

"What's up, baby!" she screamed.

"Hey, baby girl! How they treatin' you up at MSU?" Eli asked.

"We gotta talk. What's up this weekend? I'm coming home."

"Cool, baby. Can't wait to see you. Oh, I took Eboni to this all-you-can-eat seafood restaurant down at the beach, and all we talked about was how you would love it, being the die hard seafood lover you are. When are you getting in?"

"Friday night. Catching a ride with this junior after her last class around three o'clock."

"Okay, we can ride down to the beach Saturday, and you can eat till your heart's content, cool?"

"Man, that sounds wonderful, because this food is whack. I want Ma to have some serious grub ready when I get there too. Is Eboni going with us?"

"Naw. She works on Saturdays. Micah is probably free, though. I'll check with him."

"Oh, that would be so great, throwin' down with my boys. What about my brother?"

"Never know with that workaholic," Eli said.

"Right, right. Ma said he's going to be a millionaire or bust."

"It's all her fault that brother works like that, but Mamalexis is my girl and she knows it too. Beat my butt so bad one day when we were kids, I started to pack my things and move in with y'all because I thought she must be my mother. That's when I stopped calling her Miss Alexis and started calling her Mamalexis. My own mother never beat me that bad. My mama had the nerve to tell your mother to feel free to do it again if I needed it. You know I never needed it again, right?"

"You don't even have to tell me about no Alexis whipping. Lawd, change the subject."

"Okay. Let me tell you how to work the buffet. Get up Saturday morning and eat a big stack of pancakes," Eli explained.

"That's dumb if the restaurant is all-you-can-eat. Don't I want to be hungry when I go?"

"Let me finish. You're going to eat the pancakes early, and that's going to stretch your stomach. Then you're going to chill for a minute. Then you're going to go in the bathroom for about an hour. Dump it all out, then you have a big fat empty stomach. Now you have room to sample most of the food. It's so much you can't get to it all."

"Wow, your logic just amazes me," Zakia said.

"Just do it. It works. Have I ever steered you wrong before?"

"Never, brah."

"All right, then. Call me when you get home Friday. I'll let you know about Micah."

"Okay, later."

It was Zakia's first time home from college. Everybody came to Alexis's Friday night to see her. Raquie was like her sister's second skin. They were so glad to see each other. Raquie was up under her the whole night, just enjoying being around her again. Zakia loved it.

The delicious meal Alexis had prepared for Zakia and all her friends who came to see her on her first weekend home from college was gone Saturday morning. There wasn't a trace of it in the refrigerator or Zakia's stomach. Per Eli's instructions, when she got up, she fixed herself a big, hearty stack of pancakes and ate every bite. She was stuffed, then she talked on the phone until sleep started coming down on her.

"I got to go, girl. Need to take a nap."

"Okay, but call me before you leave, and finish telling me about all the gorgeous Manna men," Eboni said from her desk at work.

"I will."

"And don't hurt nothing. Pace yourself, because as much as you like seafood, you could do some damage."

"Is it that good? I can't even think about it right now from all those pancakes your man told me to eat," Zakia said.

"It's that good, girl, so be careful down there. I'll catch up with you guys later."

After her nap, Zakia got up and gathered her textbook, notebook, and a novel in case she got bored doing homework. She also took the cordless phone, some magazines, and a can of Lysol. She headed to the bathroom because she planned to be there for a while, just as Eli had instructed. She was looking forward to the seafood.

"Raise the window to let in some fresh air, and light a scented candle while you're at it," Alexis yelled through the bathroom door.

"Ha ha, funny, Ma," Zakia said, laughing at her mother, who could never resist messing with her every time she packed up and moved into the bathroom.

An hour passed before she came out. She felt great. She called Eli.

"What time are you coming?"

"In about an hour. I have to pick Micah up from the garage. He's dropping his ride off to have it serviced," Eli said.

"Okay. I'll be ready. This food better be all that too."

"Trust me, baby. You're gonna love it."

Eli and Micah came in to get Zakia because Alexis didn't allow men to honk the horn for her daughter.

"Hello, Mamalexis," Eli greeted.

"Hi, Mamalexis," Micah said.

"Hi, boys."

"Where's Zach?" Micah inquired.

"At work. That boy is going to be a millionaire by the time he's twenty-five years old," Alexis said proudly, shaking her head.

Zakia came into the kitchen where they all were.

"Hey, y'all, I'm ready. Ma, have you ever heard of this place they're taking me to? What's it called, Eli?"

"The Sea Wharf, down by the beach," Eli said.

"Oh yeah, I heard it was pretty good."

"I hope so. See you later," Zakia said as she kissed her mother on the cheek.

"Want us to bring you something back, Mamalexis?" Micah asked.

"No thank you, baby. Just feed this bottomless pit of mine. She acts like there's no food at that college."

"That mess they serve us to eat should be used as bait," Zakia said.

"It can't be that bad," Alexis said.

"For real, Ma. I want a doctor's excuse that says I can't eat the food they serve, and maybe they will keep the room and give me the board money so I can buy my own food. It's that bad. Me and the girls I eat with mix it all together, close our eyes, hold our noses, put the food in our mouths, and just swallow. We don't allow our taste buds to even know what just passed through. It's ridiculous. Come on, y'all, I'm getting sick just thinking about it," Zakia said, walking out the door with Eli and Micah behind her.

"Have fun," Alexis said.

"See ya later," they all said.

During the hour-long ride to the Sea Wharf, they talked about MSU.

"You're gonna still bust them As, right?" Eli asked.

"That or Mamalexis gonna bust her butt," Micah said.

"MSU is not Booker T by a long shot, and Ma is just going to have to understand. If I don't get all As, which I already know I'm not, you guys are going to have to help me make her understand. She didn't go to college, so she doesn't know what I'm going through," Zakia said.

"No, she went to night school, worked, and raised twins, plus us most of the time, so you better not tell her nothing about what she doesn't understand," Micah warned.

"That's right. Don't get crazy, baby. I believe she'll still jack you up. I can still feel her wrath from back in the day," Eli said.

"Dag, you're right. How the heck did she do all that?" Zakia wondered.

"Mamalexis is bad, so you have to be too. Don't worry, you'll be fine," Eli said. "So has anybody been sniffing up on you?"

"Man, the men ain't no joke. I can't tell who's serious or not. This basketball player named Malik stays up in my face. My roommate says it's just because I'm a challenge. Like he can get anybody he wants, but because I could care less about him, he's trying to act like he wants me."

"Don't get played again. Xavier messed around and got Dana pregnant, but I can't blame the brother. That chick threw it on him. He couldn't help it," Micah reminded her.

Zakia gave Micah a look that sent chills through his body.

"That brother loves you, girl," he said, attempting to ease the tension.

"Xavier Slade, Dana, and their baby can go jump in the lake. Bump them. That's why he busted his knee and couldn't get a scholarship. His grades sure couldn't get him into college," Zakia vented, still angry that her man "accidentally" got somebody else pregnant in high school because she wouldn't give him what he wanted. At least that was according to the sick logic the guys used in an effort to calm her down when it happened. The logic angered her as much as the fact that Dana was pregnant by Xavier.

"Forget about them, babe. You're in college now, and you're not just another pretty face. You got skills. Just don't forget what you know," Eli said.

"I know. I'm not greedy. All those men talking in both of my ears at the same time confuses me. I need one man to keep the others away."

"Make it a good one," Micah instructed.

"How can I tell a good one from a bad one? They all look good. Dang, they look good," she said as she closed her eyes and visualized a group of men standing by the door of the student union.

"Let him choose you," Micah said as Zakia snapped back to attention.

"Yeah, check out his approach. You'll be able to tell if he's foul or not," Eli added.

"You'll know. We trained you well," Micah encouraged.

"That's right. I know a whack mack when I hear one," Zakia said.

"But remember, even good brothers can still get weak at times, especially when the women are serving it up on a silver platter. Love ain't got nothing to do with it," Eli said.

"Whatever," Zakia responded, rolling her eyes at him.

The food at the restaurant looked and smelled very appetizing. Zakia ate until she thought she would pop. She made four trips to the buffet. It was all Eli said it would be and more.

"Dang, girl!" Micah said as she attempted to get up for the last time.

"Shut up," she said. "I told you that's not food they serve us in college."

"But you can't store it all up for later," he said.

"I can try."

When she tried to get up, she couldn't. "Oww, my stomach," she said, leaning forward, face scrunched up, grabbing her stomach. "I can't walk."

"So does that mean you're finally done?" Eli asked.

"I'm done."

Eli paid the bill, and Micah left the tip. "Let's go. Grab her arm," Eli told Micah.

Micah grabbed her right arm, and Eli had her left. Her human crutches helped her walk out to the car, where they laid her in the backseat,

"That's just plain pitiful. Don't make sense for somebody to eat like that. And where does she put it, with her skinny self?" Eli asked.

"It goes straight to those big feet of hers," Micah said as they made sure she was safely strapped in the backseat.

She was moaning. A half hour later, she was snoring.

"Listen to her snoring like a natural man," Eli said.

"Hey, Zakia," she heard Micah call from her semiconscious state, but couldn't answer. She could hear everything but was too miserable to talk.

"She's out cold, man," Eli said.

"Good, 'cause she would cuss my butt out if she knew I had gotten Simone pregnant," Micah said.

"Naw, man," Eli said.

"Yeah, man."

"What are you going to do about Pam?"

"I want Simone to have an abortion, but she ain't hearing it."

Zakia heard the whole conversation but didn't let on that she was listening, continuing to snore even though she was awake. They let her in on most things, but Pam was her friend, so she knew they didn't want her to know this bit of information.

"What did Simone say exactly, so we can figure out

where her head is and convince her otherwise? Shoot, this is like Zakia and Xavier, déjà vu, except with you and Pam this time. I might not be up to it. I got my own issues with Eboni trying to get pregnant. Zach has the right idea. Women are for later. For now, it's got to be work, work, work. Get established and make money," Eli said.

"That's why Sheba gave up on that brother a long time ago. He's driven and has no time for women, and now I see why. A baby is like a monkey wrench, messing up a good plan," Micah said.

"So do you think Simone can be convinced to cooperate?" Eli asked.

"She said she's not killing her baby."

Good for her, Zakia thought.

The ride home seemed extra long for Zakia, since she didn't say one word the entire time.

"Z, wake up, baby. You're home," Eli yelled as he pulled up in front of the house.

She got straight up, and without a word got out of the car, giving both of them the cold shoulder. She slammed the door without even saying thank you.

Chapter Three

As hard as she tried, at the end of the first semester of her freshman year, Zakia had one A, two Bs, and two Cs. She was devastated. Unlike Ruby, who was rejoicing that she had received only one F, Zakia was scared out of her wits to tell, much less show, her mother her grades. She was distracted. She had too much freedom. It was her crazy, partying roommate getting high all the time in their dorm room. She blamed the world, but the truth was she had just lost focus.

It was all the men who did not take no for an answer. If they wanted something, they didn't let up until they conquered it. She was fighting for dear life her first semester. The men were bold and smooth. Malik was a six-foot-four, creamy, sauntering basketball player who was much sought after by the women, but he had made Zakia his target. She resisted all she could. One day she was in the cafeteria line, and quietly as a panther he glided up behind her and kissed her ever so gently on the back of her neck. She jumped straight out of her skin.

"Are you crazy?" she snapped, jerking around so that he could clearly see her anger.

Initially, she could resist him while she was in tomboy mode, but Malik saw the princess in Zakia and knew just how to bring her out. Always, after a few minutes, his overwhelming charm drained her of all her power to resist him. Why couldn't she remember anything her boys had taught her when she needed to? She tried to rely on common sense.

"Malik, you have a girlfriend. I would hate to have to beat somebody's butt because they thought I was after their man," Zakia said with all the sternness she could muster.

He grabbed her around the waist and pulled her close to him in the cafeteria line. The sorority women were checking them out as Zakia pushed him off her and almost punched him, knowing that he was making women she didn't even know hate her.

"Look, I would really appreciate it if you kept your hands off me," she said, meaning every word.

"Okay, baby, okay. Big Daddy is so sorry for making you feel uncomfortable. Look, I'm having a party at the town house Saturday. You and Ruby should come on over," he suggested.

Malik was a junior who lived in a two-bedroom town house with his roommate, Melvin. She could not understand why he wanted her when all these women were willing to do any- and everything for him, while she was willing to do nothing.

"Okay, okay, okay. Now back off," she said.

He laughed. "You better come or I'm gonna come get you."

"I said okay," she replied as she picked up her tray and went to join Ruby and some other girls from the dorm. She could feel the heat from the hard stares the sorority women gave her as she walked past their table.

The town house was three blocks from campus. Zakia, Ruby, and the girls they ate with walked over to the party that Saturday night. There was music, card playing, backgammon, food, beer, hard alcohol, marijuana, cocaine, and folks yelling, "Party ovah heah!"

College students are cool but not too focused, Zakia thought.

"Loosen up and have some fun," Ruby said, "or I'm gonna sic Malik on you. Here, drink a beer."

"Girl, beer looks like pee, and it's nasty," Zakia said.

"Just do it like you do the cafeteria food. This Olde English is the bomb. Drink the rest of this one to loosen up," Ruby instructed, handing her the can.

"You're not going to leave me alone until I do, are you?" Zakia asked.

"Gonna bug you all night. Come on, roomie, I got your back," Ruby replied.

Zakia took the can and quickly emptied its contents in an effort to avoid the taste. It went straight to her head, and because she was completely drug- and alcohol-free, she was instantly high. She began to loosen up. She was dancing, grooving, and becoming lighter and freer. Malik was all over her, and she reciprocated. She was getting higher off the smoke that filled the room, which drove all her inhibitions away. Zakia was no longer herself. She could do whatever she wanted. She let out a loud yell as if to let everything locked up inside of her out.

The party people yelled back. She yelled again and experienced a release that made her feel freer than she had ever been. They yelled back again. When she went off yelling and dancing out of control, Ruby and Malik knew something was wrong. Malik grabbed Zakia and led her upstairs to lay on his bed. Ruby ran up the stairs behind them.

"What are you doing?" Ruby asked Malik.

"Just letting her lay down, that's all," he said, lifting her legs onto the bed.

"Yeah, right."

"I wouldn't take advantage of her like that, Ruby. Give me a break. I wouldn't want it like that."

Zakia sang loudly as she lay on the bed with her eyes closed, oblivious to where she was, not hearing the conversation for the loud music.

"Yeah, right. She's to'e up," Ruby said.

Zakia continued to sing at the top of her lungs.

Ruby, worried about her roommate, looked at Malik.

"She'll be all right," he said, sensing her concern.

Zakia was still singing, louder and louder.

"Listen to her," Ruby said.

"Just let her stay here and sleep it off. I'll walk her back to the dorm in the morning," Malik insisted.

"Please! She's so messed up she wouldn't even remember if you took advantage of her."

"I'm telling you, I wouldn't take advantage of her like that."

Now Zakia was moaning and groaning. They looked at her, then at each other. Malik tried to look as innocent as possible. Ruby looked deep into his eyes for what seemed like an eternity.

"Aaww heck naw! Come on, walk us back to the dorm *now!*"

The next day, Zakia vowed to never do drugs or alcohol again. Malik came to her room that afternoon to make sure she was all right.

"How're you doing today, baby?" he asked, genuinely concerned as he sat in the chair at her desk. Ruby was still asleep.

"Fine. Never again, though. That was not me at all."

"I know, but did you have a good time? Tell the truth," Malik said.

"It was okay. I wouldn't do that every weekend. Or like Ruby, every day, if she could."

"Yeah, she's crazy, but she's got your back. That's good. But she's so wild. You need a man to have your back, baby. Come on. Let me be your man. Let me take care of you. I understand what you're all about, and that's why I love you. We can help each other."

Breaking down, Zakia asked, "What about Vashti?"

"History, baby. Closed chapter, the past, gone, over."

Zakia contemplated what being with Malik would mean. It would definitely eliminate one major distraction by keeping other men at bay. She decided to go for it.

"Okay, Malik."

Chapter Four

Zakia witnessed college females, like the women in her neighborhood back in Richmond, being traumatized by men who did not realize that it was not morally acceptable behavior to have harems in the United States. Zakia made it clear to Malik that she would not be disrespected in such a way. The thought had never entered Malik's mind that Zakia would be his only woman, just his main one. All of the others would understand that and respect her as such, never letting her find out about them if they wanted a piece of him. However, Zakia was so focused on her classes, scholarship, and subsequent employment that Malik often felt neglected. He missed the attention and perks he got from other women. Some of them would do anything to get with him, but after he got Zakia, he decided he would keep her.

It was mutually over with Vashti. She had become sick of the reports from her sorors. The only thing that had changed about Malik was his official girlfriend. Zakia had no peace in her spirit about Malik. She dismissed the uneasiness she felt from other women. She knew that the root of the stares was that they wanted her man.

"Look, Malik, I know I don't have a lot of time to give you all the attention you need, and I'm cool with just being your friend," Zakia told him as he walked her to class one day.

He thought about it for a split second, but not wanting to take a chance on a less needy brother taking his place, he reassured her. "What are you talking about? You are my woman and my friend and you always will be."

They grew to depend on each other and to really love each other as friends. They were both good, beautiful people who happened to find themselves in an environment that didn't always bring the positive characteristics out of a person socially; however, they could see the goodness and inner beauty that the other possessed. They decided to stay together.

Zakia and Malik broke up and got back together many times during Zakia's freshman year. The main reason for many of the breakups was that Zakia would learn that Malik was messing around with another woman, especially during basketball season when groupies were a dime a dozen.

One afternoon before a home game, Malik went to Zakia's room to get a good-luck kiss.

"Let me hear you cheering for me tonight. I'm going to hit three threes in a row just for you, baby," he promised.

"Oh, didn't I tell you? I'm going home after my last class today. My mother's birthday is tomorrow."

"What? But I have a game tonight."

"And you have your own cheering section. I'm sure somebody will be screaming your name."

"Why can't you go after the game or in the morning?"

"Gotta catch a ride when I can," Zakia said.

Malik pouted all the way to the gym.

The post-game celebrations were the most opportune times for women to hug and kiss Malik in public. This irritated Zakia a great deal, but there wasn't much she could do about it. She was no fool and preferred not to give these women the satisfaction of being able to love on her man in front of her. She wanted to stay and support him, but he loved the attention so much that he actually told her to get used to it because NBA groupies were way worse than college ones. He said that this was practice for her. She thought he was a fool to think she would just stand by and get used to him hugging and kissing on women in her presence, especially when she could tell more was going on than just congratulations. She asked him if he was serious.

"They are fans, baby. We just won the game. They're happy. It's no big deal."

"Call me after basketball season is over, Malik."

Malik wasn't too disappointed because he would now be free to oblige his fans. So he took her advice, confident that he could charm her back after the season.

Basketball off-season wasn't off-season for his other women, but there was no reason to be openly flirtatious, so Malik was more subtle. Still, the flirting was obvious.

One April afternoon during off-season, Zakia, Malik, and Melvin, Malik's roommate, were having lunch together in the cafeteria. Malik was still in the line when Zakia and Melvin found a table and sat down. Zakia saw Malik wink at a female as she blushed and giggled and began whispering to her friends standing in line. Before he could even make it to their table, she saw a different female slip a piece of paper in his back pocket.

"Melvin, what's up?" Zakia asked.

"What's up with what?"

"You're a good-looking guy, you play ball, you have no steady woman. How can you keep these hussies off you and Malik can't?"

"You can keep whoever you want to keep off you. If they are up on you, it's because you want them to be," Melvin said.

"That's true," Zakia agreed.

Malik finally made it to the table and sat down with his back to his admirers.

"Let me see the paper that hussy gave you," Zakia said.

"What paper?" Malik asked, feigning innocence.

Melvin smirked as he bit into his sandwich.

Zakia and Ruby decided to move off campus their sophomore year. They followed most of the upper-classmen to the town houses where Malik and Melvin lived. One weekend Zach, Eli, Micah, Raquie, and Eboni came for a visit.

"Nice crib, twin. You're moving up in the world. Where's Malik?" Zach asked. Malik had met Zakia's family and friends over the summer, and everyone approved of him, including Alexis.

"Later for that dog."

"Oh Lawd, here we go again," Eli said. "What did he do now?"

"It doesn't even matter, but I see why y'all like him. Y'all all alike."

"Not my baby," Eboni said, sitting on Eli's lap, wrapping her arms around him and kissing him.

"You better hold on to him, 'cause these hussies will try to take him right out of your arms," Zakia told Eboni.

"Let's go check them out, Micah," Zach said. "Call Malik, twin. We're not in your drama."

Zakia broke down and called Malik after much persistence from Zach. He came right over. After he rallied all of their support, they went to Zakia on his behalf and pressured her into giving him one more chance. She buckled under the pressure, believing that he really loved her in spite of his weakness for women, and she eventually took him back.

Zakia's junior year was better. Malik had matured and was concentrating on his future. Unfortunately, due to the fierce competition he was cut during the NBA tryouts. He had to find a job. He didn't have to look very hard or far before he was offered a basketball coaching position at MSU. In spite of his new position, Malik was depressed because he'd been so sure he would make the NBA. Zakia was not sensitive enough to cater to his emotional needs when Malik ended up back on Manna's campus after he was cut. She was preparing for her own graduation the following year, focusing on landing a good job. Zakia's insensitivity to Malik's depression caused him to seek solace elsewhere.

Being back on campus brought out Malik's old tendencies, along with his depression. Even though he was now a physical education teacher and a coach, Malik didn't feel that students were off-limits. One particularly persistent groupie named Candice had been a thorn in Zakia's flesh. She was slick and subtle as a snake and just a little bit too friendly toward Zakia.

"Feels like something crawled up in me and died when Candice is around," Zakia told Ruby one day.

"Watch that heifer," Ruby warned.

One day just two months before her graduation, Zakia stopped in to say hello to Malik, who was still sharing the town house with Melvin, who had gotten a job with a local record company as a producer. Her stomach turned when she found a gold necklace on Malik's dresser that was adorned with the name *Candice*. She picked up the necklace and went into the bathroom.

"Malik, come here, please," she called out as she put on the necklace.

He came into the bathroom where she was standing by the toilet.

"What's different about me?" she asked with her hands on her hips, posing as he checked her out from head to toe.

"I don't know," he said.

"Do you like my necklace?"

His eyes got big as quarters, and before he could do or say anything, she yanked the necklace from around her neck, breaking the clasp, dropped it in the toilet, and flushed it. He was still standing there paralyzed until he felt the pain of a wooden brush across his face. He immediately snapped out of it and grabbed her as she dug her fingernails into his flesh. He picked her up, threw her across his shoulder, carried her into his room while she was beating him on his back with her fists, threw her on the bed, and locked her in the room alone.

"You lowlife piece of crap!" she yelled. "I knew the last time I shouldn't have taken your sorry butt back. I hate you. You make me puke! You think you so fine. You a sorry dog, that's what you are. I should have never come back. I threw my dang pills away to make sure I didn't come back, but no, I listened to Raquie and Zach and Eli. 'Give him another chance. He's gonna make it up to you.' Bump you! I should slice you up and give each of your women a piece of you!"

Zakia stayed focused until graduation. Zach talked to Malik and advised him to stay away from her and to face the fact that it was over. There was no more coming back. Malik knew it was over for good this time. Zakia would be ready to move on after she graduated, so he reluctantly let go.

After graduation, Zakia had several job offers in Baltimore, where she planned to stay. Although she had been nauseous, she had put off taking a pregnancy test. Now that she had her bachelor's degree in marketing, she had to know for sure if she was pregnant, since she would not try to raise a child alone in a city that was not her home. As strong as she was, she couldn't face pregnancy without her family in Richmond. She was ready to start her career, but the results of the pregnancy test were positive. She had to put her career on hold and move back to Richmond. She hated Malik with every fiber of her being, blaming him for this major setback in her life.

Chapter Five

Contrary to popular belief, the opposite of love is not hate. The opposite of love is indifference. Hate is love that has been hurt. Hate cares. Indifference does not care.

Zakia hated Malik. However, after seeing Micah with his son, Jaron, she couldn't fathom the concept of abortion for herself. She loved life too much and couldn't bring herself to deprive an innocent child of his. The child she was carrying was innocent. She was the guilty one, and so was Malik. If they had to suffer the consequences of their actions, then so be it, but her child would not suffer. She wanted nothing to do with Malik, not even for her child's sake, and believed that she could give the baby enough love to make up for his not having a father.

Zakia could not stand to disappoint her mother. Alexis was truly devastated that her daughter had gotten pregnant before she could get herself established and instead had to come back home. She had gotten used to living alone. Zachary was working and out on his own. She didn't hide her disappointment well, and Zakia vowed to be out of her mother's house the first chance she got. Even though she received all the love and support she could ever need from her family and from the Execs as well, she felt like a failure.

Ignoring Zakia's request not to do so, Alexis called Malik to let him know that he was going to be a father. She believed a man was supposed to take care of his children. When Malik found out, he drove down to Richmond, and when Zakia opened the door, he handed her a dozen red roses. She knocked the roses out of his hand, sending the vase, water, and flowers all over the porch. She spit in his face, then slammed the door. *He will never lay eyes on this baby,* she vowed.

Malik begged, pleaded, and cried and had everybody in the village talk to Zakia. She was becoming indifferent toward Malik. Slowly, her family and friends realized that she said what she meant and she meant what she said. Malik did not exist. She threatened that she wouldn't speak to whoever let him know anything about her and her baby. They believed her, and nobody told Malik when his beautiful son, Ezekiel, who was the spitting image of him, was born. Whenever he called, he was advised to let it go. Over time he did just that.

Zakia was on a mission. She had been sidetracked, delayed for a bit, but she was back and with a beautiful healthy baby boy for whom to provide. Ezekiel was her pride and joy. He was a curse-turned-blessing because the baby was truly an angel from heaven. With a vengeance, Zakia picked up right where she had left off when she found out she was pregnant.

Her excess weight fell off quickly, and she was back in the interview suits she had bought before the pregnancy. She aggressively pursued positions that had potential for advancement, impressing interviewers with her intelligence and energy. She had many offers. Finally, she chose a position with a local advertising agency that did a large percentage of the print ad work in not just the city but the state. She loved her job at Ascension Advertising. She worked long hours, going above and beyond the call of duty on all of her assignments.

The villagers were very helpful with baby Zeke. There was never a shortage of babysitters. Raquie was now at Manna State University, equipped with knowledge and wisdom, and determined to be at the top of the class of 1988. When she was home, she never said no when Zakia needed her. As Zeke grew older and started walking, he and his Uncle Zach became inseparable.

Zakia got three promotions in four years for landing some of the toughest accounts in the state. She was creative, diligent, and committed to client satisfaction. Indeed, she was a workaholic. However, she was also a good and devoted mother. She spent quality time with Zeke, and he was thriving as he developed into a wonderful little boy.

One night Zakia and Eboni decided to go out. Club Ritz was on the outskirts of Richmond, in the swanky part of town. The patrons were upper-middle-class buppies. The men were suave, and they were generous. They reminded Zakia of mature Manna men. She had been there, done that, and decided to just enjoy the evening and go home. Several men brought her virgin drinks and danced with her all night. She had maintained her vow of being drug-

and alcohol-free since the incident during her freshman year of college. Zakia and Eboni had fun and enjoyed the attention so much that they planned to go again the following Friday.

When Eboni went to the ladies' room the following week, a man slid into her seat across from Zakia and looked deeply into her eyes.

"That seat is taken," Zakia said before he could introduce himself.

"I know. I'll return it when it's time. I just wanted to tell you that you appear to be a very classy lady, and I was wondering if you were attached," he said, getting right to the point.

"No, I'm not."

"Good, neither am I. Are you from around here?"

"Yes," she answered, wondering why she felt compelled to respond to this complete stranger's questions.

"What high school did you attend?" he asked

"Booker T," she said.

"I graduated from your archrival, Dunbar," he said.

She dared not ask him if he knew Xavier. "Did you play any sports?" she asked instead.

"Not really, more of a bookworm."

"Oh, I thought I might have seen you at a game," she said, playing off her curiosity.

"Wait a minute. You were a cheerleader, right?"

"How did you know that?"

"I had a hobby of always picking out the prettiest cheerleaders. I thought when I first saw you last week that you looked vaguely familiar. I couldn't remember where I had seen you before. I've been thinking about you all week. And just when you mentioned sports, it came to me where I had seen you. You haven't changed a bit, still pretty as ever."

"You saw me here last week?" she asked, flattered.

"Yes, I did."

She thought it best not to ask why he didn't speak to her then. Eboni was coming.

"Hello, I'm Eboni," she said, introducing herself to him while extending her hand for him to shake.

"Hello, Eboni," he said, shaking her hand as he got up.

"Oh, and I'm Zakia Wilkes," Zakia said, extending her hand.

"Jay Carter. It's been a pleasure," he said as he gently kissed the back of her hand, sending tingles through her body. He handed her one of his business cards. "Give me a call. Maybe we can do lunch."

She took the card and read it: *Jay Carter, Chief Financial Officer, NuTech Computers.* He worked for one of her firm's clients.

Chapter Six

All day Saturday Zakia thought about how Mr. Jay Carter had charmed her. Eboni called Saturday night to give her some advice.

"You call that man first thing Monday, girl," Eboni said.

"And look desperate?"

"No. Interested, not desperate. Just call him. Use reverse psychology. He won't be expecting you to call Monday because you won't want to seem desperate, but when you call all bold and confident, not desperate, he won't know what to think."

Zakia was holding her head, shaking it with her eyes closed, listening to Eboni explain her theory.

"Eli's the philosopher and you're the psychologist. Why aren't you two married?" Zakia asked. Eli and Eboni lived together and had a six-year-old daughter named Essence.

"Just call him Monday."

• • •

By the time she got to work on Monday, Zakia still didn't know if she was ready for dating. Should she wait or call him? How did it work nowadays? She called.

"Hello, Jay Carter's office," said a pleasant female voice.

"This is Zakia Wilkes. Is Mr. Carter available?"

"One moment, please."

After a few seconds, she heard a very enthusiastic "Well, good morning, Ms. Wilkes."

"Good morning, Mr. Carter. How are you?" she responded with just as much enthusiasm.

"Just wonderful all of a sudden. How are you?"

"Fine, thank you. Did you have a good weekend?" Zakia asked.

"Actually, I worked in the yard, since the weather was nice. I was thinking about our conversation the whole time. I really enjoyed talking to you."

"Yes, it was nice."

After a brief pause, Jay said, "Do you have a busy day today?"

"Not particularly."

"Are you available for lunch?"

"I have no plans."

"Where are you located?"

"In the King Tower."

"Right up the street. How convenient. Would you like to meet me at the restaurant next door to your building?" Jay asked.

"Sure. What time?"

"What's good for you?"

"How about high noon?"

"See you then."

Zakia felt a rush she hadn't felt in a very long time, and panic began to set in. *Am I ready for this? I got my peace back. I work like a dog, but my peace is worth it. Ezekiel is four years old, surrounded and smothered in love, Malik is history, and I have family and friends who love and support me and I them. Why complicate things? I can always find an escort for my corporate functions whenever I need one. I finally got my life back on track with nothing missing and nothing broken. Sex really is overrated. I would much rather have my peace.*

She called Jay back and was put through.

"Hello, Jay. I'm sorry. I don't think it will be a good idea to meet for lunch."

"Why not?" Jay asked.

"I just don't," she said in an unsure, I-do-want-to-but-I'm-afraid-to tone.

"You need to eat, right?" he asked.

"Yes."

"Well, that is all I am proposing, Zakia, that you eat."

What harm can one lunch do? she thought. "Okay, Jay."

"So I'll see you at noon?" he said.

"Okay."

Jay and Zakia had an immediate connection that was confirmed during their lunch conversation. Their backgrounds were different, but they had a lot in common.

"I'm looking forward to meeting Zeke," Jay said.

"He's great," Zakia said with all the pride and love a mother could unleash in those two words.

"I'm sure he is. Look at his mother," Jay said.

• • •

For the next two weeks, they met every day for lunch.

"I would love for you and Zeke to come with me to my parents' for a cookout this weekend," Jay said during one of their lunch dates.

"Sounds great," Zakia agreed.

Jay's relatives were the warmest, nicest, most loving people Zakia had ever met. They made her and her son feel like a part of the family. When she brought Jay home to meet her own family, Alexis took Zakia into the kitchen to speak to her in private.

"Now, that's what I'm talkin' 'bout," her mother said.

Jay and Zakia spent a lot of time together. The communication was stimulating. They talked about back in the day, their careers, and the future. They grew and learned from and with each other. Soon they were spending all of their time together. They flew to New York for a weekend to shop and take in dinner and a play. This felt comfortable to Zakia, and finally, the wall she had built around her heart began to break down.

Jay and Zakia had been dating for seven months. Within the last two, Jay had begun to drop marriage crumbs to see if Zakia would bite. She noticed the hints and completely disregarded them. Even though she was very much in love with him, the wall around her heart wasn't completely down yet. She had borrowed Eli's "If it ain't broke, don't fix it" motto. But as she and Jay grew closer, and with everything going so well in her life, the time eventually came when Zakia found herself entertaining thoughts of marriage. She decided to bite the next time Jay threw out a crumb.

One day while Jay was helping her to prepare dinner,

he said, "We're not getting any younger. Do you have anything you want to accomplish before you hit thirty?"

There's that crumb I've been waiting for, she thought. "Sure. I just recently realized that in spite of my upbringing and all I've been through with Zeke's dad and making my way in the world, that success is sweeter when you have someone to share it with," she said, borrowing from Billy Dee Williams in *Mahogany*.

"That is so true, baby. And when you can find someone you are compatible with, someone who understands and appreciates you, whose goals coincide with yours, someone you love and trust, you would be crazy not to do whatever it took to hold on to that person," Jay said, echoing her sentiments.

"I agree."

Jay was a man who was always prepared. He reached in his pocket and pulled out a three-carat diamond solitaire ring. He got down on one knee and took her hand. As he slid the ring on her finger, he said, "Zakia, will you marry me?"

Zakia was not breathing as all this took place. Jay had managed to surprise her. She didn't expect to get an actual proposal that day, just to start talking about marriage. It was the beginning of a new decade, the nineties, and time to move on, time for a new life. She looked at the ring, then at Jay, and said yes.

Their wedding was elegant and exquisitely quaint in Jay's parents' sprawling backyard. Since Zakia had a child, she didn't want to have too many bells and whistles. Eboni and Raquie stood up for Zakia, and Eboni gave Eli the eye during the ceremony. Jay's brother was the best man, and Zach escorted Raquie. Rahlo gave his daughter away. At the reception, each Exec took Jay to the side and gave him a personalized speech about how special Zakia was and how special they expected him to treat her.

Chapter Seven

Zakia and Zeke moved into Jay's bigger, nicer house out in the suburbs. They decided to keep Zakia's house as investment property. They agreed to also maintain his house as investment property after they finished building their dream home the following year. Within their first few years of marriage, the value of their portfolio increased significantly. Their life together was off to a great start.

After their new home was built, Zakia decided to start entertaining coworkers. She was lining up perfectly with corporate America, following the rules, playing the games, and winning. She hosted the office Christmas party two years in a row. She had the favor of her bosses, and she had earned it.

When Zakia became pregnant, the computer technicians from her job came in and set up an office in her home so that she wouldn't miss a beat during maternity leave. She was very productive at home up until she went into labor.

Zakia gave birth to a second son. He was beautiful and fit perfectly into her ideal world. He was called JJ for Jay Jr. Zeke adored his little brother, and Jay had never been more proud.

"How did you get another boy? You know Essence was supposed to be a boy," Eboni said one day.

"Girl, I'm lining up, living right. Things work out when you live right and just let it come to you. Your man needs a revelation on that."

"He's too comfortable, girl. Every time I leave him, he just waits, knowing I'm going to come back."

"Then don't go back until he marries you."

"I try, but you know I love that man. Okay, I'm going to hold out the next time."

"I hear ya."

"But I'm really happy for you," Eboni said, hugging her friend.

"I know you are, girl. Thanks!"

Two months after JJ's birth, Zakia returned to her office downtown with far less zeal than when she had left. She kept the office set up at home for the days she didn't want to deal with the traffic. Her bosses agreed with the arrangement, since she was just as productive at home as she was in the office. The setup worked very well, but with each passing year, Zakia lost a little more enthusiasm for her work.

Jay was becoming a very skilled investor. He decided to break out of his safe real estate and mutual fund mode to really take some risks. He had a good feeling about a small software company whose financials looked great and whose earning potential looked even greater. He decided to take a chance and invest substantially in the company's stock, and it turned out to be a smart move. The company took off, and Jay saw his investment triple. He was already confident, but being married to Zakia for the last five years had given him an assurance that he had never known. Eventually, Jay had the boys' college tuition to any school in the country safely invested until it was needed.

As the years passed and they grew and acquired and conquered, a funny feeling started to grow inside of Zakia. Her excitement about life was decreasing the more her family increased. She decided to take inventory of her life. She had it all and then some. She had beautiful, healthy children; a wonderful, loving husband with whom she was always in sync; a great job; financial stability; loving, supportive family and friends; her mother's approval; and excellent health—yet she was missing something. She had no idea why, but there was a void in her that none of what she had—and she had everything materially—even began to fill.

Zakia was too much of a doer to just let the feeling get the best of her, so she began to investigate and try different things to fill the void. She tried working out, and even though she was starting to look and feel better physically, the void was still there. She traveled to new places alone and with her family. She talked her husband into renting a Winnebago, and they drove across the country and back. The boys had a blast, and so did Jay. Zakia had fun; however, the void persisted. They cruised as a couple to the Caribbean, and Zakia went to Europe alone to shop. Still, the cavity remained.

While flipping through magazines, Zakia got the

notion that a newly decorated home would help to fill her emptiness. She hired an interior designer, and they spent months redecorating the entire house. She gave much of her old furniture away. She gave a party for her family and friends once the house was ready, but afterward she was still missing something.

Zakia volunteered at the homeless shelter. She read books. Nothing helped. The family went to church, and everything was the same old, same old. She had been going to Fig Tree Baptist Church with Jay since they had gotten married because his father was a deacon there. The church was more than a hundred years old, and the service format hadn't changed in all that time.

Not even church did anything to lift the cloud hovering over Zakia. Ironically, the emptiness was beginning to weigh her down. The more she acquired, the heavier she felt. She didn't know what it was, nor could she shake the feeling.

Jay was into his work and investments, but Zakia knew he noticed his wife becoming distant. She wanted sex less and less, and Jay often asked if she was sick. While watching TV in bed one night, he reached for her and she turned away.

"What's wrong, baby?"

"I don't know."

"How do you feel?"

"Fine."

"When was your last physical?"

"Less than a year ago. Clean bill of health."

"I'm worried about you."

"I'll be fine. I just want to go to sleep right now."

Jay wasn't one to press, and having no idea what was

wrong or what to do about it, he continued to focus on his work and his investments. Life was wonderful for Jay. If he kept doing what he was doing, being a supportive husband, an involved father, and providing a stable life for his family, he believed things would get back on track for his wife and everything would be fine.

Chapter Eight

One cold and rainy Saturday afternoon, Zakia was in the mall wandering in and out of stores, buying things she didn't need. Shopping no longer had the thrill or satisfaction it once held for her. She decided to have everything delivered, and when she was finished, she just sat in the mall people-watching. Thoughts about her life and what she had accomplished filled her mind. Everything had worked out according to plan. With wit, wisdom, hard work, determination, and commitment, she had overcome the obstacles of life. Feelings of accomplishment evaded her, however, as depression tried desperately to grab her.

As she sat and thought, her stomach growled. The big, hot, soft pretzels were her favorite. She bought one and returned to her seat on the bench preparing her pretzel with cheese and mustard. A woman came and sat down beside her. She was an older woman with gray hair and brown eyes, dressed in what could have been five layers of ragged, frayed clothing, closely resembling a bag lady. *Bag ladies didn't usually frequent malls*, Zakia thought. Besides, this woman's shopping bags were new, and the woman looked clean and smelled fresh. Zakia spoke to her, suddenly feeling awkward about eating in front of her.

"Good afternoon, ma'am. May I buy you a pretzel?" Zakia asked.

The woman had been looking at Zakia prepare her pretzel. "No thank you, sweetie. You know Jesus loves you," the woman told her.

Zakia bit her pretzel, smiled at the woman, and nodded as she chewed.

"No, I mean He really loves you, and He has all the answers you need," the woman said as she handed Zakia a tract. "You've been searching for something, haven't you?"

Zakia stopped smiling but kept listening. She took the tract, still chewing, not talking, looked straight into the woman's warm eyes, and silently nodded.

"God wanted me to let you know that He has what you are looking for."

Zakia was entranced.

"Would you like to have your void filled, sweetheart?" She nodded more vigorously.

"Come to my church tomorrow, and God will meet you there with exactly what you've been searching for. The address is on the tract. Do you think you can make it?"

Zakia couldn't stop nodding, still speechless.

"I'll be looking for you," the old woman said as she got up and walked away.

Zakia watched in silence as she left. When she disappeared into a store, Zakia turned her attention to the tract.

She read every word about how Jesus died for her. She already knew about some of what she read, but now it was taking on a new significance. She felt better but was unsure about things. She wanted more.

Now that Zakia's initial shock over the exchange had passed, she wanted to talk to the lady. She roamed the mall looking for her, but the old woman was nowhere to be found. Zakia left the mall and on her way home decided to see if she could find the church whose address was on the tract.

What she found was a beautiful, large, dome-shaped building that reminded her of a performing arts center. She was really curious about what was inside. She saw lights on through the glass door and decided to check it out. The door was locked. She walked around to the side of the building and tried another door. It was open. She entered the lobby. There was no one to be seen. She spotted another set of doors that led deeper inside the building. She opened one and peeked into the most gorgeous modern-day sanctuary she had ever seen. It looked to seat about fifteen hundred people. Instead of pews, there were comfortable-looking individual chairs arranged in auditorium fashion. The pale green abstract pattern on the chairs matched the cloth-paneled walls, which blended with the carpet, creating a warm and inviting ambience.

In the middle of the sanctuary sat a huge platform that held expensive-looking camera equipment. It was dark, but the glow from the security lights and exit signs provided enough light that Zakia was able to see. She was moved by the sleeping room and had a strong desire to see it awake. Yes, she would definitely be back the next day. As she left the sanctuary and entered the hallway, people were coming toward her.

"May I help you, sister?" a forty-something gentleman in a sweat suit asked, smiling.

Zakia was nervous, not knowing if she was trespassing.

"No. I was trying to find the church. A lady gave me this tract and invited me to come tomorrow, and I just stopped by to see if this was the right place," she explained, holding up the tract.

"You are in the right place. Please do come back tomorrow for our praise and worship service and then be blessed by the Word of God."

"Thank you, I will."

"Have a good evening, sister," the nice gentleman said. Then turning to another brother, he said, "Lock up, John. I'll see you tomorrow."

Zakia left with a feeling of excitement and anticipation. Looking at the tract for service times, she decided to go alone to the eight o'clock service to check things out. That way she could be home in time to go to Fig Tree Baptist Church with her family at eleven o'clock. Jay would understand.

"How are all of my handsome men?" she asked, kissing each one of them.

They just silently looked at her.

"Honey, I met this lady in the mall, and she invited me to her church. I rode by there, and it looked interesting. They have two services, so I decided to check out their early one while you get the boys ready. I'll make sure I'm back in time for Fig Tree Baptist," she explained as she got a slice of pizza.

"Oh, a new church now. Okay, Z. Hopefully, one day soon, you'll find what you're looking for," Jay said.

"Thanks for your patience," she said, kissing him on the cheek, sparking something they had both missed. Her new excitement gave her new energy and new appeal. "I'll be upstairs."

Jay hurried the boys to finish their pizza and clean up.

Zakia was greeted at Faith in the Word Christian Center with a smile and a warm hug. The music was different, inspirational, uplifting even. She loved good music. It soothed her, especially when she was a part of it. She had a decent background voice and had sung alto in the Fig Tree Baptist gospel choir. She never wanted to sing solo, but the backbiting the soloists did to get parts was ridiculous. The competition was fierce, and the dramatics of some of the choir members all but led to fistfights. She was losing her desire and love for the music, so she got out. Yet the music was her saving grace, since not much else went on that was truly inspiring at church, so she opted to just enjoy listening to the music on Sundays. She did miss being a part of the choir, though.

Zakia chose a seat in the middle of the sanctuary. The atmosphere was charged with something that was causing her dull, achy void to feel like it was dissipating. The choir sounded like angels singing. They even looked like angels. The music soothed her empty soul. Less organ and more harp produced more worship and less show than she was used to. Then the Word came forth. The pastor was young, in his thirties, and of average build. Instead of a robe, he wore a very sharp, conservative, dark-vested tailored suit. Pastor Patterson talked about how God reached down and pulled him back from the verge of a nervous breakdown. He talked about being a drug addict and an alcoholic, yet when he made Jesus the Lord of his life, he lost all desire to indulge. Zakia thought it was utterly amazing for a person, especially a pastor, to tell all his business like that. She knew alcoholics and drug addicts who served on the usher board, in the choir, and on the trustee board at Fig Tree Baptist who thought it was acceptable to drink and smoke Monday through Friday and especially on Saturday as long as they made it to their post on Sunday. Listening to Pastor Patterson, she began to understand that it was that kind of hypocrisy that was causing her emptiness.

She sat there with her eyes wide and heart, ears, and mouth open as he went from scripture to scripture proving by the Word of God every point he made. She had been given a Bible when she arrived, but had trouble keeping up because she didn't know where many of the scriptures were located. A lady sitting next to her noticed her frustration and whispered to her.

"You can purchase a cassette tape of the message after service if you don't get it all now."

"Oh, thank you," Zakia said, relieved, then just sat back and listened.

The Word that came across the pulpit had her head spinning, heart fluttering, spirit jumping, and legs shaking. When the invitation was given to join the church, Zakia found herself right in front of the preacher. She didn't even remember walking up there. It was as though she had been transported supernaturally to the altar. She accepted Jesus as her Lord and

Savior, making the decision to live her life for Him according to the Word of God. Then she and about twenty other new born-again Christians were escorted to a room where prayer counselors were waiting for them. After they were all lined up, the woman she had met in the mall the day before came up to her.

"So glad you made it, sweetie."

The woman was now dressed in a beautiful flowery print dress, makeup, and a silver-gray wig. Zakia burst out crying as she hugged her ever so tightly. The woman held her and rubbed her back as Zakia squeezed her even tighter.

"It's all right, sweetie. You are fine now. It's time to get what you've been searching for. I'm Sister Jenkins. Are you ready?"

"Yes. Yes, ma'am," Zakia said between sniffles.

Sister Jenkins handed her some tissue. As Zakia wiped her face, Sister Jenkins began to explain the Baptism of the Holy Spirit.

"Now that you have made Jesus Christ your Lord and Savior, the next step is to receive the power of the Holy Ghost so that you can live victoriously. Do you know what that is?"

Zakia shook her head.

"Do you believe that you are saved now because of what Jesus did for you on Calvary?"

Zakia nodded.

"Did you have to do anything other than believe to receive your salvation?"

Zakia shook her head. She knew she was saved, and all she had done was accept the pastor's invitation to receive Jesus.

"Well, you receive the power of the Holy Spirit the same way, by faith. Okay?"

Zakia nodded.

"I'm going to pray with you to receive the power of the Holy Spirit, and when you believe you receive it, open up your mouth and begin to speak. Just let out whatever comes up. You will not understand it, but keep speaking in tongues. That is your heavenly language. It is your brand-new, born-again spirit praying the perfect prayer to God. When that is happening, you are operating in the highest power. Understand?" Sister Jenkins asked so sweetly, holding both of Zakia's hands.

Zakia nodded.

"Let's pray. Dear Lord, thank You for saving this sweet child. You have snatched her out of the hands of the enemy. She belongs to You and will serve You all the days of her life. Equip her, Lord, and anoint her right now to walk on top of any situation or circumstance that arises in her life. Let her light shine brightly as she walks upright before You. Move on the inside of her precious Holy Spirit. Give her peace that passes all understanding. As she receives Your glorious power from on high, let her prayer language come forth. Amen. Now open your mouth and speak, sweetie," Sister Jenkins instructed.

Zakia opened her mouth, and her tongue began to flow. Because of her open heart, she received her prayer language instantly.

Zakia prayed the perfect prayer, totally surrendering to the Holy Spirit that was overtaking her. She flowed for a few minutes as Sister Jenkins continued to hold both her hands, interceding for her. Afterward they hugged. Zakia looked at her.

"What just happened to me?"

"You were just born again and filled with the Holy Spirit of God, and your evidence was that special prayer language you just spoke. It will empower you to live this new life in Christ."

"Wow! Now what do I do?" Zakia asked, pulling herself together.

"Get into that Word. Feed your spirit. Read your Bible, come to church, and listen to Word tapes. Faith comes by hearing. That is the only way you will grow spiritually."

"Oh, I have to get the tape of today's message. Do you know where I can find it?"

"Yes. The bookstore is to the right of the front of the sanctuary."

"Oh, thank you so much. Thank you so very, very much," Zakia said as she squeezed her again.

"Have a blessed week, sweetie."

"You too, and thank you for inviting me," Zakia said as she left.

She found the bookstore and bought one hundred dollars' worth of products. As she stood in the cashier line, she realized something. She stood completely still. She closed her eyes and began to smile. The emptiness was gone. Her void had been filled.

Zakia sped home to tell Jay what had just happened. She was listening to one of the cassette tapes she had purchased and didn't hear the siren; however, the flashing blue lights got her attention through the rearview mirror. She pulled over, her happiness unaffected. While waiting for the policeman to come to her car, she began to pray in tongues.

"In a hurry, ma'am?" the policeman asked.

"I'm so sorry, Officer. I just left church and am so excited to get home to my husband to tell him all about it," she said, genuinely enthused.

"Well, slow down so you can make it there in one piece. Have a nice day," the policeman said as he tipped his hat and went back to his squad car.

"Thank You, Jesus! Thank You, Jesus! Thank You, Jesus!" Zakia praised God all the way home.

Chapter Nine

Jay, Jay! Baby, where are you? Jaaaayyyy!" Zakia cried out joyfully as she dropped her bag and went from room to room looking for her husband.

"What's wrong, baby?" Jay asked, running to his wife.

She grabbed him and hugged and squeezed him. He hugged her back.

"What is it, baby?" he asked again, only a little less alarmed.

She spoke to him in her newly found language.

"Huh?"

"Baby, I went to that church, and it was totally awesome. The people greeted me at the door with friendly smiles and warm hugs. The music was just so uplifting, and the preacher, oh wow, the preacher was so awesome. He was walking up and down the aisles as he preached . . . and he preached, you hear me, I am telling you, he preached! In all the Sunday school and church I've been to, I never ever heard anybody preach like that. It was absolutely liberating. I feel so free, so rejuvenated, so brand-new. Oh, and guess what? I joined and was taken to the back room, and I spoke in tongues. That's what I just spoke to you. They said tongues would be my power. So guess what? Guess what? I was speeding and a policeman stopped me and I started speaking in tongues and the policeman told me to have a nice day and he didn't even give me a ticket," Zakia said all in one breath.

"Huh?"

"I found us a new church, baby."

"What's wrong with the old one?"

"It's not about what's wrong with the old one, it's about what's right with the new one, baby. You got to check it out."

"Baby, I am not looking for a new church," Jay said.

"You have to check it out, Jay."

"Zakia, I have dealt with all of your other ventures and adventures, but now you are talking church. You have crossed the line. My dad is a deacon at our church, for crying out loud. And you just up and joined some other church. You have really, really gone too far this time."

"But, Jay . . ."

"But Jay nothing. Now, let's get ready to go to our church."

"But . . ."

"This discussion is over."

They went to Fig Tree Baptist, and absolutely everything seemed wrong about it to Zakia. Deacon Morris flirted with Sister Ann while his wife ushered. Two of the choir members were rolling their eyes at each other. Brother Braxton smelled like alcohol. The male choir director's eyebrows looked like they had been waxed. The offering bucket came around four times. People were sleeping while Rev. Fisher preached, and he didn't open the Bible, just read from notes. She couldn't wait to go back to Faith in the Word Christian Center, with or without her husband.

Zakia took the next day off work to go over to her new church. She spent the day learning about it. She learned about all the ministries and the weekly Bible studies. They even had a Bible Institute where she could earn college credit. She realized that she had so much to learn, and she couldn't wait to get started. She spent another few hundred dollars in the bookstore. She bought several versions of the Bible, concordances, commentaries, cassettes, and videotapes. She bought caps and T-shirts bearing the slogan "What Would Jesus Do?" for the boys. All week long as she studied her material, she bugged Jay to go to church with her the following Sunday.

"Look, baby, you can do whatever you want. I don't have time to go with you on all your little trips. This is one I am not going on. I have been at my church all my life. I was born there, and I'm going to die there," he said, sounding like his father.

"Please, Jay, just once. Come with me next Sunday, and if you don't like it, I promise I won't ever bother you about it again."

Jay went to church with her the following Sunday hard-hearted and closed up. Based on his conventional upbringing, he was expecting a traditional-looking building with stained-glass windows.

"Where's the steeple?" he asked as they entered the church.

"Oh, Jay, just wait until you hear the preacher. You are going to forget all about that kind of stuff."

Jay had a bad attitude the whole service. The boys thought the place was cool, but Jay thought that crazy language the congregation was speaking sounded spooky, and he couldn't wait to leave. He didn't even hear the Word as it went forth because by then he was sound asleep. He had developed the ability to sleep with his eyes open to avoid his mother's nudges as a child.

"I'm awake," he said, alarmed when Zakia poked him because of an awesome revelation the pastor had just shared, which Jay had totally missed.

When the invitation was given, Zakia was waiting for Jay to answer the altar call. He did not move. He looked at his watch. *How can he not go up there? I want to go up there again.* She nudged him.

"Quit it," he snapped.

Zakia didn't understand why Jay wasn't affected like she was. They had always been in accord. They were a team and flowed in perfect harmony. Even when they argued and disagreed, they always found a compromise. This one should have been easy. It was the real deal that spoke for itself. Why couldn't Jay see it? As they walked to the car, she gave him the third degree.

"Why didn't you go up there?"

"For what?"

"Didn't you like it?"

"No."

"Why not?"

"Zakia, save it. We'll talk when we get home."

Nothing else was said on the drive home. When they got into the house, the boys went to their room to change clothes. As Jay and Zakia were in the master suite changing, he sensed her about to burst and decided to beat her to it.

"What the heck kind of church is that, and what was all that crazy talk, like you come busting up in the house last week talking?" he yelled.

"It's our power, baby. It stopped that officer from giving me a ticket."

"Bull! You probably batted your eyes at him like you did at me, and that's why he didn't give you a ticket."

"Now you're talking crazy."

"I'm serious. You think some crazy talk stopped a cop from giving you a ticket. Well, I think you sweet-talked your way out of it, but that's all right: use what you got to get what you want."

"Come on, Jay, be serious."

"I am serious. Now, look, you promised that if I didn't like it, you wouldn't bother me about going anymore. I didn't like it! Do you hear me? Now I expect you to keep your word and don't ask me to go back," he said with an adamant finality.

Zakia didn't know what to say, so she just grabbed her new Bible case with all of her material in it and went to the office downstairs to study the notes she had taken.

Zakia could not stay away from Faith in the Word Christian Center. It seemed that every time the doors opened she was there, whether it was for weekly Bible study or just to visit the bookstore during the day. The people were so full of genuine love for God and hunger for the Word, which was exactly what she needed to fill her void. The more she filled it, the more it needed filling. She read and prayed and read and prayed. She studied like she was in school, comparing line upon line and precept upon precept. She was neglecting her family, her work, and her house, and when she did pay attention, all she talked about was the Word, but nobody wanted to hear it. This frustrated both her and those she tried to talk to. The Execs avoided her because she was absolutely no fun anymore.

The Cowboys and Redskins were playing. The gang was at Zachary's house to play cards and watch the game on the big screen. Zakia still tried to hang out with her friends, and when they played cards, she would shout "Hallelujah" when she got a good hand and "Thank You, Jesus" when she won. She didn't realize that it made them uncomfortable. She didn't want to be a hypocrite, but she learned that she couldn't avoid those in darkness. She felt she needed to be around them so that her light could shine and draw them. After all, Jesus hung out with sinners.

"Hey, look. 'Jesus loves me, this I know, for the Bible tells me so.' You don't have to keep telling us, Z," Eli said, trying to shut her up.

"Yeah, chill, twin. You playing and praying all at the same time is messing up my concentration," Zachary admonished.

"You know, twin, if I were you, I'd get rid of that wicker furniture in your sunroom. Wicker is too close to wicked for me. You don't want anything evil in your house, now, do you?" Zakia asked sincerely.

"Now she's calling my furniture evil. Girl, I'm really beginning to worry about you," Zachary said.

"I thought you study to get smart. You done got dumb,

Z. You need to leave that Bible alone. It's making you crazy, baby," Eli said.

Zakia just ignored their insults and continued to pray for them.

Months passed, and to her family, Zakia was getting worse instead of better. She was alienating everybody who loved her in the name of getting them saved. She called out their sins and told them that their adultery, fornication, smoking, drinking, cursing, and gambling were going to land them in hell. Everyone avoided her except her sons. Zeke and JJ understood what she was saying. She took them to the eight o'clock service, leaving Jay behind. Eventually, she stopped going to Fig Tree Baptist altogether, not making it back from Faith in the Word in time, so Jay went alone.

Chapter Ten

Zakia joined the Faith in the Word mass choir. Her desire to be a part of the creation of such a wonderful atmosphere overwhelmed her. Rehearsal was only one day a week, which gave her time to take a Bible class or two. She was also considering joining the soul-winning ministry. Zakia was aware that her methods of leading folks to Christ had been less than effective, and she deeply desired to sharpen her skills. Fitting these new activities into her schedule, along with the boys' activities, became a real juggling act.

Because her zest for advertising had all but disappeared, she was missing a lot of time from work. She had been analyzing her family's portfolio and was seriously entertaining the thought of being a stay-at-home mom. Convincing Jay was the tricky part.

"Honey, I've been thinking. There is a lot going on. Our portfolio is stronger than ever. Our assets alone are generating enough income to cover our expenses, and the boys' college fund is working for us. I really feel this is a good time to be a stay-at-home mom."

"What about early retirement?" Jay asked.

"Have you looked at our investments lately? You should work for Wall Street, baby."

Knowing they had been very fortunate that his risk-taking had yielded high returns, he had no argument. "Are you sure you'll be fulfilled without your work?"

"Oh, I'm positive."

"I hope this does it for you, Zakia. I've been tolerant and patient with you. You have me going to church alone, and that's just not right. Maybe without so much on your mind you'll see clearly and come to your senses."

"Oh, thank you, baby," she said, hugging and kissing him. *Maybe I'll learn how to convince him that he's the one who needs to come to his senses about church,* she thought.

As much as Zakia planned to be home by not having to report to an office, all her extra time was spent at church. Jay was not pleased. While she was working, he had over-looked something he was used to having. His mother, having been a housewife all his life, was always there for her family, so he knew what to expect from a stay-at-home wife. He complained to Zakia that things were not working out as he expected. Zakia still wasn't home, her housekeeping didn't meet his expectations, and they still didn't talk to each other like they used to. They were speaking two different languages. He flat out refused to go back to Faith in the Word to learn this new language she was speaking, truly believing that everything was perfect before she found her new church.

It wasn't long before the Fig Tree Baptist women

noticed Jay attending church alone and began to speculate. His family was respected in the church, but that didn't stop the rumors. It was said that he and his wife were getting a divorce because Zakia had joined a cult. The women were lining up for when that rumor was confirmed.

"Good morning, Jay," one of the women sang in a sweet voice to match her big, bright smile as she approached him one day.

"Good morning," Jay said, returning her smile, not sure of her name.

"Is your wife doing okay? I haven't seen her in a while, and I didn't see her name on the sick and shut in list?"

"She's fine. Thank you for asking. Excuse me," Jay said, walking away to avoid any other inquiries about Zakia.

"Looking mighty sharp, Jay," said another woman as she moved in a little too close for Jay's comfort. She began to straighten his tie, causing him to take a step back.

"Thank you," he said, straightening the tie himself as he stepped around her and kept walking to the finance room.

Jay served on the finance committee of Fig Tree Baptist because of his business savvy.

One evening Jay attended a meeting held at the home of the finance secretary. After the meeting was adjourned, she asked Jay if he could stay a while longer to give her some personal investment advice. Jay couldn't resist the stock game and obliged. She gave him the prospectus of a company in which she was considering investing.

"No, no, no. This company will fold before the year is out," Jay said.

"Oh my. I would have lost everything."

"Call me before you do anything in the future."

"You bet I will."

And she did. Jessica called him often, at work initially, since it was supposedly about business. Then she started calling at home. Zakia didn't notice. She was deep into her Bible classes, ministry meetings, and choir rehearsals. She was always at the church, which gave Jay more time to provide investment advice to Jessica.

When Jay got home after work, he would invariably smell nothing cooking. Nobody was ever home. One evening he called Alexis.

"Mamalexis, do you know where my family is?"

"They're not here. Did you call the church?"

"You know, this is getting old. I thought Zakia would have snapped out of it by now."

"Maybe it's the real thing. I mean, I went over there to check it out. If my child had been lured into some cult, I would have promptly blown the whole building up, then turned myself in," Alexis said.

"So what did you think?" Jay asked.

"Well, what was being preached was the truth, and one thing about my child, she was always in search of the truth. The real deal. She always had that need to know."

"Yeah, well, she doesn't act like she needs to know how *I* feel."

"She'll come around. I talked to one of the counselors, who told me that new born-again baby Christians are so excited about the newfound things of God that they sometimes throw caution to the wind, believing God has their back, and go out to single-handedly save the world. It made sense and described Zakia perfectly. I decided not to blow the building up," Alexis explained.

"If you say so. Thanks, Mamalexis."

"Sure, baby. Hang in there."

"I'm trying."

Jay continued to give after-hours financial advice to Jessica, who followed through on one of Jay's tips and received a windfall that was beyond her imagination. She insisted that Jay come to her house to help her celebrate.

"Thank you so much!" she said, hugging and squeezing him with excitement when he arrived at her apartment.

"You're quite welcome," he said as he received her gratitude.

The hug lasted a little longer than their usual Christian embraces. Jessica finally pulled away, appearing shy, causing Jay to feel like he had made her uncomfortable.

"So did you take your own investment advice?" she asked as she led him to the sofa.

"What kind of investor do you think I am? Of course I did."

"How'd you do?"

"I doubled what you did."

"Oh, Jay!" she exclaimed as she gave him a big hug and a kiss on the cheek. "I'll get the champagne. We have to toast your brilliance," she said, going into the kitchen.

"Let me help you," Jay said, feeling good to be needed.

As they drank champagne, they talked about how to reinvest. Jay was becoming very comfortable, and after so much champagne, he began to imagine that Jessica was Zakia.

"This is it, the last of the champagne," Jessica said, emptying the bottle evenly into both of their glasses.

They held up the glasses, toasted, and sipped the remaining champagne as she looked deep into his eyes, drawing him into her. He moved closer to her, and she met him with a long, deep kiss. Jay imagined his wife as they removed their clothes and made love.

When he woke up hours later, groggy from all the champagne, he was very remorseful about what had happened. He thought he had taken advantage of Jessica.

Things were exactly the same between Jay and Zakia. He started feeling less and less guilty about his infidelity . . . until Jessica called Jay at work three weeks later and informed him that he was going to be a daddy.

"I don't expect anything from you, Jay, but I do plan to have my baby and raise him or her in the church. You have been wonderful, and thanks to you, I am doing fine financially. We'll be fine."

"I wouldn't turn my back on a child of mine, Jessica. Give me some time to figure things out."

"Of course, darling. Take all the time you need."

That evening Jay decided to tell his wife everything. Zakia was brushing her teeth when Jay came into their bedroom and stuck his head in the bathroom.

"We need to talk when you're done," he said.

"Okay," Zakia responded with a mouthful of toothpaste. She rinsed and spat, then came into the room wiping her mouth with a hand towel.

Jay was sitting on the side of the bed and patted the spot beside him for her to sit down. Zakia was relieved that Jay didn't appear to be upset with her for again not cooking dinner. She thought he probably grabbed something on his way home from work, which was why he was late. He had stopped complaining about a full-course meal not being ready every day, so he was probably eating out more often, having figured out that she wasn't the housewife type. That was good. Less pressure on her.

"Zakia, Jessica is pregnant."

"Who?"

"Jessica Stone. She's the finance secretary at Fig Tree Baptist."

"So?"

"It's mine."

The revelation that he was having an affair sent her into a state of shock. She froze as thoughts of Ezekiel's daddy, Malik, and his cheating ran through her mind. She was numb and couldn't speak, so Jay continued.

"You are obsessed with the church, neglecting me and your family, alienating your friends," Jay said. "Is that the kind of God you want to serve, one who makes you lose everything important in your life?"

Shock turned to rage. She mustered all the strength she had to speak.

"Get out," she managed to say without bursting into tears.

It only took him minutes to pack a few things. He left her sitting on the bed still in shock.

Chapter Eleven

God, how? Why? Where did I go wrong? I obeyed Your Word. I believed You. I don't understand. What is going on?" Zakia cried out.

She felt nothing, heard nothing. She was numb. She must have missed something, but she was too depressed to find out what it was. She just lay in her bed feeling betrayed. Jay's words rang in her ears, "Is that the kind of God you want to serve, one who makes you lose everything important in your life?" Jay's question caused her to think hard for the first time in a long while. Her family had been treating her differently, like she was strange. Her friends seemed to always be irritated with her. She began to question her actions, her faith, and her life. Her mind wandered, she lost focus, and she felt drained.

The next day, Jay called Alexis and confessed everything, making sure Zakia was getting the support she needed. Upon learning that Jay had moved out, Alexis immediately went to console her daughter.

"You need time, baby. Just trust the fact that you have

everything already on the inside of you that you need to make the right decisions."

"I do need to figure things out."

"Do you want me to take the boys home with me?"

"Would you?"

"Of course. You just get yourself together and figure out what you're going to do."

A few days later, Zakia was still down. She heard the phone ring but allowed the answering machine to pick up.

"When you hear the beep, you know what to do. And remember, God loves you and we do too," the machine said.

"Z! Pick up. I know you're there. Pick up, sis. It's me, Raquie," she said.

Zakia reached from under the covers and picked up the phone. "Yeah," she said in a dry, lazy voice.

"Hey, sis, what it be like?" Raquie said cheerfully.

"It be like nothing with me, what it be like with you?" was Zakia's lifeless response.

"Mamalexis told me about Jay. You okay?"

"No, I'm not okay."

"Do you need me to come home?" she asked. Shortly after graduating summa cum laude from Manna, Raquie had taken a job in New York.

"Naw, baby, there's nothing you can do. I just need to sort through some things."

"Well, you do whatever you have to do. You want to talk about it?"

"I'm just confused. Jay said something before he left that made sense, and now I don't know anymore."

"What did he say?"

"He asked me if I wanted to serve a God that makes you lose everything important in your life."

"Wow. That's deep."

"My whole life doesn't make sense anymore. Maybe I should go back to work. I need to keep busy to fight these negative emotions, but I don't want to see people. I don't know anything anymore."

"You can do both, you know."

"Both what?"

"Go back to work and not see people."

"How?"

"The Internet. Lots of people are doing it."

"Been there, done that."

"Yeah, but you still had an office downtown and you saw those people. They knew you and you knew them. I'm talking about no physical contact at all. And in this buck-wild, very exciting entertainment industry."

"Go on."

"I contract with webmasters, graphic designers, online hosts, and distributors that I've never met. And there's plenty of work available, especially for somebody with your expertise. Right now I'm working on landing this contract to create a Web site for Jazz Jafari. Ever heard of him?"

"Yeah, I've heard of him. I like his sound."

"Well, that brother needs a fresh cyberpresence like yesterday, and I'm going after it. I could probably use your help with the proposal. If I could say I have the top advertising executive in the state of Virginia waiting to work with Jazz, that might put me over the top. What do you say?"

"You know I'm here for you if you need me. Besides, I probably need to step away from what's happening here and be productive elsewhere until I figure things out."

"That's what I was thinking. It's all about what's best for you, sis."

"I've been away from the game for a while now."

"Hey, it's like riding a bike. And the fact that all your market research and reports will be done online in the comfort of your own home, you can call your own shots. However you want to work it, sis. You're the pro."

"Sounds intriguing. What the heck? I'm in."

"Are you sure? Don't feel obligated. I can always get it done. I just want you all right."

"No, this will be fun. Send me whatever you have on Jazz, and I'll start my research."

"See, you're going to be fine, sis. You're the best, and you only deserve the best."

"You're just biased, but thanks anyway. Love you, baby."

"Love you too."

Raquie sent a package overnight. Zakia logged on to the Internet and went to some sites her sister had recommended. She was paying particular attention to the graphics and making notes about traffic.

As part of her research Zakia thought about interacting directly with the market by participating on the message boards and chat rooms to find out exactly what the fans were willing to pay for and how much.

She read some of the fan messages to Raquie's other celebrity clients and noted how personal and confusing it got. They were very creative, though. Posters were actually arguing and cussing each other out about certain entertainers. They even had cyberparties, complete with food and decorations described in their posts right down to the smallest detail.

Zakia was totally absorbed in the Internet until around

three o'clock in the morning, when she got up from the computer to go to the bathroom and noticed the time.

"Dang, it's that late? Let me log off and get some rest."

The next morning Zakia was back in cyberspace, surfing the Net. She was on there all day. This means of escape was working to some degree because she wasn't hurting as bad. Raquie called that evening.

"Hello." Zakia answered the phone only semi-depressed.

"That's not much better than yesterday. Did you get on the Internet?" Raquie asked.

"Yep, wild stuff, but with the information you sent me and the stuff I found online, I have some good ideas for a proposal."

"That's great. So you're really in?"

"Yeah, why not?"

"I'm so glad to hear that, Z, because I was going to try something that I would only try with you."

"Like what?" she asked, intrigued.

"I'm going to a party tonight, and Jazz Jafari is going to be there. I was going to really build you up and suggest that he call you so you can work your magic on him. He should call you so it will be at his convenience and you won't have to deal with trying to get through to him. If we can get him on our side, he can help us get past that brick-wall manager of his."

"His manager's tough, huh?"

"You know how those gay perfectionists are. He represents a lot of the up-and-coming artists and has a rep for being difficult to work with."

"I know the type."

"I know you do. So that's the plan. Get Jazz Jafari on our side."

"You work it on your end, and I'll work it on mine."

Zakia turned on the computer and found a jazz message board where posters were discussing Jazz Jafari. She decided to make up a screen name and join the chat, but that would have to wait until the next day because she had choir rehearsal. When she looked at the clock, she saw that she was more than an hour late. She decided not to go. She stayed home and did some more research until late into the night. She needed a concept to ensure that she got the information she needed from the posters on the message board. While she was strategizing, the phone rang.

"Hello," she answered.

"Hello, may I speak with Zakia Carter?" a beautiful, smooth, sensuous male voice said.

Zakia took the phone from her ear and looked at it. Then she put it back to her ear and said, "Speaking."

"This is Jazz Jafari."

"Well, hello, Mr. Jafari."

"Your sister said that you would be expecting my call."

"I was definitely looking forward to it."

"She tells me that you're an advertising guru."

"When I'm done, they'll be playing your music everywhere, including the grocery stores to the truck stops to the elevators."

He laughed. "I'm impressed. Maybe you should talk to my manager."

"If you can set up a meeting, my sister will be happy to meet with your manager. With an agreement between them, I can come in with all of my ideas."

"I'll set it up."

"That would be great."

Chapter Twelve

Zakia broke a nail dialing her sister's number.

"Hel—"

"Raquie! Get ready, girl. I talked to Jazz Jafari, and he's going to set up a meeting between you and his manager."

"Way to work it, sis."

"You had already set him up. I didn't even say that much. Now you have to go in for the kill."

"Is that teamwork or what?"

"We've always been in sync like that. I know you're going to land that account, so I'm going to tighten up my part of the proposal," Zakia said.

"You know, I hadn't considered working with you seriously before this, but we might have something here," Raquie said.

"Indeed we might, little sis. Indeed we might."

Zakia suffered from tunnel vision. She hadn't been to church since Jay left three weeks ago. What he had said about losing everything still bothered her. She had lost a great deal, and until she could make some sense out of it all, she wouldn't go back to Faith in the Word. She still had her tapes, her Bible, and her notes, but because being there had contributed to her loss, she didn't want to go back. A choir member called to make sure she was all right.

"Hello, Sister Zakia. This is Sister Cheryl. We haven't seen you at church lately. That's not like you. Is everything all right?"

"Everything's fine, Sister Cheryl. I have to take a break for a while. I'll call the church and let them know so they won't worry about me."

"Sure, honey. Is there anything we can do?"

"Just continue to pray for me."

"Sure will, sister."

"Thanks, Sister Cheryl. Stay blessed."

With no family, job, or church activities in her life, Zakia turned all of her attention to helping Raquie get the Jazz Jafari account. She came up with the screen name Jazmania. She logged on to the Internet, clicked on the link to the jazz site in her favorite places, and read to see what was going on. A poster by the name of Keystroker had just posted.

Keystroker: has anybody found anything on jazz jafari?

Sexyphone: Nothing. All I found was his label's site, Milli Records, and all they have is how you can order his CD, but no details on him. I just don't get it.

Keystroker: how can he not have a web site? how are we supposed to know all of his personal business?

Sexyphone: Maybe he's working on it.

Keystroker: they need to hurry up. i want to know is he married? does he have children? where's he from? what's his favorite color?

Sexyphone: Does he have any pets? Is he going on tour? We wanna know!

Perfect timing for Jazmania to make her debut post.

Jazmania: Hello, everyone.

Sexyphone: Hello, Jazmania. Welcome to the board.

Keystroker: hey, jazmania. I like your name. are you male or female?

Jazmania: Female, and I like your name too. I've been reading your posts for the last couple of days. I find you all very fascinating.

Keystroker: thanks. so what brings you here?

Jazmania: I see you guys have a lot of questions about Jazz Jafari. I may be able to get some answers for you.

Keystroker: yeah? how you gonna do that?

Jazmania: His management is working on his cyberpresence. He should have his own Web site in the near future. I'm a part of his development team. I came here to see what the fans want so that we can give it to you.

Keystroker: are you for real?

Jazmania: I kid you not. I talked to him yesterday. I'm preparing a report for his Web site designer. If you guys let me know what you want to see, we can work to get it up on his Web site.

Keystroker: is he married?

Jazmania: You can click on my profile and e-mail me all of your questions. I'll do my best to get you answers.

Sexyphone: See, she's lying. She doesn't know Jazz Jafari.

Jazmania: I have no reason to lie. If I answer one question, I'll have to answer them all. If I get all the questions at once, we can put all the answers to your questions up on his Web site so that all of his fans who may not be logged on right now can see.

Zakia was thrilled to have so many e-mails. They were all very positive, with lots of questions, comments, and suggestions. She added all of the new information to the proposal and sent it overnight to Raquie. This deal was all but sealed. She called Raquie to tell her to be on the lookout for the package and to get an update.

"Hey, sis, have you heard anything from the Jazz Jafari camp?"

"As a matter of fact, I have. His manager left a message just today. Said Jazz himself recommended me to begin promoting him on the Internet."

"Get outta here. Have you talked to him yet?"

"Not yet."

"Oh, that's good. I'll e-mail you my part of the proposal to look at before you talk with him. You'll have the entire package tomorrow so that you can really impress him when you meet."

"Wow. You've been busy."

"Yeah. I like interacting with the posters. Tell his manager I could host a chat between Jazz and his fans. He can be there to observe."

"Yeah, a chat on his Web site that we design. That should run up the number of hits on his site."

"I told you we were in sync."

Chapter Thirteen

Zakia was thrilled when she learned Raquie had landed the Jazz Jafari deal. She immediately e-mailed the marketing information to Jazz as Raquie had requested. She continued logging on to the message boards in an effort to gain more insight into what Jazz's fans wanted. One day while she was online, she received an unfamiliar e-mail.

HELLO ZAKIA DARLING. I HAVE BEEN ADMIRING YOU FOR MANY YEARS. I THINK IT'S TIME WE GOT TOGETHER. PLEASE RESPOND IF YOU ARE INTERESTED.

Zakia, not recognizing the e-mail address, read it and thought it was a joke. She responded: VERY FUNNY. YOU FORGOT TO SIGN YOUR NAME.

YOU KNOW MY NAME, MISS THANG. SO HOW IS MALIK? was the response.

Zakia was shocked. She sensed the tone of the e-mail, and it was not a funny one. She decided not to reply. But the e-mails kept coming.

Zakia was getting very uncomfortable with cyberspace. She thought it was one of Malik's women from college who had discovered her e-mail address. That had to be it. Why would someone keep bringing up Malik? She hadn't seen him in years. It was disconcerting to have a cyberstranger know her personal business. She tried to dismiss the e-mailer as some lonely, deranged woman who needed a life.

Then the e-mail arrived that stopped her world cold:

IF EZEKIEL IS AS FINE AS HIS DADDY, I AM GOING TO MAKE HIM THE MOST BEAUTIFUL DRAG QUEEN ANYONE HAS EVER LAID EYES ON.

Zakia went straight to Alexis's house and got Zeke and JJ. She didn't mention anything about the e-mails because she knew her family would think she was just on another trip. She was through with the Internet. Raquie and her team could handle Jazz's Web site without her.

Over coffee at Alexis's kitchen table, Zakia assured her mother that she was ready to take the boys home and get on with life.

"Ma, this world is so crazy. It's hard to know what to believe anymore. You've always been there for me and raised me the best way you knew how. I love and appreciate you for that. But now I'm responsible for my life and my children's lives until they're grown. Studying God's Word has taught me a lot, and I have to get back to that while showing the boys how to get what they need from the Word of God," Zakia explained.

"I agree with you there, baby. This world is crazy and out of control, not at all like when I was growing up. I went to church on Sundays, not on weekdays, so I sent you and your brother to Sunday school. I was not taught or even encouraged to study God's Word to get what I needed. I was taught by my mother, who worked cleaning white folks' toilets to support her children because our whoremongering daddy wouldn't. She taught me to work hard for what I wanted and needed."

"Is that why you were always on our daddy to support us, because Granddaddy didn't support his children?"

"He helped make you, then he was going to help take care of you. My mother was cold, hard, and bitter, having to do it all herself. I was in some ways similar and did not want that for you, but I didn't know how to show you anything different."

"You did your best, Ma. Now I have to do my best for myself and the boys. I wasn't upset that I slept with Malik and had Zeke out of wedlock because it was against the Word of God. I was upset because getting pregnant messed up my career plans."

"I couldn't give you what I didn't have, baby. All I knew is what I saw. I did eventually forgive your dad for Raquie when I saw how close you girls would always be. Someday you'll have to forgive Malik," Alexis said.

"I have, Ma. I *know* better now, so I have to *do* better. Studying gives me satisfaction, the kind that helps me to let go of anything negative. Nothing I've done in my life has made me feel I was doing the right thing as when I was studying the Word."

"If you want your family and marriage, then you have to do more than study. You have to work—and I mean work hard—for it," Alexis advised her daughter. "And don't forget, it was all that studying God's Word that got you in this situation in the first place."

"I know, Ma. That's why I have to keep studying. I was on to something when my marriage came under attack. That tells me that the enemy was trying to distract me from what I was doing. And he did in a big way. That, or God allowed it to happen so I could realize that balance really is the key to life. The more I learn, I find out just how ignorant I am. It's amazing that the more studying I do, the dumber I feel because I realize just how much I don't know."

"I do know that the devil is busy and that too much of a good thing can be just as devastating as too much of a bad thing," Alexis said.

"See, Ma, that's what I'm trying to do. Take the common sense you've given me, add some Bible sense, and make some sense out of my life."

Her mother believed her and gave her an encouraging hug.

"Pack it up, boys. Let's go home. I miss my men. I'm one man down, but the two I have left are the best two ever made," Zakia said exuberantly. She wanted to pull what was left of her family together and establish a firmer foundation on which to continue raising her sons, regardless of the outcome of her marriage. The stalker's e-mails had also made her want to keep them close, tucked safely under her protective wing.

Zakia was distracted and busy with the boys during the day, but the thoughts about the e-mails continued to haunt her at night. At first, she'd been sure it was one of Malik's college women, but how could any of them know the name of their son, since she had him after graduation and in another state? She didn't know what to think. How could she trace an e-mail to its original sender?

Mentioning the stalker's e-mails to her family, even

to Raquie, would make her seem paranoid, but the fact of the matter still remained. This stalker had threatened her child in a horrible way, and it was not in her nature to take something that serious lightly.

Zakia and her sons were inseparable except when the boys were at school or with Jay at his parents' home. When she didn't have the boys, she was preoccupied with the stalker's e-mail. She wanted to find out who knew about her and Malik and especially about Zeke. She contacted a local Internet company that she found in the yellow pages and made arrangements to take the printed e-mails in to have them analyzed.

Upon arrival for her appointment at CySpace Masters, the receptionist had her wait while she called for one of the consultants to come assist her. Zakia was seated in the lobby when the elevator doors opened, and she looked up when she heard, "Ms. Carter?"

She was stunned to see her old high school sweetheart. "Xavier Slade," she said. "I heard that you were in California. What in the world are you doing here?"

"Zakia Wilkes. Oh, excuse me. Zakia Carter now. Look at you," he said, taking all of her in at a glance. "I see life has been good to you."

"You look good yourself," she said. "Are you the consultant?"

"At your service."

She felt sort of relieved thinking that since he wasn't a total stranger, he would be more sensitive to her dilemma and do a better job of helping her find the culprit.

"Good. I have a serious problem," she said.

"Well, come on up to my office and tell me all about it."

She followed him into the elevator. As they ascended, he asked about the Execs. They talked about old times and continued to bring each other up-to-date in his office. Much time passed before she mentioned a word about the e-mails. Zakia felt comfortable enough to let him know that she was separated from her husband, and she noticed his caring concern. That made her even more comfortable about sharing the e-mails.

"Well, the reason why I'm here is to find out about these e-mails," she said as her stomach growled. "Excuse me. I skipped breakfast."

"Well, it's almost noon. Let me treat you, and we can discuss the e-mails over lunch . . . unless you have another commitment," Xavier said.

"We can do that. I am kind of hungry."

They went to a cafeteria-style restaurant near Xavier's office building. Nothing was said in line as they contemplated which items to select. Once they were seated, they had a nice time but still didn't discuss the e-mails. Zakia felt herself opening up more. She learned that Dana, the girl Xavier cheated with, was now living in California and was married with two more children besides Xavier's daughter.

"Not that it's any of your business, Xavier, but my sons have different fathers. I just thought I'd share that to let you know I now understand how what happened in high school between us happened. Life teaches you a few things if you live long enough. No hard feelings," she said, sticking out her hand for him to shake.

"Wow! You never gave me an opportunity to explain, just wrote me off, then shipped off to college, and that was that. I always wanted to talk to you about it but figured you were gone forever. Now here you are, more than twenty years later and looking the same," he said.

"Nowhere near the same, but thanks for the compliment."

They finished lunch and went back to Xavier's office. Finally, they got to the business at hand. As Zakia explained the whole ordeal, they ruled out any of Jazz Jafari's fans. Even though they had her e-mail address, there was no connection between Zakia and Jazmania. Xavier kept copies of the printed e-mails and instructed her to forward a few of them to his e-mail address for further analysis. She agreed, and their meeting was over. He walked her all the way to her car.

"I'll call you as soon as I have an answer," he said.

"Thanks, Xavier. I really want to get to the bottom of this as soon as possible."

"I understand. Soon, I promise."

Xavier and Zakia talked on the phone every day, with Xavier assuring her that they were getting close to finding the culprit. Then the conversation would turn personal. He asked to take her out, but she wouldn't go out with him because she was married and couldn't date, even though her husband had impregnated some woman from church. Xavier was becoming a great friend to talk to, though, and Zakia was becoming his social dependent. One day he asked her if she had received any more e-mails from the stalker. When she checked, she had several that horrified her with their sordid homosexual details involving her son. She printed them and went straight to Xavier's office in tears.

She hadn't been to church in so long that her senses were beginning to dull. Her antennas needed some tuning. Xavier said he had some special equipment at home that might help him to determine the e-mails' origin and suggested she accompany him so they could get to the bottom of the problem. She rode with him.

In his apartment, she was a nervous wreck.

"Relax, Z. We'll figure it out. Here, sit down at the computer," he said, then pulled up a chair and sat beside her.

He started to rub her back, and it felt good to her. She began to relax and closed her eyes. He pulled up even closer, and she smelled his intoxicating cologne. He began to talk in computer language she didn't understand, and it made her head ache, forcing her to focus on the attraction between them instead.

"See the return path and the user agent identification gives us an indication, but not precisely of the e-mails' origin," he said, noticing that she wasn't paying attention. He began to massage her shoulders.

"Oh, baby, you are so tense," he said.

Feeling the stress leaving her body at his touch, Zakia closed her eyes and enjoyed the massage. He rubbed her shoulders and neck. He started at the top and went all the way down her back and then up again. It was nothing less than erotic. She was quietly moaning. When he kissed her on the lips, she snapped open her eyes and slapped him as hard as she could.

He jumped up, grabbing at his face.

"I'm sorry, Zakia. I shouldn't have done that. You are just so beautiful."

"Take me back to my car."

Not a word was said all the way back to his office, where he let her out beside her car. She got in and sped off not knowing whom she could trust.

Chapter Fourteen

Zakia went back to Faith in the Word. That was the only place she felt safe anymore. She did not get involved again with any of the ministries. She just sat up under the Word and fed her spirit the wisdom of God as she took inventory of her life.

She no longer allowed fear to drive her to take matters into her own hands as she prayed for resolution to the stalker issue. She would let God handle it. After she let go of the situation, Xavier left a message informing her that he had e-mailed her the stalker information she was seeking. Zakia sent it to Raquie, explaining the whole ordeal for her to investigate further. She was spent and resolved to simply trust God. Her sister promised to use her Internet resources to resolve the matter.

Zakia had been sick every morning for a week and could no longer avoid the inevitable. She scheduled an appointment with her gynecologist to confirm what she had expected for the past few weeks. She was three months pregnant. She knew she was, but with Jay's infidelity along with everything else that was going on in her life, she chose not to face it until she had to. The time had come. She called Jay at his parents' home and asked him to come over.

"I'm three months pregnant," she said.

"What? That's great!"

"Great for who?"

"For us."

"What are you talking about? You have two women pregnant at the same time. How can that be great for anybody?"

"That's what I was going to tell you. Jessica lied. She isn't pregnant. Never was."

"Does that change the fact that you slept with her?"

Jay hadn't even thought of it that way because he was so relieved that Jessica wasn't pregnant.

"No, but now we have a second chance. We can make it work. Make it better than before."

"Do you really believe life is that simple, Jay?"

"It can be, Zakia, if we put the effort back into it like we used to."

"Jay, there is no excuse for what you did to us. I accept responsibility for neglecting my family, but I cannot get over the fact that you showed no remorse about sleeping with someone else. I moved on with my life without you at that point."

"I was a complete jerk, baby. Totally confused. I know you can forgive me. Look at all that we have, and now we have a baby on the way."

"You will always be in your children's lives, but I don't need you."

"But, baby . . ."

"Please leave. I'm tired."

Jay left not knowing what his wife was actually going to do. He would just have to follow her lead.

Zakia woke up refreshed from a good night's sleep. There wasn't even any morning sickness. She felt better than she had in a long time. Now that Jay had been told, she would plan her future without him. She got the portfolio and began to analyze her financial status. They were in great financial shape. Even without Jay, she didn't have to go out and get a job if she opted not to. After working with Raquie on the Jafari proposal, she had found yet another avenue to generate income and still be there for her sons. God was providing.

As Zakia worked her plan, she studied and prayed without ceasing. She grew with God as deeper and deeper revelation came. She was maturing in the things of God, and her life was becoming more balanced. Realizing from her own experiences as a sold-out-for-Jesus Christian that temptation was forever present and anybody could fall—real saved folks as well as unsaved folks—she became more tolerant of others. As a result, her friends came back, spending more and more time with her. Through no effort of her own, the Word of God always seemed to pop up in their conversations. Most of the time it was her friends who brought it up. One day Eli and Eboni stopped by to bring her some Heavenly Hash ice cream.

"Oh, thank you so much. I was craving this stuff so bad," Zakia said, ripping off the top of the carton and eating right out of the quart container.

"I told you we should have gotten a half gallon, you

talking about her weight," Eli said to Eboni, watching Zakia go for it.

"You were right, baby," Eboni said. "Oh, guess what, Z?"

"What?" Zakia said with a mouthful of nuts, chocolate chips, marshmallow, and chocolate ice cream.

"Tell her, baby," Eboni instructed Eli.

"She's making me legal," Eli said as Eboni held out her hand to show Zakia her engagement ring.

Zakia stopped eating and started screaming. She put down the ice cream and hugged Eboni, both of them screaming and jumping around.

"I don't know why you're making all that fuss. By law, we been married," Eli said.

"Please come to church with me," Zakia begged.

"Okay, baby?" Eboni asked Eli.

"Why not? I'm hooked now. Whatever you ladies want," Eli surrendered.

Zakia and Eboni screamed again.

She was leading them one by one to Christ.

Zakia was rubbing her stomach and folding clothes when Raquie called.

"Sis, did you know Melvin Hickman in college?"

"No, I don't think so," Zakia answered. With so much going on in her life, she only recalled recent places, people, and events.

"Are you sure?"

"Yeah, why? Who is he?"

"He's the stalker who's been sending you e-mails."

"Melvin Hickman," she said as she tried to recall everyone she had met in her life. "Oh, wait a minute,

Melvin Hickman!" she shouted when the revelation hit her.

"So you do know him?" Raquie asked.

"He was Malik's college roommate."

"Now, that would be interesting. He's Jazz Jafari's manager."

"What?" Zakia said, stunned.

"Have you gotten any more e-mails?" Raquie asked.

"Girl, I closed the account. The whole thing was threatening my existence. I was worried and paranoid all the time. I couldn't put all that stress on my unborn child. I gave it to you and God to handle. But it can't be the same guy."

"He went to Manna. It's him. I'm glad you came to me. You can only trust who you can trust."

"Yeah, I learned that the hard way. When I let God handle it and He told me to give it to you, I've had peace ever since."

"Well, God handled it. It took a while, but we finally came up with Melvin Hickman. He was slick enough not to make it easy by any means, but his patterns led us to him."

"Has he been confronted?"

"Not yet. I wanted to see if you knew him first to determine if there was a reason for his behavior, or if you were a randomly chosen victim. Do you have any idea why he would be sending you such e-mails?"

"For kicks? I don't know. Actually, we didn't have much to say to each other the whole time that we were in college. He seemed to have something against me, but a few people did, so I didn't pay it any attention. College was totally different from high school for me. Popularity was not important. Getting prepared for the real world was my top priority, so I dismissed Melvin and anybody else who didn't like me. That was their problem," Zakia explained.

"What got me suspicious of Melvin is that after all that work was done on Jazz's Web site, he canceled the contract. We never got a dime for all that work, and I couldn't understand why. I finally talked to Jazz about it, and all he could tell me was his manager insisted that they go with somebody else. He said Melvin insisted that he concentrate on the music and let him do his job," Raquie said.

"Really?"

"And get this. Jazz said that AIDS must be affecting Melvin's mind."

"AIDS?"

"Yep."

"He has it?"

"That's what Jazz said. Was he gay in college?"

"Girl, Malik would never have a gay roommate."

"Are you sure?"

"Stop tripping me out."

"When is the last time you talked to Malik? Do you know what he's been up to all these years? Apparently, Melvin was popular in the gay world."

"Raquie, girl, there is not a gay bone in Malik's body."

"I say we find out for sure. Can you handle it, with the baby and all?"

"Now I have to know."

"How can we find him?"

"The last point of contact I had with him was when I found out I was pregnant with Zeke. That was twelve years ago."

"I know Mamalexis had his contact information because he called all the time asking about Zeke, but you were so adamant about him not being in your lives we finally convinced him to go on with his," Raquie said.

"Well, I have to know now. I'm going to see if I can find him."

"Oh, now, if anybody will find him, you will. In the meantime, what shall we do about Melvin?"

"Let me find Malik first."

"Cool. I won't make a move until I hear from you."

Zakia hung up, then called her mother.

"Ma, do you have a number for Malik?"

"Somewhere, why?"

"I have to get in contact with him."

"Why? Is it Zeke? Has he been in an accident? Does he need blood?"

"No, Ma, nothing like that."

"Then why do you need to contact him? You finally come to your senses after all this time that a boy should know his natural father?"

"Something like that. Can I get the number, please?"

"I'll call you back. I have to look for it."

"Thanks, Ma."

Ten minutes later, Alexis called Zakia back.

"I have the number for you, and just so you'll know, I have kept in contact with Malik over the years. The man was interested in his son, so I kept him up-to-date. I didn't tell him your personal business, just that you were fine. He's married with one daughter, and he still lives in Baltimore. I hope you can work it out so that Zeke can get to know his father. There was never a good time to bring this subject up, but since you're calling him, maybe now is the time," Alexis said.

Whew! I knew he wasn't gay. He can't be, with a wife and child, Zakia thought.

"Thanks, Ma. Maybe you're right."

Zakia called and talked to Malik for the first time since she slammed the door in his face.

"Hello," Malik answered.

"Hello, Malik. This is Zakia," she said very professionally.

"Well, hello. How are you?" he responded, not hiding his excitement.

"Fine, and you?" she responded, still professionally.

"Fine. How's my son?" he asked.

"Ezekiel is great."

For a moment, Malik was silent. "Does he know about me?" he asked quietly.

"We haven't talked about you, but maybe it's time we did."

"Past time. I want to meet him."

"That can be arranged."

"When?"

"Let me talk to him, and I'll get back with you."

"Great!"

"Ma told me you were married with a daughter."

"Yeah, it finally hit me that I had blown it with you, so I moved on."

"You ever tried the gay thing?"

"What? What did you say?"

"I think you heard me."

"Heck no. Why would you ask me something like that? Wait a minute. Zeke isn't gay, is he?"

"No! That's not it at all."

"Then where did that come from?"

"Okay. It's a long story, and I may tell you more about it someday, but the bottom line is Raquie and I think Melvin Hickman, your old college roommate, is gay and has been stalking me on the Internet."

"Oh wow!" Malik said, but not totally shocked, as Zakia had expected him to be.

"What? You sound like you know something about this. You better tell me. If it's him, he has threatened Zeke, to turn him into a drag queen, and all sorts of sick stuff. What do you know about that pervert?"

"If he comes near my son, I will break him in half. Zakia, I had no idea. He kept it hidden all through college. All I knew was that he was a good athlete. He had a few women. He was just quiet and sensitive and serious about school, like you, so I had no reason to suspect anything like that. You know we continued to be roommates after we graduated. He was really there for me when you cut me out of your life. I really loved you, and that's when he let me know that he was gay and that we should be together. I just about threw up on him. I went off and told him to stay away from me. That psycho blamed you for coming between him and me. How can you be friends with something as sick as that? I haven't seen him since."

Taking it all in, the picture was becoming clearer in Zakia's mind.

"Well, Raquie has all the evidence that he is the one sending me the threatening e-mails. He doesn't know that we know yet. I told her not to confront him until I talked to you. I'm glad I did. Now what are we going to do?"

"We are going to confront him. Where is he?"

"He's in New York City, and Raquie said he has AIDS."

"Awww man." Malik paused. "Well, dang. What do you expect? We have to confront him."

"When can you go to New York?" Zakia asked.

"Whenever."

"Let me fill Raquie in and get back to you."

"Okay. We'll get it straightened out, then I can have a relationship with my son."

Chapter Fifteen

Zakia flew to New York the day before they were to confront Melvin. Malik was driving up the next morning. They were to meet at Raquie's office.

Zakia and Raquie were there when Malik arrived. When he saw Zakia, he grabbed her and hugged her for a long time. She hugged him back, feeling nothing but warm and caring friendship coming from him.

"Congratulations," Malik said, referring to her pregnancy.

"Thank you," Zakia said.

"When are you due?"

"Soon, so we have to get this resolved," she said.

Zakia and Raquie filled him in on the turn of events.

"When we called Melvin's office to make sure he was in before we went over there, we were informed that he was in the hospital," Raquie explained.

"Hospital?" Malik responded.

"Yeah. He has full-blown advanced AIDS," Zakia said.

"Well, then we'll confront him at the hospital," Malik stated.

Zakia and Raquie looked at him, pleased that he wasn't deterred. They were all in agreement that Melvin needed to be confronted. They all felt that he shouldn't die thinking that he got away with something.

Malik, Zakia, and Raquie took a taxi to the hospital. When they entered Melvin's room, he was alone, dozing.

"Melvin, wake up," Malik said.

Melvin opened his eyes and saw Malik. He smiled.

"I knew you'd come. I knew you loved me," he said.

"Oh heck no. It ain't even like that, Melvin. Never was. I thought I made that clear the last time we talked."

"Then why are you here?" Melvin asked.

"Hi, Melvin. Remember me?" Zakia asked, stepping into his view.

"Who are you?" he asked.

"Hi, Melvin. How's Jazz's Web site going?" Raquie asked.

"What do you want?" Melvin asked, trying to maintain his composure.

"You've been stalking me on the Internet. You threatened my child, and I want to know why," Zakia said.

"Why?" he asked. "I don't know what you're talking about."

"Save it, Melvin," Malik said. "You don't have to admit it. We just didn't want you to die thinking you got away with anything. We know all about your gay lifestyle. Heck, we're looking at it right now. You have no power. You think because you won't admit it, that gives you some power? Are you trying to get in one last dig before you croak? Good thing you're dying, or I would kill you for threatening my son. But looks like that's already been taken care of, right, Melvin? How powerful are you feeling now?"

Melvin began to cry.

Malik was repulsed. "Come on, y'all. Let's get out of here," he said.

Raquie was ready to leave the pathetically depressing scene. They knew the truth when they got there, and his confession or denial wouldn't change anything. She turned to leave with Malik.

Zakia was moved to tears herself. An overwhelming feeling of compassion came over her, leading her to minister to Melvin. She went closer to him.

Raquie and Malik turned to her.

"Come on, Z. He won't admit it," Raquie said.

Zakia ignored them. She had something to do before she left. Looking deep into Melvin's weak eyes with love and compassion, she touched his soul.

"Melvin, whether you admit it or not, I forgive you. I'm sorry you're sick. I don't want you to die, but we all have to sometime. What I do want is for you to live better in your next life. It will be spent in heaven, or it will be spent in hell. This hell you are experiencing right now is nothing compared to the hell you will experience when you die. Melvin, in spite of everything, I want you to be saved so that you won't have to experience any more hell. If you believe and if you want me to, I can pray that you will be set free from hell forever. How does that sound?"

Melvin nodded.

"Do you believe God is real and is everywhere, including in here with us right now?" she continued.

He nodded.

"Do you repent of your sins?"

He closed his eyes and nodded.

"Say it. I repent, Jesus," Zakia instructed.

"I repent, Jesus," Melvin obeyed with his eyes still closed.

"Do you believe that God sent His son, Jesus, who shed His blood and died on the cross for your sins?"

He nodded again.

"Do you believe that God raised Jesus from the dead and that He's alive today?"

Melvin continued to nod and cry.

"Do you accept Jesus as your Lord and Savior?"

He was crying uncontrollably as he continued to nod vigorously. Zakia held his hand and wiped his eyes with a tissue.

"Father, in the name of Jesus, we come to you asking for forgiveness for Melvin. As he comes before You now, totally humbled and submitted to You, he accepts Jesus as his Lord and Savior. Therefore, the precious shed blood of Jesus washes away all of his sins, and he has been set free. He is free from the enemy and will now spend eternity with You. We know You forgive him, Lord, and so do we, for You have instructed us to forgive those who trespass against us so that You can forgive us. Your mercies are new every morning, Lord, and we thank You for them. We pray Your grace and mercy, peace and understanding over Melvin right now. In the mighty name of Jesus, amen."

"Amen," Melvin managed to get out.

Zakia gave him a big hug, and he hugged her back. She walked over to the door where Raquie and Malik were just standing, staring. She turned to Melvin and waved good-bye.

"Thank you," he said.

She nodded and smiled at him.

As they left the room, they all heard him say, "I'm sorry."

They were silent all the way back to Raquie's office.

"Now, how wild was that?" Raquie asked, flopping down in her chair.

Zakia and Malik sat at the small conference table in her office.

"Finally. Closure," Zakia said.

"Yeah. That must have been rough on you," Malik said.

"A nightmare."

"Well, now that you know that there is nothing gay going on in or around me, how's my son?"

"Extremely blessed."

"When can I meet him?"

"I'll talk to him, then I'll call you."

"Thanks, Z."

"It's time."

"Yes, it is. Man, what a day, what a day. I think I'm going to get me a room, hang out in the city tonight, and head back early in the morning," Malik said.

"My flight isn't out until the morning either," Zakia said.

"Hey, cool, you guys. There are a few places you should check out while you're here," Raquie said.

"What a great way to end such an unpleasant ordeal," Zakia said.

Zakia and Raquie met Malik at his hotel for dinner. They ate at a fine seafood restaurant in the hotel which featured a wonderful piano player. Zakia had been craving seafood and was not embarrassed to order two entrées, blaming her appetite on the baby. After dinner, she almost felt like she had on her first trip to the Sea Wharf. They had an enjoyable evening together, eating, listening to good music, and talking about everything.

"Want to go to a club?" Raquie asked.

"Do I look like I want to go to a club, sis?"

"Not you, Miss Christian," Raquie said, looking at Malik.

"I must be getting old. This has been a long day, and I have to drive back in the morning, so I'll pass, but thanks for the offer," he said.

After the last set, Malik got up. "It has been truly a pleasure dining with you ladies this evening."

"The pleasure was all ours," Zakia said.

"I'll be waiting on pins and needles for that call," Malik reminded her.

Zakia just smiled. She wanted Zeke to get to know this man who had matured into a wonderful, responsible person. Malik walked them to the car, hugged each of them good night, and went back to his room.

"Yep, Raquie, it's time for Zeke to get to know Malik," Zakia said as she struggled to fasten her seat belt.

Although she had never allowed them to meet behind Zakia's back, Alexis had told Zeke about his daddy. When they finally did talk, Malik and Zeke fell instantly in love with each other over the phone. Malik promised that if it was okay with his mother, he would pick him up after school on Friday and take him to Baltimore to meet his stepmother and half sister. Zeke was thrilled. Zakia agreed, and Malik did as he promised. Malik's family, who attended a Word of Faith church, which thrilled Zakia, loved Zeke, and Zeke loved them. He was tickled pink to have a little sister, and five-year-old Bianca was thrilled to have a big brother. Zeke was developing into a wonderfully balanced young man.

Chapter Sixteen

As Zakia's pregnancy progressed, her family and friends supported her as they always had. Jay was right there with her on all of her doctor visits.

"So Zeke and his biological father are getting pretty close, huh?" he said during one of the trips.

Zakia reassured him. "You are Zeke's father. No biology can change that. Malik is a happily married man. He has a wonderful family who happens to get along very well with our son."

When time came for Zakia to give birth, Jay was right there helping to deliver their third son, whom they named Ahmad. Jay thought for sure Zakia would take him back after the baby was born, but Zakia stayed with her decision. She called her girlfriend and high school cheerleading co-captain, Nikki, for spiritual encouragement when she needed it. Nikki Harris had married Sam Riley, her high school sweetheart, who had become a drug user. Over the years, Nikki and Zakia had learned to support each other using the Word of God and prayer.

Before church one Sunday morning, the phone rang.

"Something good is going to happen to you today, sis," Nikki said.

"Nikki! How are you, girl?" Zakia responded.

"Blessed! I can't talk. On my way out the door, but I just had to let you know that the Spirit of God told me to tell you to expect something good to come your way today," Nikki said.

"Okay, sis. Have a blessed day. We'll talk soon," Zakia said.

"Yes. I really, really need to talk to you to let you know what God has been doing in my life," Nikki said.

"I'll call you soon," Zakia said.

Ahmad was the fastest-developing child Zakia had. One Sunday when she took him to his Little Lambs class before donning her robe, his teacher told her that he sang the loudest on all of the songs. Zakia thought that her rehearsing around the house attributed to his love for music. While she was singing in the choir, she looked out and saw her husband. Jay was in the Faith in the Word congregation on his own. He had stopped trying to come back home a year ago, and Zakia had moved on with her life. She was doing contract work for Raquie from home, and her life in Christ was working for her. After service, Jay was standing by her car in the parking lot.

"Will wonders never cease," she said as she approached him.

"Hey, Zakia. That was a powerful Word that went forth, huh?"

She was stunned, having never heard her husband speak in such terms.

"You go, boy," she said, teasing him.

The boys had been trailing Zakia.

"Daddy!" Zeke and JJ said in unison, surprised to see Jay.

Ahmad broke away from Zeke and ran to his father. Jay scooped him up, giving him a big hug and kiss.

"Hi guys. How've you been?" Jay asked.

"Okay," Zeke said.

"I miss you, Daddy," JJ said.

"I miss you, too," Jay said, turning to Zakia. "Can we take the boys to Mamalexis's and you and I go somewhere and talk?"

Zakia simply nodded.

Jay took Zakia to the restaurant where he had had the revelation that she would be his wife on that wonderful day she first called his office. Brunch was being served. Zakia remembered the first time they had been there and smiled.

"What were you doing at Faith in the Word?" she asked.

"I'm thinking about joining."

"Good God Almighty!"

"I knew you would be pleased."

"Pleased is an understatement."

"I'm also thinking about my family. I miss you, Z. I've watched you, and you got it going on, girl. You are handling it. I want to come home. Can I come home?"

Zakia was in deep contemplation. Her only concern about taking Jay back had been his attitude toward her church. She had forgiven him for his infidelity, but two different churches just would not work. Jay thought she was thinking about his infidelity. She was taking too long to respond.

"Look, I messed up, but I was only unfaithful that one time. The folk at Fig Tree Baptist won't let me forget it. That's why I started coming to Faith in the Word. And you were right, baby, the church is everything you said it was."

He dispelled all of her apprehension with that outburst, and she finally responded.

"Told you," she said, smiling.

"Can I come home?"

"I, too, understand that because of my lack of balance, I drove you to do what you did. It was hard for me to accept because I thought I was doing the right thing serving the Lord. I now realize how insensitive I was to you and our family. I'm not justifying what you did, I'm just saying I understand. I would love nothing more than for you to come home."

"That's good, baby. Thank you. I've missed you so much. I love you."

"I love you too, Jay."

Jay was rising up to kiss her right in the middle of the restaurant, but her cell phone rang and stopped him. She pulled it out and looked at the caller ID.

"It's Raquie," she said, pressing the answer button. "Hey, sis, what's up?"

"Hey, sis. Jazz Jafari called to tell me that Melvin died."

"Dang. Well, at least he was saved."

"You saw to that."

"Thanks for telling me. I'll let Malik know."

"Tell him I said hi."

"Okay, sis. I'm having brunch with my husband right now," she said.

"Yes! I hear ya, Z. That's wonderful. Work it out, girl. You can do it. That's my big sister."

"Okay, sis. I love you. Bye," she said, laughing and hanging up. "Where were we?" she asked her husband.

Jay rose up, and she met him halfway. They kissed across the table, melting away all hardness and healing all pain, then they sat back down, and he looked deep into her eyes.

"You understand that it's time for us to put our family back together?" Jay asked.

"I understand that perfectly," Zakia answered.

"Okay. Then if we're done here, let's go tell the boys," Jay said.

"I can't wait to tell them, but why don't you come over this evening? I need some time to myself to pray. I also need to call Nikki to tell her the good news," Zakia said.

"That's fine," Jay said.

At home, after Zakia prayed, she called Nikki.

"Girl, I have a wonderful surprise for you, but first I want to hear what God has been doing in your life down there in the ATL. I know you're being blessed," Zakia said.

PART TWO

Real Saved Folk

Atlanta, Georgia

And Jesus answered and said, Verily I say unto you, There is no man that hath left house, or brethren, or sisters, or father, or mother, or wife, or children, or lands, for my sake, and the gospel's, But he shall receive an hundredfold now in this time, houses, and brethren, and sisters, and mothers, and children, and lands, with persecutions; and in the world to come eternal life.

MARK 10: 29–30

Chapter Seventeen

Finally, the last piece of furniture was in place. The driver of the moving van presented Nikki Riley with a receipt to sign. Once she had checked it over and scribbled her name on the bottom, he left, and Nikki was alone. She looked around at the boxes that needed unpacking, the pictures that had to be hung, and the clothes that needed putting away. Despite all the work ahead, Nikki looked forward to making the new apartment a happy home for her family. The children had helped put a few things away, but now they were all on top of the unmade bed fast asleep in one of the bedrooms. As she looked in on them, she smiled, for they had made it, but not without some drama.

It had been a long day. The eight-and-a-half-hour drive from Richmond, Virginia, to Atlanta, Georgia, would have been easier had Nikki had some help driving. Long-distance driving was not her forte. Her ex-husband, Sam Riley, usually handled all of the driving when they traveled, while she made all of the arrangements. None of their three children were of driving age, so the Lord had appointed her to handle the trip, which she did with relative ease.

Nikki's oldest child and only son, Taj, was quite responsible for ten years old. As they drove down Interstate 85, he drifted in and out of consciousness, trying to stay awake to keep his mother company. He was worn out from helping to get his hysterical sisters into the minivan as they attempted to leave Richmond. Nine-year-old Shay and six-year-old Mia had been clinging, hugging, crying, and slobbering all over their grandfather Jim in Nikki's parents' living room before they left for Atlanta.

Jim Harris was the definition of grandparent, a child's natural ally. If his grandchildren wanted something, he bought it, no questions asked. Nikki insisted that the kids be made to earn some of the gifts, which always started an argument between her and her dad.

"They're just kids. They don't have to work for anything. Your mother and I are supposed to give them things to make them happy. Besides, I'm grateful for two things: that I can afford to buy them things and that I'm around to see them enjoy the things I can afford to buy them, so let me enjoy myself with my grandchildren, please. Thank you," Jim would say, and that would be the end of it.

Nikki's relationship with her father had become a little strained since she had given him grandchildren. He seemed to usurp her authority because of her strict discipline every chance he got. Her ex-husband, Sam, had been a silent partner on that issue and just allowed Nikki to do whatever she deemed appropriate in all situations, since he was otherwise occupied with his so-called recreational drug use, which eventually led to their divorce a year ago. Sam was in denial about the seriousness of his addiction. Even when Nikki questioned him about his drastic weight loss, he reasoned it away.

"I'm intentionally losing the fat that my muscle turned into when I stopped working out like I used to when I played football. Once I lose all the fat, I'll join a gym and rebuild my muscles and get that solid frame back that you love so much," Sam explained. At one point, his six-one frame held two hundred ten pounds, but that was a long time ago.

Nikki had grown weary of the lies and deception and finally left him, but only after years of counseling, which led to nowhere. He only went to counseling to appease her. Sam just would not see the danger he was imposing upon his family. Finally, she mustered all the faith and strength she had to divorce him and begin again. Even after the divorce, Sam still believed that she would come back to him.

As his family prepared to leave Richmond for Atlanta, Sam went to the home of his ex-in-laws to see them off. He just stood and watched, not fully comprehending how Nikki was able to leave him and her roots, as the dramatic scene unfolded right before his eyes.

"I don't want to go!" Mia screamed.

"I love you, Granddaddy," Shay sobbed, holding on to Jim's neck for dear life.

Nikki realized it would take some very gentle coercion to get the girls away from their granddaddy and into the car. "Come on, girls," she said softly. "We have to go. Granddaddy will be down to visit us, maybe next week, knowing him. He'll probably be there in time to help us unpack. Come on now."

There was no attempt to let go. Jim was holding on just as tight as the girls. Nikki decided she would have to physically pry the girls away from their granddaddy. Nikki pulled Mia up into her arms and carried her outside. Jim, wiping tears from his eyes, followed them, assisting Shay, who was dragging her feet.

Taj, Sam, and Nikki's mother, Jean, were all standing by the minivan, which was packed, gassed, and ready to go. Taj, trying to be a man and fight back his tears, helped Nikki put the girls in the backseat as they continued to reach for their father and grandparents. After kissing everybody one last time, Taj got in the front passenger seat.

"Bye. Love you. See you. Come visit. We'll call you when we get there," Nikki said as she pulled off, waving to the teary-eyed people standing in the driveway.

As they merged onto the interstate, Nikki smiled. She tried to hide her joy as she looked at the kids. The girls were in the backseat wailing like their world was coming to an end. They were hugging each other almost hysterically. Taj looked like he wanted to cry too. In spite of it all, Nikki laughed. She'd stepped out on faith and left. God was indeed her strength.

As Nikki walked around her new bedroom a few hours later, she was overwhelmed with thanksgiving, excitement, and hopefulness for a bright future. She knew deep down inside that whatever God had in store for her was so awesome that it was going to make everything she had been through to get to Atlanta worth it.

Chapter Eighteen

It was a glorious summer morning. The loud ring of the cell phone startled her awake.

"Huh? Huh? What?" Nikki asked, waking up, adjusting to the unfamiliar room. For a second, she wondered, *Where am I?* The phone rang again, jarring her memory as she answered it. "Hello."

"So you actually did it. You up and left your family and friends. What are we supposed to do now? We don't stand a chance in this dog-eat-dog world without you here praying for us," the female voice said.

"What's up, cuz? What? You thought I was joking about moving? Besides, I can pray for my folks from anywhere," Nikki said, recognizing her cousin Rae Peterson's voice.

"Yeah, well, we need you here," Rae said.

"Why? You all do whatever you want to do. You don't listen to me. Sam didn't and you either."

"I do. Matter of fact, something you said to me had to keep me from killing somebody last night."

"Rae, girl, what have you gone and done now?"

"See, I got this page to go make a drop, and when I showed up and gave them the hundred-dollar rock, they said they only had fifty dollars. I told them to give it back so I could cut it in half, and they tried to leave with the whole thing after only paying for half, talking about they good for it. It was two sorry, punk crackheads that I keep saying I'm going to stop dealing with, but I keep going to get that money. It got to the point where I had to pull out my piece and put it to the head of the one who wouldn't give me my stuff back."

"Did he give it back?"

"Heck yeah, he gave me my rock back. The other one took off running when he saw my nine-millimeter. I cussed him out, took my stuff, and drove off. I did throw the fifty dollars out the window as I pulled off," Rae explained.

"Wow, an honest drug dealer," Nikki said sarcastically.

"Hey, at least nobody got hurt."

"But somebody will get hurt eventually, Rae. Haven't you learned anything? How many people have to die before you get it? What is wrong with you? Selling drugs, carrying guns."

"Nikki, I didn't go to college, I didn't finish high school . . . How am I supposed to support my kids? I only weigh one hundred ten pounds, I'm fine as I wanna be, but I don't like men, so I can't get paid that way. My street sense and my nine-millimeter are the only things that keep me alive."

"And my prayers."

"That's what I'm saying. How could you leave us?"

"Rae, you're a responsible adult, and you have to find a better way to survive."

"Yeah, well, I'm doing the best I can. Living ain't cheap."

"Who are you telling? My rent is just as much as a mortgage."

"Dang, so you're all settled in?"

"Hardly. We just got here, so we have a lot of work to do."

"Well, I just called to see if you made it there okay. I'll let you get to work. Keep in touch, cuz. I really do listen to you when you get your preach on, though."

"Yeah, right."

"I do. I'm saved. I said all of those confessions you had me make. I just don't know how else to make enough money to live and support my kids."

"Well, at least you're saved. I'll talk to you later, cuz."

Hanging up, Nikki prayed for God to keep her cousin, to show her a better way to live. Rae was a painful reminder that not everything in her life was moving in the right direction. She loved her cousin and felt that talking to her whenever she called would help bring the Lord into Rae's life in a real way. Nikki shook her head as if trying to get rid of the bad thoughts and ran her fingers through her short dark hair. She jumped out of bed and praised the Lord when she realized this was the first day of her new life. Nikki ran into the girls' room. They were already awake, unpacking their clothes. She grabbed Mia, picked her up, spun her around, and squeezed her until she squealed.

"Thank You, Lord. We made it! Praise You, Jesus! Glory to God! Hallelujah! Praise You, Father! If I had ten thousand tongues, I couldn't thank You enough, Father! Praise You, praise You, praise You, praise You, praise You!"

The children were used to their mother "getting her praise on." She had taught them that her victory was in her praise. They liked it when she was in praise mode. Then they knew everything was all right, not like when she was quiet and deep in thought, playing with her hair with a serious look on her face. They worried when she was quiet and not smiling because it was her nature to smile and talk all the time, especially about the Word of God.

Nikki walked through the apartment, maneuvering around the boxes that the movers had left. The apartment was perfect. During Taj's spring break, he and Nikki had gone to Atlanta to secure a place to live. They were extremely prayed up. They had been very specific with God in their request about apartment size, location, and environment. Nikki had told Taj, a prayer warrior like his mother, a joke about a mouse coming face-to-face with a lion. The mouse prayed, "Lord, please let this be a Christian lion." The lion prayed, "Lord, thank You for this food," and ate the mouse. The mouse got exactly what he asked for. From then on, Taj became very specific in his prayers.

Nikki had taken Taj on her apartment-hunting trip because he was growing into a wise and mature young man. She wanted him to realize how important he was to the family. Taj knew his mother well and was very sensitive to her. In the beginning, his sensitivity was out of survival. To avoid that quick backhand of hers, he had to figure out what he could and couldn't get away with. But for the past few years, seeing all the stress and pressure she was under, he studied her to learn what he could do to relieve some of her burdens, because he loved her so much.

Good grades made her happy, so Taj made sure he did well in school. Nikki also loved to laugh, so he became quite the comedian, making her laugh so hard her stomach hurt. He was the man now. He knew what she liked, and his job on the apartment-hunting trip was to help her find it. They both knew the Regency complex was the perfect location for them when they first stepped into the unit that would be their home. It was spacious, open, and bright with all the modern conveniences. There was plenty of storage space, and it overlooked the playground so that Nikki could keep an eye on her brood from inside.

"I'm going out to get some breakfast. What kind of croissants do you want?" Nikki asked the children.

"I want bacon, egg, and cheese," Shay said.

Hearing the question, Taj came into the girls' room. "Me too," he chimed in. "Can I have French toast sticks too? I'm going to need some extra energy with all the work we have to do today."

Such a man. I am so proud of him, Nikki thought. "Sure, baby. Anything else? Let's see, hash browns, juice, milk, and coffee for me, of course."

"That's it for me, Mommy," Taj said.

"I want sausage, egg, and cheese," Mia said.

"Okay, I'll be right back. Put the chain on the door, and don't open it for anyone but me," she instructed.

Nikki was back at the apartment complex in about twenty minutes. She pulled the minivan into a parking space beside a couple just getting out of a Honda.

Oooh, my neighbors, she thought as she got out and retrieved the bags. She wanted to find out what type of people lived around her. Her experience up until that moment had been that folk in Atlanta were very friendly. There was a lot of southern hospitality in the air, so she felt comfortable approaching the couple.

The man was opening the door to an apartment downstairs. An icebreaking opportunity, she thought.

"Hello, I'm your new neighbor, Nicole Riley, but everyone calls me Nikki." Her hands were full, so she couldn't offer a handshake, but she continued. "I hope we didn't disturb you too much with all the moving yesterday," she said, smiling from ear to ear, friendliness, excitement, and joy gushing.

They both just stared at her.

Nikki's first thoughts were, *Why are they looking at me so seriously? He's nice-looking. What runway did she just step off? She is not his wife. Why aren't they at work in the middle of a weekday? Mind your business, girl.*

After the fashion-model woman finished checking Nikki out from head to toe, she finally said in a serious tone, "Well, you had to move in."

The man appeared irritated and said nothing.

Nikki sensed the tension and decided not to pursue a conversation.

"Well, have a nice day," she said, still grinning as she made her way up the steps. The couple just nodded.

The children were waiting in the living room, ready to dig into the croissants.

"Let's eat!" she said.

They attacked the food like they hadn't eaten in days. It tasted even better than usual to the hungry crew. After they had eaten every speck of breakfast, they went back to unpacking.

With the sounds from the radio to energize them, the children enjoyed the labor, folding and hanging up clothes and decorating their rooms with their toys and stuffed animals. They sang and danced as they got their new home in order. Once again tired and hungry, they stopped working around seven-thirty and went out for burgers, fries, and shakes. They came home and watched TV until they all fell asleep.

The next morning, Nikki again went out to get breakfast. On her way back, a different person was coming out of the same unit that she had seen the couple go into the day before. He was smiling.

"Hi. How're you doing?" he asked.

"Fine, thank you," Nikki said, smiling back, trying to be as friendly as he appeared to be. Although he hesitated as if he wanted to talk to his new neighbor, this was not a good time for her with kids to feed, so she kept walking.

The weather was gorgeous, perfect for a leisurely stroll, so after they ate, Nikki and the children decided to explore their new neighborhood. The friendly neighbor was out washing his car. They exchanged hellos before Nikki and the children started their walk. Taj and Mia led the way while Nikki and Shay hung back and talked.

"How are you feeling, baby?" Nikki asked her older daughter.

"Good. I like our apartment. I miss my friends in Virginia, but I can write them," Shay said.

"You can even call them on weekends and talk as much as you want, since my cell phone package includes free long distance on nights and weekends," Nikki said.

"Thanks, Mommy. I can't wait to make new friends here too."

"That won't take you long, precious, not long at all."

They strolled along, checking out the Mazdas, Volvos, some nice Fords and Chevys, a few Cadillacs, even BMWs. Plants were hanging out on some of the balconies. Children who seemed to be Mia's age were playing at a second playground on the other side of the complex. She tapped her mother on the arm.

"You want to go meet them?" Nikki asked.

"Maybe later," Mia said as she simply observed them swinging and playing on the jungle gym.

When they made their way back, the friendly neighbor was removing the wax from his fire-engine-red Mustang. He made eye contact with Nikki, and they both just smiled this time.

The apartment was beginning to look like home. Now that all the dishes were put away, they could give the fast-food restaurants a break and fix a home-cooked meal. The next morning, Nikki went grocery shopping. She let the children sleep and locked the dead bolt, leaving the extra key in the lock on the inside in case of an emergency. She had learned a long time ago not to take the children grocery shopping if she wanted to stay within her budget.

After she got in the minivan, she remembered she had left the shopping list on the kitchen counter. As she headed back toward her apartment, the friendly neighbor came out his door in shorts, a T-shirt, and flip-flops. He was clearly athletic. His skin was the color of black coffee with a hint of cream, and he was about six-two with muscles everywhere. He looked like he didn't have a care in the world and nowhere to go. Nikki wondered why he wasn't at work. He looked young enough to live with his parents, but that wouldn't make sense because she had seen the couple around his age go into the same apartment the other day.

Mind your business, girl, she thought before saying, "Beautiful day."

"Sure is," he responded, flashing a huge smile.

Nikki wanted to ask him what he did for a living, but resisted the urge.

"Well, have a good one," she said as she ran up to the apartment to retrieve the list. When she came back out, he was reaching inside his glove compartment. He looked up, and they smiled at each other. Then she was gone.

Nikki spent two hundred dollars at the grocery store. That should hold them for at least a week. Yeah, right. She'd have to go back in a couple of days for milk, if nothing else. Taj drank it like it was water. He said he had to grow, and milk was going to make it happen.

When she got back, her neighbor's red Mustang was gone. *Where's my smiling, friendly neighbor now to help me take these groceries upstairs?*

Chapter Nineteen

The children were up and dressed. Each of them made several trips to the car to retrieve all of the grocery bags. After they put the food away, they put the last of the empty storage boxes in the van to take to the Dumpster.

"I think it's time to check out Way Maker Ministries. If it's anything like it seems on TV, that will definitely be our new church home," Nikki informed her crew.

She had been a faithful partner with WMM for almost three years. Tapes and books from the ministry filled her bookshelves in Virginia, since she couldn't resist ordering just about every product they offered. WMM was a major factor in her choosing Atlanta as their new home.

After calling and getting directions, they all piled into the minivan and made their way to the Dumpster, then the church. Upon arriving at the church, they saw a few people walking around who appeared to work there, but no services were being held, so they decided to leave. Nikki was satisfied that they knew how to get there and that it was a relatively easy trip. They continued to ride around, locating the necessary shopping spots. They ended up on a highway not far from their apartment and saw a mall located off an exit. They checked it out and found it had everything they could possibly need: movie theater, bookstore, and nice places to eat. Having a good sense of their surroundings, they headed for home.

Later that day, Nikki fixed a feast of smothered pork chops, mashed potatoes with gravy, collard greens, corn on the cob, and hot buttered biscuits to offset some of the fast food they had overindulged in. The meal turned out wonderfully. They ate so much, all they could do was fall out in the middle of the living room floor in front of the TV. They watched the Disney Channel until they all fell asleep right where they lay.

The sun rose gloriously on Sunday morning. It seemed to have an extra special shine to Nikki.

"Let's go!" she shouted in all of her excitement. "I can't wait to get on the inside of Way Maker Ministries. Come on, kids, get in the van."

They grabbed their Bibles, pencils, and pads, and the girls brought cute little purses. Shay had done her own as well as her sister's hair. She was very talented in creating fashionable styles decorated with bows, twists, and ties to hold their braids in place.

During the TV broadcasts, Nikki had noticed how members of the congregation dressed and she knew casual attire would be appropriate. The two girls wore the same-colored sundresses except that Shay's had flowers and Mia's had butterflies. Mia's sandals were flat, but Shay had talked her mother into letting her wear a small heel. Taj looked handsome in his polo shirt, khaki shorts, and closed-toe sandals. Although he and Shay were the same height, she was slightly taller when she wore her heels, forcing him to subconsciously tiptoe when he was next to her. Nikki, too, dressed comfortably in a sundress and sandals. They quickly filed out the door and got in the minivan.

"Buckle up," Shay instructed.

After seeing a crash dummies commercial and learning that you could get a ticket for not using seat belts, Shay assumed the responsibility for making sure her family rode in safety. Even if they were already buckled up, Shay said it anyway. It became a habit. Sometimes they needed the reminder, sometimes they didn't. But they got it whether they needed it or not. That was her job.

Nikki was pleased with them when they acted responsibly. Shay, like her brother, sought to make her mother happy, mostly because she couldn't stand it when Nikki yelled at her. So Shay, too, studied her mother to learn what it was that she had to do to keep her calm and content.

When they pulled up on the campus of WMM, they were amazed at what they saw. There was a sea of vehicles on acres and acres of land, people galore trying to get into several buildings, as well as an army of parking attendants and policemen directing traffic. There were lines and lines of people looking like they were waiting to get into a music concert.

When she called earlier to find out what time service started, Nikki was told seven o'clock, nine o'clock, and eleven o'clock on Sunday mornings and seven o'clock on Wednesday evenings. She chose the nine o'clock service because it wasn't too early or too late. The scene outside so excited them that they could hardly wait to get on the inside. Some people were dressed up in suits and hats, while others were dressed down in jeans, T-shirts, and sneakers. Never had she seen that at her old church, Richmond Baptist. The men always had on ties and jackets. You could hardly see the pulpit for the hats that more than half the women wore.

Nikki was directed to the children's church to deliver the kids to their appropriate classes. Shay and Taj were in the same class, since they were only a year apart in age, and Mia's class was across the hall. Once they were all settled, Nikki went over to the main building and got in one of the lines that led into the sanctuary. The lines went out of the exit doors and wrapped around the building. Nikki carefully followed the instructions that the ushers yelled at the worshippers and flowed right in with the crowd. She got pushed through the door, down the hallway into the sanctuary, and into a seat. The music ushered them in. The crowd was praising and worshipping God.

This is what the Bible means by entering into His gates with thanksgiving and into His courts with praise, she thought. It all flowed smoothly, even though there were so many people. Being one in the Spirit was the only way order could be kept—and flowing in obedience to the instructions of the ushers, of course.

Once settled in her seat, Nikki looked around. As she took it all in, joy came out of her in the form of uncontrollable tears. She let them flow freely, laughing out loud, shouting, "Hallelujah." Lifting her hands in praise, clapping, rocking side to side, and stomping her feet, Nikki realized she had never felt so close to God before. This was nothing like the praise and worship at her old church. She knew she was home. Following the praise team, even though the songs were not familiar, she joined in the praise and worship. She cried some more and thanked the Lord for bringing her to Way Maker's.

After praise and worship was over and the congregation squeezed into their seats like sardines, Nikki managed to regain control of herself and her tears. Ushers were walking the aisles with tissues and offered her some. Wiping her eyes, she took in more of her surroundings. The sanctuary was exactly like it looked on TV, with wooden pews, stained-glass windows, and live plants and flowers decorating the pulpit. The band was to the left of the choir, and TV cameras were all over. The baptismal pool was behind the choir, and there was a balcony. It was a traditional sanctuary except for the cameras, although a much larger, more modern place of worship was under construction nearby. It hit her that this was the scene that she had been viewing every week on TV for the last few years. The revelation almost overwhelmed her, and she rocked back and forth in her seat thanking Jesus.

After the announcements and other preliminaries, she began to settle down. Pastor Freeman arrived and Nikki froze. She could not take her eyes off him. Here in the same room with her was her link to everything her heart desired. She closed her eyes and remembered watching him on TV at home in Virginia, then opened them to see him right there in the flesh. He had always spoken directly to whatever she was going through at the time, providing comfort and direction. At first, she had thought that somehow he personally knew about her, her divorce and fears about single parenting. Then she realized that he did not, but that the Holy Spirit ministering through him knew her and loved her dearly. She kept opening and closing her eyes until the tears flowed again as the revelation of where God had brought her embraced her. She had been delivered, and her future was brighter than ever.

When the pastor got up to preach, all the people disappeared in Nikki's mind, and no one was there but the two of them. After a few minutes, Pastor Freeman disappeared too, and only Nikki and the Word of God that was coming out of his mouth were there. The Word had taken on a life all its own. It was no longer just a man standing there talking directly to Nikki who began filling her, molding her, and anointing her for whatever God led her to do. The most powerful force there is, the Word of God itself, was ministering to her, pouring itself right into her spirit. It was the most transforming experience of her life.

At the end of the message, Pastor Freeman was ushered out ahead of the crowd, and Nikki watched him leave. She felt numb. After service, as the crowd pushed her out the door, she staggered toward the minivan. Then, realizing she had not picked up the children, she turned around, still dazed a bit—what the pastor called drunk in the Spirit—and headed back to get in the line at the children's church.

By the time everyone was retrieved, she was almost back to normal.

"How did you like church?" she asked on the drive home.

"It was great," Taj said.

"We had fun," Mia jumped in. "We read our Bibles, watched videos about Jesus, played games, and won prizes. Look what I won," she said, showing Nikki a pad and pencil set. "Thanks for making me learn my books of the Bible, Mommy. I won because I knew the four Gospels."

"I loved it too, Mommy," Shay said. It took a lot to impress Shay. If she loved it, that said a lot to Nikki. "How was your church, Mommy?"

"Just plain awesome. I can't wait for the next time. I heard somebody say that the weekly Bible study is just like Sunday service. I'm so looking forward to Wednesday," Nikki said.

Getting something to eat and relaxing were next on their agenda. They went to a pancake restaurant because Nikki was too keyed up to cook. The food was pretty good and made everyone feel full and sleepy.

"I'm going to lay down for a couple of hours. What are you guys going to do?" Nikki asked as she opened the door and they all filed into the apartment.

"I'm sleepy too," Shay said.

"Me too," Taj agreed.

"Me three," Mia said, yawning.

Everyone quickly changed clothes, found a comfortable spot, and went straight to sleep. Nikki dozed off, dreaming about how she was, without a doubt, sure that God had brought her to the right place.

Chapter Twenty

Nikki spent the day on the phone, getting instructions to register the children for school. She learned that they needed to visit the health department to get their immunization records certified. She gathered all of the appropriate papers, and they were on their way.

Outside, her smiling neighbor was wiping down his car again.

What does he do? Nikki's curiosity was getting the best of her. "Hi. My name is Nikki Riley. This is my son, Taj, and my daughters, Shay and Mia," she said, offering her hand to shake.

"I'm Randy Jordan. Nice to meet you," he replied, shaking her hand.

Quickly thinking of something to say, Nikki asked, "Randy, do you know a good barber? Since we just moved here, I have to find one for my son."

"My roommate cuts hair."

"Really? Does he cut yours?" Nikki asked, checking

out his haircut and concluding that if his roommate cut it, he was worth a try. She wondered if that cute guy with the girl was his roommate.

"Yes, he cuts mine."

"Is he expensive, and does he make house calls?" Nikki asked jokingly, but really wanting to know. "What's his name?" she continued before he had a chance to respond to her previous inquiry.

"Kevin," Randy said, hesitating before answering the other questions. There was a pause as Nikki examined Randy's haircut again.

"What do you think, Taj?" Nikki asked her son.

"We can try him out," Taj said, nodding.

"Will you ask him if he will cut Taj's hair for me, please?"

"Sure, I'll ask him when he gets in tonight."

With that settled and noticing that the writing on his T-shirt read "RHS Football Coaching Staff," she asked, "What's RHS?"

"Riverdale High School, where I teach," Randy answered.

Finally! Mystery solved. He's a teacher, and they have the summers off. That's why he's walking around here with nothing to do all day. "What do you teach?" she asked.

"History," he said.

"Interesting. You coach football too?"

"Yeah. I coach the wide receivers."

"Cool," Nikki responded, visibly impressed. She always thought teachers and coaches were the most important people in the world. She knew many young men who survived the streets only because of their high school coaches. They replaced a lot of the absent fathers and helped get some of the players into college, many of them on scholarship. And teachers in general, but especially high school teachers, had the toughest job in the world. To motivate high school students to do well and prepare them for life had to take a special type of individual.

"Where are you from?" Randy asked.

"Virginia," Taj answered.

"Richmond, Virginia," Mia said, "and I want to go back. I miss my granddaddy."

"That's our cue to leave," Nikki said. "See you later, Randy."

"Bye. Nice meeting you," he said.

They got in the minivan, directions in hand, and headed to the health department. After all of the shots and tests were taken, they had to wait for the records to be updated. Finally, they left with all the required paperwork completed.

"That took forever. Let's go get something to eat," Nikki said as they headed to the car.

As they were walking into the apartment, Nikki heard a door shut downstairs. She hesitated and looked to see who it was. She spotted the first guy she had met, this time accompanied by a young boy. She went in the apartment thinking, *He has a son about Taj's age.*

Later that night, there was a knock on the door. When Nikki looked through the peephole, she saw a vaguely familiar face. She opened the door with the chain still on to get a better look at the big, good-looking guy. He resembled a linebacker and wore shorts and a T-shirt, showcasing his thick neck, broad chest, and muscular legs. Between the tall and thin basketball type and the shorter, more muscular and strong football type, she preferred the football type, being drawn to strength. Her ex-husband, Sam, had been that way when they first met, before he let his body deteriorate from drugs.

"Hi. I'm Kevin Washington from downstairs. My room-mate said your son needed a barber." He spoke without smiling.

"Oh," she said, closing the door, removing the chain, and opening it all the way so that he could enter. "Come in."

Kevin came in without saying a word and stood stiffly by the door as Nikki locked it. She turned to him and snuck another quick complete view.

So serious, Nikki thought. "Hi, I'm Nikki. My son needs a haircut like yesterday," she said, trying to loosen him up.

"I have time now," Kevin said, still serious.

He doesn't mess around, she thought. "How much do you charge?" she asked.

"Six dollars."

"Okay. Can you cut it here?" she asked, thinking that was a good deal, hoping she would get more than her money's worth in terms of quality. Haircuts back home had gone up to ten dollars.

"Sure. I'll go get my clippers. I'll be right back," he said as he turned and let himself out.

A few minutes later, when he returned, Kevin looked around her living room and said, "Wow! It's like night and day." He was obviously impressed.

"What is?" Nikki asked.

"Your apartment compared to ours," he said.

That's a refreshing touch of honesty, she thought. "Thanks, I guess," she said, not wanting to sound presumptuous.

"No, this is nice. It's hooked up," Kevin said, still not smiling.

This is a serious guy. "Well, thank you very much. Now, where do you want to cut my son's hair?"

"The kitchen will be fine. The light is probably better in there than anywhere else."

"Okay. Taj!" she called.

Taj came out of his room, and seeing Kevin, he moved close beside his mother.

Putting her arm around her son's shoulder, she introduced them. "Taj, this is Kevin, our neighbor and Randy's, who we met earlier, roommate. He's here to cut your hair."

Kevin came over, and they solemnly shook hands.

"Hey, man, how you doing?" Kevin asked.

"Fine," Taj said.

"Are you ready to do this?"

"I guess," Taj responded, shrugging.

Taj sat in a chair in the kitchen as Kevin draped him. When he started combing through Taj's hair, Nikki got out of the way. She could see them from across the breakfast bar while she organized some things in the living room. She couldn't help but notice how intense Kevin was. *He and his roommate must get along really well because they appear to be total opposites. Randy seems friendly, smiling all the time, while Kevin seems so serious. I haven't seen him smile yet. Probably got a jacked-up grill.*

The haircut turned out pretty well, so Nikki gave Kevin a ten-dollar bill and told him to keep the change.

"Thanks a lot," he said, packing up his tools.

Taj was sweeping up his hair off the floor.

"Have you ever been to Way Maker Ministries?" Nikki asked Kevin.

"No. Where's that?" he asked.

"You don't know where Way Maker Ministries is, as close as you live to it?" Nikki asked, shocked, then hoping she hadn't offended him.

But Kevin was cool. He kept on with what he was doing. "Nope," he said, never looking up.

"Where are you from?" she asked.

"Macon, thirty minutes from here. Born and raised, all my life," he said.

"What church do you go to?" she asked.

"Actually, I'm looking for one. I go with Randy to his church sometimes, but I haven't joined," he said.

"Why don't you come with us? Just to check it out, since you're searching," she said.

"I'm game," Kevin said.

"This Sunday? We normally try and go to one of the early services," Nikki said.

"Call me and remind me. I'll give you my number."

"Cool," she said.

Kevin wrote his phone number on a piece of paper and left it on the counter. "What's your number?" he asked.

He wrote down Nikki's number, put the sheet in his

pocket, and heading toward the door, he said, "Good night, and thanks again for the tip."

"Have a blessed evening, and thanks for making the house call."

Chapter Twenty-one

It was becoming common for Nikki's family to get up early on Sunday mornings, have breakfast, go to the second service, come home, and jump back in the bed for a nap. They still had the whole day ahead of them to enjoy and were well rested if they wanted to explore. Kevin was supposed to go with them to church, but he didn't answer when Nikki called. After church, just as Nikki was dozing off, the phone rang.

"Hello?"

"Hmm, hello. Hmm, this is Kevin. From downstairs."

"Hey, Kevin."

"I called to apologize for not going to church with you this morning. I went out of town and thought I would be back in time. I just got back. Did you go?"

"We sure did."

"How was it?"

"Awesome. We are all up here recuperating from it."

"Sounds like you had a good time. Sorry I missed it," Kevin said.

"I'll have to tell you all about it later," Nikki replied.

"Okay. I just wanted to let you know I didn't intentionally not go. I'll talk to you later."

"Okay, Kevin, maybe later on this evening. I'll call you when we get ourselves together."

"Deal," he said.

"Bye now," she said, and was fast asleep in no time flat.

After her nap, Nikki was refreshed and decided to cook a big dinner and invite her new neighbors for some fellowship. She praised, prayed, and hummed along to Fred Hammond as she prepared the evening meal. She missed having adult conversation and decided to let the children eat first and then invite the guys up afterward so that she could talk to them about the happenings in Georgia. She ate with the children in case the guys couldn't come. After dinner, she called downstairs.

"Hello."

"Hello. May I speak to Kevin?"

"Speaking."

"Hey, it's Nikki. Whatcha doin'?"

"Watching the game," he replied.

"Have you guys eaten yet?" she asked.

"Naw, man," Kevin said. "We're trying to decide what we're going to do about dinner now. Probably ride out for a burger or some hot wings or something."

"When's the last time you had a home-cooked meal?" Nikki asked.

"I couldn't even tell you," Kevin responded.

"That's not good. Why don't you and Randy come up here for a home-cooked meal?"

"Be right up," Kevin said, and hung up the phone.

Nikki hung the phone up laughing. A few seconds later, she heard a knock. She saw Kevin through the peephole and opened the door, still laughing.

"It must have been a long while. Wash your hands and go on in the kitchen and help yourself. Where's Randy?" she asked as they walked into the apartment.

"He was all into the game. On my way out the door, I told him you invited us to dinner, and he said bring him a plate back."

"Uh-uh. No way. This is not a take-out joint. Come, sit down, relax, and enjoy, right here," Nikki said.

Kevin washed his hands in the kitchen sink and dried them on a paper towel. Although Nikki preferred for people to wash their hands in the bathroom, she let it go and forgave him this time, but made a mental note to mention it the next time. She went into the kitchen behind Kevin and handed him a plate. As she took the top off each pot, she went over the menu.

"These are the collard greens," she said. She replaced the lid and uncovered the casserole dish. "Here's the macaroni and cheese." Removing the top from the roaster, she unveiled succulent beef short ribs, roasted to perfection with a beautiful glazed barbecue sauce. "And your bread is here," she said, uncovering perfect golden brown buttered rolls.

As she turned toward the refrigerator, she glanced at Kevin, who was standing behind her looking over her shoulder at the food. His tongue was literally hanging out of his mouth, his eyes as big as quarters. She burst out laughing. He looked so funny . . . cute but funny.

"Excuse me," she said, still laughing as she moved

past him to the refrigerator. He took one step back to let her pass. She opened the door and took out a dish. She said, "And this is the potato salad."

"If it tastes half as good as it looks, I'm in for a treat. It looks absolutely scrumptious, as my grandmother would say," Kevin said.

"Well, go for it. We've all eaten, and you can just help yourself."

"Thank you very, very much," he said as he filled his plate.

Nikki poured him a glass of fresh-squeezed lemonade and set it on the dining room table.

"If it's not hot enough, you can run your plate in the microwave for a couple of minutes," she said.

Tasting one of the ribs, Kevin threw his head back and shook it from side to side. "Hmm, hmm, hmm. Lord, have mercy. It's delicious just the way it is," he said, licking the barbecue sauce off his lips.

"Do you need anything else?" Nikki asked.

"No thank you. This is perfect. Sit down and relax. You worked hard in this kitchen today," he said.

"All right," Nikki said, taking a seat at the dining room table as she waited for Kevin to sit. She couldn't wait to tell him about church.

"This is so nice of you, Nikki."

"No problem. We have plenty, and the kids will be tired of it after tomorrow. One day of leftovers, then I'm throwing food away, with all those starving people in Africa."

Kevin laughed. "If getting rid of leftovers is a problem for you, please call downstairs so we can help you out."

She chuckled at him.

"The food is already blessed, but you might want to do your own praying," she said, sounding like a mother.

She felt good sitting there with this young man and actually began to relax for the first time in a long, long while.

Kevin blessed his food, but before he put the first bite in his mouth, he said, "So tell me all about church."

Thankful for the opening, Nikki dived in headfirst. "We joined today. The first time we went I was too caught up in it all. I hadn't cried that much in I don't know how long. I needed that cry too."

Kevin looked at her, puzzled, and she discerned that he was wondering why she needed to cry.

"I was able to release some stuff I had been carrying for a long time," she continued.

Kevin nodded, understanding, still chewing and listening intently.

Satisfied that they were on the same page, she said, "Okay, okay, I'll start at the beginning. First, when we got there, actual policemen—I mean, uniformed guys— were directing traffic. Then they had parking lot attendants telling you exactly where to park. It was so organized. They've got their stuff together. Thousands and thousands of people were coming and going. Lines and lines of people were waiting to get into the different children's classes and into the sanctuary. You have to conclude that any place that has that many people standing in line voluntarily has to have it going on."

"Oh yeah, I remember hearing something about that church now that you're describing it. I guess I never picked up on the name before," he said.

"I figured you had to have at least heard about it in

passing, you living so close and all. Let me tell you. I was tripping looking at the pastor in person, then closing my eyes and imagining I was in Virginia watching him on TV, then opening my eyes again."

"That must have been wild."

"It was fantastic. Felt like I had stepped into the TV. And the Word was just awesome. You have got to go and experience this for yourself."

"Next Sunday, I promise," Kevin said right before he put his last bite in his mouth.

"Good. Would you like some more to eat?" she asked.

"No thank you. That was delicious. I honestly can't remember the last time I had a meal that good," he complimented her after he finished chewing.

"Thank you, sir," Nikki said, almost blushing. "We have some ice cream . . . vanilla."

"Dag, you go all out, don't you? Maybe later. I'm just too stuffed to eat another bite right now," Kevin said.

She nodded and smiled, feeling comfortable with her new friend. "So what do you do?"

"I teach high school biology."

"At the same school as Randy?"

"Yes. We've always done the same things, encouraging each other since we were kids. Good friends are hard to find."

"That's true."

"So what was your major?" Kevin asked, assuming she had gone to college.

"Accounting."

"Tough major," he said.

"But worth it," Nikki said. "Accountants can always find work."

"Where do you work now?" he asked.

"I don't. I have my résumé ready to take over to the church tomorrow. I don't want to work right now. Maybe after school starts. I have enough to maintain for a while. I need to be here for the kids, to make sure they are settling in all right. Know what I mean?" Nikki explained.

"Sure. You shouldn't have any trouble finding a job when you're ready. You're in demand," Kevin said.

"And so are you. Young, strong, intelligent black men are needed in the classroom. That's exactly what our children need to see."

"And I love it," Kevin said.

"Do you coach football too?" Nikki asked.

"I coach the defensive backs . . . my guys against Randy's guys."

"That should be fun," she said.

"Oh man, we have a ball. Ever since pee-wee football, he's been trying to catch the ball and I've been trying to stop him. We always knew we'd end up doing exactly what we're doing."

"Maybe you'll get to take it to the college level."

"Why stop there? We should go on to the NFL. We may not have made it there as players, but as coaches, you never know."

"Your faith can take you wherever you want to go. Mine brought me here," Nikki said, thinking there was no place else she'd rather be at that particular moment.

"You know, talking to you, I see the possibilities."

"Seeing them is the first step. Can you see yourself eating some ice cream now?"

Kevin sat back and rubbed his stomach.

"Actually, I'm still full," he said, "but I'll take a rain check. Let me help you clean up."

"That's okay. I got it. You sure about that ice cream?"

"I'm sure. Thanks again for dinner. I'm gonna go mess with Randy and tell him what he missed."

"Glad you enjoyed it. See you later," she said, laughing and walking him to the door.

Chapter Twenty-two

"Mommy, we're going to need some more milk today," Taj said as he held up the almost empty carton to show Nikki when she came into the kitchen to cook breakfast. He was the first one up, and not knowing when his mother would be preparing breakfast, he ate cereal, almost finishing off the milk.

"Boy, I'm going to buy you a cow for your birthday. After breakfast, I'm going to run up to the church to drop off my résumé at the personnel department. I'll pick up some milk then."

Shay came into the kitchen and gave her mother a big hug. She set the table while Nikki cooked.

"You all stay here and chill, and I'll be back as soon as I can, okay?" Nikki said.

"Sure, Mommy. We'll be okay," Taj said.

"Yeah, take your time," Shay agreed.

"You all are so responsible. I really appreciate how well you've been behaving. You're the most precious darlings in the world, and I thank God for blessing me with you," Nikki praised.

They grinned at their mother's kind and loving words. Their behavior was no accident, but a direct result of how they were being raised.

Nikki went into her room to get dressed. She wasn't sure what to put on. After staring in her closet for a few moments, she decided on a long olive-colored dress, complemented by a lightweight beige jacket, with olive flats. She wanted to look business-casual. Her short, low-maintenance haircut was a blessing at times like this when she wanted to look sharp and stylish without a lot of work.

Once dressed, she felt ready to conquer the world. Upon arriving at the church, she went to the front desk and informed the receptionist that she was there to deliver her résumé to the personnel director. Just then a woman walked in the door and stood beside Nikki and began talking to the receptionist.

"Any messages for personnel, Sister Tonya?" the woman asked.

"No, Sister Erica," Tonya said.

An alert Nikki zeroed in on Sister Erica.

Extending her hand, Nikki said, "Hello, Sister Erica. My name is Nicole Riley."

Erica shook Nikki's hand. "Hello, Sister Nicole," she said.

Nikki saw an opening.

"I am an accountant with fifteen years of experience. I just moved here from Richmond, Virginia, and am very interested in working here at the church. I have been saved and living for Jesus for six years. This is my résumé and letters of recommendation," Nikki said, handing Erica the information.

Erica smiled as she took the package. Nikki felt she had made a good first impression.

"Walk with me to my office," Erica said.

"Thank you," Nikki said, overjoyed for the favor she was being shown.

They walked down the hall to Erica's nice plush office. Soft inspirational music was playing in the background. Nikki looked around. She observed a beautiful wall painting of ladies dancing, flowing in subtle pastel colors. The flower arrangement on the file cabinet displayed the same colors. The textured wallpaper had a softly arched pattern, and the color blended perfectly with the rest of the décor.

"What a lovely office," Nikki complimented.

"Thank you. Please have a seat," Erica said as she retrieved an employment application from the files.

Nikki noticed how professional, stylish, and beautiful Erica was. Her makeup was flawless. She felt a connection to the double-breasted olive suit and two-tone matching pumps that Erica was wearing. They had chosen the same color scheme, and Nikki thought that was a good sign.

Erica handed her a clipboard with a paper attached, and Nikki noticed her perfect French manicure.

"Take a few minutes to complete this application, and I'll be right back."

"Thank you," Nikki said, feeling really welcome.

When Erica returned, Nikki handed her the completed form. Erica scanned it as she sat down. As everything appeared to be in order, she looked directly into Nikki's eyes.

"So tell me about yourself," she said.

Wow, Nikki thought, *am I being interviewed? This is sudden. I had better be totally professional, but what do church people want?*

She knew what corporate America wanted and could handle herself in a secular interview, but this was different. Before she panicked, she decided to let the Holy Spirit lead. She relaxed, sat back, let the peace of God overtake her, and began.

"After my divorce, God led me to move my children here from Richmond. My last job in Virginia was with the federal government in accounting. I also did a lot of volunteer work at my church."

Nikki hesitated before going on, debating whether she should get more personal. Erica was very patient. She quietly gave Nikki all the time she needed and really made her feel comfortable. Nikki proceeded.

"I have been a partner with Way Maker Ministries for years. I've always considered it my second church home. I asked God to bring me here, and He did. I am so thankful to be here, and I am looking forward to getting involved."

"Have you joined the church yet?" Erica asked.

"Yes."

"Have you started new-members classes?"

"Not yet. I just heard the announcement about it at church on Sunday. That was my next stop."

"Good. The classes will give you the vision of the ministry and introduce you to all the different areas in which you can serve."

"That sounds great. Thank you."

"How many children do you have?" Erica asked, changing the subject.

"I have three, one son and two daughters. My son, Taj, is ten. Shay is nine, and Mia is six. Do you have any children?" Nikki asked, feeling more and more comfortable with this woman.

Erica paused, then sighed.

"I lost my then six-year-old son, Emmanuel, to a drunk driver five years ago. He was my only child, and I couldn't have any more," Erica revealed.

Nikki couldn't imagine anything like that happening to any of her children. Her heart went out to Erica.

"You must have been devastated," Nikki said, full of compassion.

"Hell. I went through pure hell. The teenage driver was killed also. My now ex-husband was driving, and he walked away without a scratch. My marriage suffered, ending in divorce, and I was driven straight to Jesus. I've been serving Him ever since," Erica said.

"How are you doing now?" Nikki asked, genuinely concerned for this woman to whom she was being drawn.

Erica suddenly smiled. "I have a meeting in a few minutes. Would you like to get together later?"

"I'd love to," was Nikki's eager response.

"I'd love to meet your children."

"That would be great."

"Where exactly do you live?"

"I live in the Regency apartment complex. Do you know where that is?"

"Right around the corner from my house. I'm talking walking distance."

"No way!" Nikki said.

"Yes way." Erica laughed.

"Please have dinner with us," Nikki said.

"Oooh, you're talking my language now. What's a good time?" Erica asked.

"Anytime," Nikki said.

"Well, I get off at five o'clock. I'll go home and change and come around six-thirty, seven o'clock," Erica calculated.

"Perfect. What do you like to eat?" Nikki asked.

"Anything."

They both laughed.

Erica got up, professionalism back on, and Nikki rose with her, following her lead.

"I will read your paperwork, and you will be contacted should there be a match between your qualifications and the needs of the ministry. If there is not a match, then your résumé and application will be kept on file for six months. Should a position become available, you will be contacted to see if you are still interested, and if so, you will not have to resubmit an application, just update it."

"I understand," Nikki said.

"It has been a pleasure talking with you. And I'll see you this evening. Is this your correct address and phone number here on your résumé?"

"That's it, and thank you so much for taking the time to talk to me. I'll see you later."

Nikki shook Erica's hand, feeling that this was the beginning of a new and beautiful friendship.

Chapter Twenty-three

W e have to clean this place up! We're having company," Nikki exclaimed when she walked in the door.

She looked around the apartment. There were a few toys and papers out of place, but with a little dusting, vacuuming, and straightening, the place would be presentable to entertain her new friend.

"Who? Kevin?" Taj asked.

"No, Sister Erica."

"Who is Sister Erica?" Shay asked.

"She's the person who does the hiring at Way Maker Ministries. Thank You, Father, that I walk in Your favor and Your power and Your comfort. And she's coming here, hallelujah!" Nikki shouted.

"Why?" Taj asked.

"Well, because as we were talking, I seriously believe that God was hooking us up. I felt really connected to her, like we've known each other for years," she explained.

"Mom, that's not unusual for you. You talk to anybody about anything all the time. We should know. We're the ones who have to stand around and wait for you, especially when you run into people you know in the mall and start talking about Jesus. We start looking for a place to sit down," Taj said.

"Yeah, Mommy, you can go," Shay said.

"Watch your mouths now," Nikki said—jokingly because she knew it was true. "I'll be right back. I'm going to run to the grocery store. Chain and dead-bolt the door, Taj."

"Okay, Mommy."

Nikki decided to cook chicken, since every time she turned around, someone was claiming they didn't eat red meat.

Taj, too, had cooking skills. His specialty was baked chicken. His granddaddy had taught him well. Nikki bought two chickens, wild rice, and green beans she decided to season with smoked turkey. She bought a cake to go with the ice cream and some lemons because lemonade was a universal drink . . . everybody seemed to like it.

She managed all the grocery bags herself in one trip.

"Taj, hook the chicken up, man."

"Cool, Mommy! You're going to let me cook for your friend? You really do like my cooking."

"Was there ever any doubt? Truth be told, you do a better job than me with the chicken. Your granddaddy rubbed off on you. We have to call Mom and Dad tonight too. Better yet, I'll call them tomorrow and let them know how nice these people are and about dinner tonight."

"Oh, Granddaddy called while you were at the store," Taj said.

"Oh Lord. Did he have a fit because I left you here alone?" she asked.

"Of course he did. I told him we were all locked in

and you would be back in a few minutes. I tried to cover for you," Taj explained while gathering the ingredients for his chicken.

"Did it work?" she asked.

"Of course not. But don't worry, Mommy. I'll tell the judge you're not an unfit mother."

Nikki laughed at her son, wondering which one of her parents had threatened to turn her in, then decided it must have been her dad.

"He'll get over it," she said.

"He said a month is long enough to get settled and they might be down next weekend."

"I'm surprised they haven't shown up yet."

"He said he wanted to make sure we were all settled in before they came to visit."

"I do miss them, and I'm ready to see them." Nikki smiled, thinking about her parents. She believed their relationship would be even stronger with the distance between them.

After the chicken was done soaking in salt water, Taj began his masterpiece. Nikki chopped up an onion and then got out of his way. He massaged butter all over the chicken parts, then seasoned them with his granddaddy's secret recipe. He carefully placed the pieces in a roaster, sprinkled the chopped onion all around, and covered the pan for moistness and flavor. Nikki had turned the oven to 375 degrees. It was hot when Taj put the roaster in.

"I'm done," he yelled, closing the oven door.

Nikki cooked the rest of the meal, deciding to pop the rolls in the oven when Erica arrived so they would be good and hot.

They straightened up the apartment, dusting, vacuuming, and making sure everything was in its proper place.

The phone rang.

"Hello," Taj answered. "Mommy, telephone."

She picked up another extension.

"Hello," Nikki said as she heard Taj hang up.

"Hi, this is Erica."

"Hey."

"Hey, girl. Are you ready for me?" Erica asked. Nikki was happy that Erica was feeling comfortable around her.

"Ready and waiting. Come on over."

"I'm on my way."

"See you in a few," Nikki said, excited about her guest.

Erica seemed to be just about the nicest, down-to-earth person Nikki had ever met.

Chapter Twenty-four

Hello, sis, come on in. Mi casa is your casa," Nikki said as she opened the door.

"Hey, thanks," Erica said, walking in and giving Nikki a hug. "Oh, it smells good in here."

Nikki led her to the kitchen, where Taj was putting the finishing touches on his chicken by basting it.

"Sister Erica, this is Taj, my oldest child and only son. Taj, this is Sister Erica from Way Maker Ministries."

Taj put down his spoon, wiped his hands, and went to shake Erica's hand. "Nice to meet you," he said.

"Very nice to meet you too, Taj," Erica said, smiling.

"Shay, Mia, come here," Nikki called.

The girls came out of their room and stood facing Erica, waiting to be introduced. Nikki stood behind Shay with both hands on her shoulders and said, "This is my big girl, Shay." Moving over to Mia and putting her hands on her shoulders, she said, "And this is my little girl, Mia."

The girls flashed electric smiles.

"Girls, this is Sister Erica."

"Hello, Sister Erica," they sang together.

"Well, aren't you adorable little princesses? How are you?" Erica asked, bending over and smiling at them.

"Fine," they sang.

"Well, it is a pleasure to meet all of you," Erica said.

"It's a pleasure to meet you too, Sister Erica," they said in unison.

"Aw, how sweet," Erica said, genuinely moved.

"I'll call you when dinner is ready," Nikki said, dismissing the children.

Turning to Erica, she said, "I'm going to put the rolls in the oven. We should be ready to eat in about fifteen minutes. Just make yourself at home."

Looking around, Erica said, "Girl, your apartment is hooked! I love your mirrors over the fireplace."

"Thanks. They just seem to open things up for me," Nikki said as she put the rolls in the oven.

They sat at the dining room table so Nikki could jump up and check on them every few minutes. The rolls had to be perfect.

"Did you work in personnel before you came to the church?" Nikki asked.

"I've always been in personnel. I'm a people person, I guess," Erica said.

"I've always been in accounting. I'm a numbers person, I guess," Nikki said, laughing.

"Where have you been since you moved here to Atlanta?" Erica asked.

"Besides church, to the grocery store and health department."

"Oh, I have to take you out."

"Please do," Nikki said, sounding desperate.

"Do you know anybody here?" Erica asked.

"Not really. I've met some neighbors. Everybody seems so nice and friendly," Nikki said, getting up to check the rolls. Looking in the oven, she said, "A few more minutes." She got out the plates, glasses, and silverware.

"Need any help?" Erica asked.

"You want to butter the rolls?"

"Okay. Where's the bathroom so I can wash my hands?"

I really like her, Nikki thought. "Right around that corner."

She took the rolls out of the oven, got the butter out of the refrigerator, grabbed a butter knife, and set them all on the table. Erica buttered the rolls while Nikki put the food out. Once everything was ready, she called the children.

"Wash up and come eat!"

They all took their places at the dinner table.

"Would you please bless the food, Taj?"

"Sure, Mommy. Dear Lord, thank You for this food. We bless it and receive it with thanksgiving, for it is sanctified by the Word of God and this prayer. In Jesus' name we pray, amen."

"Amen," Erica agreed, visibly impressed.

As they ate, Erica told them about the church and the children's ministry. She told Nikki that she would be happy to watch the children for her if she had something she wanted to do.

"So what grade are you going to be in when school starts?" Erica asked.

"I'm in the fifth grade," Taj said.

"I'm going to the fourth," Shay offered.

"Second grade," Mia said.

"That's wonderful. I bet you guys get good grades too."

"We don't have a choice," Shay said.

Erica looked at Nikki. "Why am I not surprised?"

"Got to keep the standards high," Nikki said.

"That's our mom," Shay said, "but we love her."

They all laughed.

After they finished eating, the children went to watch TV Land. Erica helped Nikki clear the table, load the dishwasher, and clean up the kitchen. Afterward, they joined the children, who were falling out laughing at something on TV.

"TV used to be great. Nowadays, there's no telling what you might see come across that tube," Erica said.

"That's for sure. Our TV pretty much stays on the Disney Channel or TV Land. They're the safest things I've found for the kids to watch. The videos are scary," Nikki said.

"I hear you, sis," Erica agreed. She laughed with the children at *I Love Lucy*. "You guys want to hang out tomorrow? Maybe ride to the mall or something?" she asked.

"Yes," Shay said.

"Sure," Nikki answered, ready to do something.

"How about if I come to get you about the same time?" Erica suggested.

"Cool. We'll be ready," Nikki said. "And I can't wait to get involved at the church. I picked up the class schedule from the receptionist's desk."

"You will learn so much from those classes if you take them seriously. Some people take them lightly and don't pass the test," Erica said.

"What test?"

"Oh, I didn't tell you. Yeah, girl, a test that you must pass to graduate," Erica explained.

"Graduate?"

"I'm telling you, it's serious. It's a big deal. Pastor imparts the vision to you during a special ceremony. Then there's a reception afterward where all the ministries try to recruit you. It's blessed," Erica explained.

"Oh wow, I'm real excited now!"

"You're in for a treat. A lot of work, but it's all good," Erica said, getting up and stretching. "I'll call you tomorrow, make sure everything is still on. After that good meal, I'm ready to get comfortable and get in my bed, know what I mean?"

"Yes, ma'am. Hope you enjoyed it," Nikki said.

"Oh girl, I can't remember the last time I've felt this wonderful, ate this good, relaxed and laughed this much. I have thoroughly enjoyed my evening. Thanks for inviting me, and I just love the kids," Erica said, walking to the door.

"Thank you so much for coming. We have really enjoyed your company. I thank God for you."

"See you later, kids!" Erica called to them.

Each of them came and gave her a hug good-bye.

Nikki walked Erica to her car. Kevin was parking as they were coming down the steps.

"God has surrounded me with good people. That guy getting out of the car is my neighbor and Taj's new barber. He makes house calls and is inexpensive. Real nice, him and his roommate," Nikki said.

"He's kind of cute," Erica said.

"That's what I thought. He's young with a son. He and his roommate teach high school and coach football."

"Impressive," Erica said.

"Evening, ladies," Kevin spoke as he approached them.

"Good evening, Kevin. This is Sister Erica, my friend from Way Maker Ministries. Sister Erica, this is my neighbor Kevin," Nikki said.

They shook hands.

"Nice to meet you," Erica said.

"Same here," he said.

"I'll talk to you tomorrow, Nikki. Good night," Erica said.

"Bye. Get home safe."

Kevin was still standing there as Nikki watched Erica get in her car and pull off.

Aware of his presence, she turned to him. "So how was your day?"

"Good, and yours?" he responded.

"Wonderful. I made a new friend, Sister Erica, who just so happens to work at the church."

"Yeah?" Kevin said.

"Yeah. And she's the personnel director. Remember I told you just yesterday that I wanted to work at the church? Well, that had to be God hooking us up. I met her today, and we hit it right off. Nobody but God."

"Hey, I believe you, Nikki, and I'm happy for you. It's good to have friends in high places. Look, I was wondering if I could share something with you," he said.

"What?"

"It's a business opportunity. Something you can do

while you're waiting for your job to come through," he explained.

Nikki had tried many of the networking businesses. While in Virginia she explored the entrepreneurial route and had become familiar with most of the independent business opportunities available.

"Kevin, what are you selling?"

Being the open, honest, not-to-beat-around-the-bush type, he said, "Knives."

"Kutright?" she asked.

"How did you know that?" he asked, surprised.

"Got some. They have a lifetime warranty, right?"

"Right."

"Then I won't be needing any more in this lifetime."

"Well, could you do me a favor when you have some time and just listen to my presentation? I'm trying to perfect it, and that only comes from doing it. I can do it in front of the mirror, but I need some constructive criticism, some feedback. If you could be my audience one day this week, that would be great."

"How long does your presentation take?" she asked.

"No more than thirty minutes with all the demonstrations, but I can make it shorter," he said.

"What's a good time for you during the week?" Nikki asked.

"Around four-thirty, five o'clock," he answered. "I teach summer school in the afternoon."

"How's tomorrow as soon as you get home?"

"That's fine. Look, I really appreciate this."

"No problem. Hey, Kevin, when are you going to let your son play with Taj?"

"Son? I don't have a son," Kevin said.

Oops. That's what you get for jumping to conclusions,
she thought. *You are going to have to work on that, girl.*
Get the facts straight before you open your big mouth.
The kids just told you that you talk all the time, "Oh, I'm
sorry. I saw a boy about Taj's age with you the other day
and just assumed he was your son. I should know better
than to jump to conclusions."

"That was my nephew, Rashad. Yeah, I get him from
time to time to give my sister a break," Kevin clarified.

"Oh," she said. *Well, that explains that. I even gave*
that misinformation to Erica. I need to mind my own
business for real . . . I wonder where his girlfriend is. I
haven't seen her since that first day.

Chapter Twenty-five

Nikki was just getting up when the phone rang.

"Good morning, sis," Erica said.

"What a pleasant surprise. How are you?" Nikki responded.

"Great. Just calling to say hey. I'm on my way to a meeting. I really have a good feeling about this one. I might be calling you with some good news later."

"Oh wow! I can't wait," Nikki said.

"Well, pray for favor during the meeting beginning at ten o'clock."

"Oh yes. Amen. I will be praying."

Nikki spent the morning around the house, waiting to hear from Erica. When the phone finally rang, she said a quick prayer before answering.

"Girl, your Daddy loves you," Erica said.

"What? What?"

"I just got out of the meeting, and I have been instructed to advertise for several new jobs, and guess what one of them is?"

"What? What?"

"Accountant."

"Accountant. Are you serious?"

"But, girl, you are completely on your own. I have to remain unbiased and fair as I screen the applications," Erica said.

"Girl, I got this. God did not bring me this far to leave me," Nikki said.

"I will submit the strongest résumés and applications to the controller. Pray that yours is in there. I can tell you this: You're looking good so far. I mean, I haven't advertised yet, but as far as résumés go, yours is very strong. It's going to take quite a bit to top what you submitted. I got your back in prayer," Erica said.

"How long have you known about this position?" Nikki asked.

"I knew some changes were coming, but Pastor just made the official announcement this morning. Do you see God in this?" Erica asked.

"Clear as day. His timing is perfect. What do I need to do?"

"Nothing. I have your paperwork, and the job hasn't even been advertised. Just wait for your interview. You might want to go on and knock those new-members classes out ASAP," Erica said.

"Glory be to God! Thanks, sis. Are we still on for this evening?" Nikki asked.

"Absolutely."

"Good. See you then. Now I have to go pray," Nikki said.

"Good. Talk to you later."

When Nikki hung up the phone, she called the children. "We have to pray. God has created a position for me at the church. Pray that I have the new accountant position because I am the only one called, anointed, and appointed to that position in Jesus' name."

They prayed pretty much all day as they went about their normal routine until the girls went outside to play.

Around four-thirty, there was a knock at the door. Nikki looked through the peephole. It was Kevin. She opened the door.

"Hey. Are you busy?" he asked.

"Busy praying. Come in. I've got to tell you this and get you to stand in agreement with us," she said.

He followed her into the apartment.

"Didn't I tell you I was going to work at the church?" she asked.

"Yes," he said.

"Well, when I went up there and submitted my résumé, there wasn't anything that matched my qualifications, but now a newly created position is being advertised. My job. Accountant. God brought me here for that job. Now I need you to stand in agreement with me that that is my job until I start working. It has to be advertised, and others have to be given the opportunity to apply, but when it's all said and done, we shall see who ends up in that position," a confident, faithful Nikki said.

"Will that be you?" Kevin asked.

"That will be me," she answered.

"You know it, huh?"

"Like I know my name. It's called faith. Do you agree with me?"

"Heck yeah. With all those positive vibes coming off

you, if it were up to me, I'd give it to you right now," Kevin said, setting himself in agreement.

"It's a done deal. So did you come up to do your presentation?" she asked.

"Do you have time now?"

"Sure. Erica won't be here till around six-thirty."

"Cool. I'm going to run down and get my material. Be right back."

"Just come on in. I'll leave the door unlocked."

"Okay."

"Taj! Come in here," Nikki called.

Shay and Mia were still outside playing with some neighborhood children. Nikki could see them from her living room window.

"Kevin wants to do a presentation, and he needs an audience. Would you mind listening to him with me?"

"Okay," Taj said.

Taj and his mother sat on the sofa. Kevin came right in without knocking.

He sure follows directions well, Nikki thought.

He looked at them sitting on the sofa.

"Great. A real live audience. Hope I don't get stage fright."

They laughed.

Kevin set up his materials neatly on the coffee table. Nikki and Taj paid close attention as Kevin described how wonderful the knives were, then he demonstrated their effectiveness. He cut a penny in half with the shears.

"Don't try this with your regular scissors. It won't work," he said, smiling.

Nikki and Taj couldn't help but smile back. Kevin's

personality and charm were drawing them in and holding their attention.

"Can your knives do this?" he asked as he cut through a Coke can.

"Yes, they can, because I have those same knives," Nikki yelled from the audience.

"Really, Mommy?" Taj asked jokingly, knowing perfectly well she did.

"No way. These same, identical, exact knives?" Kevin said, playing along.

They all laughed. At the end of the presentation, they clapped and Kevin bowed.

"May I go outside?" Taj asked.

"Yes, you may," Nikki said, watching him bolt for the door. Then she turned her attention back to Kevin.

"That was so good that if I didn't already have the knives, I would definitely be tempted to buy them."

"Thanks," Kevin said. "Now let me really have it."

"No, that was great. You weren't nervous. You have knowledge of the product. You answered our questions— even the ones you weren't sure about—with intelligent, honest responses. I like when you took the time to look in the book to verify your answer. Lets 'em know you don't mind showing that you don't know everything and that you are willing to do the work to find out. It was really good, and I wouldn't say that if it weren't true. You're ready."

"Well, I do appreciate that."

"No problem," Nikki said.

Nikki got up and turned on the radio. As Kevin packed up his materials, he sang along. Nikki noticed his beautiful voice. *He really loosens up when he gets to know you,* she thought.

"Do you sing in a choir?" she asked.

"Not now. I did in college."

"What college was that?" she asked.

"Randy and I both went to Atlanta State University on football scholarships. And you?"

"Manna State University."

"In Maryland?"

"That's the one."

"We used to play you guys."

"Who won?"

"We did, of course," Kevin said, chuckling

"Well, you have skills off the field too. When you finally get to Way Maker and become a member—and I'm sure you will—you should join the choir. You have the voice of a soloist."

"Yeah, right." Kevin shrugged.

"I'm serious, and I'm a hard critic. Nobody ever told you that before?"

"I've been told. Now, I know some people who can really sing, and I can't touch them," he said.

His modesty was very attractive. The phone rang. Nikki went over and grabbed it. It was Erica.

"Are you ready?" she asked.

"I will be when you get here. Are you coming now?"

"On my way."

"Right on time," she said, looking at Kevin.

"See you in a few," Erica said.

As Nikki hung up, Kevin said, "Well, I'll catch you later," and headed toward the door.

"I'll walk down with you," she said, and went outside to see if the children looked presentable. When she saw Mia, she decided she needed freshening up.

"Stay here and tell Erica I'll be right out so she won't have to get out of the car," she told Taj and Shay, then took Mia back up to the apartment.

"You look like you had a good time, baby. We're going to have to wipe your face and brush that hair. Let me see your clothes," she said, standing back to look at her daughter, not noticing any dirt, but her shirt was hanging out.

"I didn't play in the dirt, Mommy. We just sat on the picnic table and played with Barbie dolls."

"No, you're not dirty, just a little sweaty from sitting in the heat," Nikki said, tucking her daughter's shirt back inside her shorts. She washed Mia's face and brushed her hair back into a neat ponytail, then they went downstairs. Taj and Shay were in Erica's car. Mia got in the backseat with them, and Nikki got up front.

"Evening, sis," Nikki said.

"Evening to you too. Have you been praying?" Erica asked.

"Without ceasing," Nikki answered.

"It's all up to you now. God has put it out there," Erica said.

"Girl, that is such a done deal we can move on to the next miracle. Where're we going?" Nikki asked.

"Well, I wanted to take the kids to Laser Land. They'll love it. Or we can go to the mall. It's up to you," Erica said.

"What's Laser Land?" Shay asked.

"An amusement center with lots of fun things to do. Want to go there?" Then looking at Nikki, she said, "We can hit the mall anytime."

"Please, Mommy, please!" Taj pleaded.

"All right," she said

They had a ball at Laser Land. They played laser tag. Erica and Taj were partners against Nikki, Shay, and Mia. Erica and Taj were faster and quicker on the trigger. They planned their attacks and hideouts and took the game more seriously than Nikki and the girls did. No wonder they won every time. They decided to drive race cars next. They eventually played every game and just ran all over the place. The time flew.

"We can't keep Sister Erica out too late," Nikki said as they regrouped at one of the benches. "She has to go to work in the morning, and you guys need to start going to bed at nine-thirty to get back in school mode. You only have a couple of weeks before it starts."

"One more game, please, Mommy," Taj pleaded.

"What did I say?"

"Yes, ma'am," Taj said.

They stopped and got some ice cream before Erica dropped them off at home. It had been a wonderful day.

Chapter Twenty-six

The apartment looked like they had lived in it for years with all the pictures hung and boxes gone. It had quickly become home sweet home. Nikki was doing some ironing when the phone rang.

"Hello."

"Hey, baby."

"Hi, Ma!" Nikki said, recognizing her mother's voice.

"You know your dad is still upset that you left his grandbabies home alone in that great big strange city that you know nothing about. His words, not mine," Jean said.

"I know, Ma. I don't remember him being that over-protective with me."

"Think about it, baby. When was he not there? When you were in high school, he didn't go to see the games, he went to see you cheer. When you didn't come home for the weekend while you were in college, he was up there to visit you. He looked like he was about to cry during your whole wedding. Every time you went into labor, no matter where he was or what he was doing, he dropped it and rushed to the hospital."

"You're right, Ma. So where were you?"

"Your dad was not dragging me all over creation following you. You made me tired just watching you rip, race, and run. And you could go, girl. Look how you just packed up and got out of here. You make up your mind and you're gone. He can try to keep up with you, but I'll be here to take care of the home front," Jean explained.

"I knew you had a logical explanation. So when are you coming?"

"I'll have to have your father call you back. Mr. Johnson from next door just stopped by, and they're tangled up in conversation."

"Okay. I'll wait until I get both of you on the phone to tell you all about Atlanta . . . or I'll just wait until you get here. It's great, Ma."

"I'm glad to hear it. As long as everything is fine, I'll wait for the details."

"Have you heard from Rae?" Nikki asked.

"Not lately, but what I've been hearing is not good," Jean said with concern.

"Like what?" Nikki asked.

"I hear she's selling those drugs."

"Yeah, I talked to her about that. All we can do is pray for her."

"Yes, pray, but don't worry about her. You don't have time to be worrying about grown folks. You worried yourself silly about Sam, and see where that got you. Besides, you have my grandbabies to raise."

"I know, Ma."

"Okay, baby. I'll get your dad to call you back later."

"Okay. Bye, Ma."

Nikki knew her mother was right about her worrying too much, but she just felt so bad. Rae was her special cousin. All hell had broken loose when Rae's mother, Nikki's Aunt Tee, committed suicide three months after Rae's older brother, Leonard, was killed in a drug-related shoot-out. Rae was only twelve years old at the time and went to live with her father and stepmother. She was so devastated from the deaths of her mother and big brother that she spun out of control. At age fourteen, Rae ran away and became a part of the drug culture. Nikki tried to find her, and when she did, she talked to her. For a while it seemed like she was getting through, but something always drew Rae back. Then Rae had a baby at age sixteen and another a year later. This seemed to settle her down a bit. She attempted to get a job and live right for her children but found that supporting a family was very difficult and expensive, so she resorted to the way her brother had taught her to make money. Thinking about her cousin made Nikki want to hear her voice.

Nikki called Rae and prayed that she answer. God answered her prayer.

"Hello?"

"Rae, it's Nikki."

"Hey, cuz. Where are you?"

"In Atlanta. How are you?"

"Hanging in there," Rae said.

"How are LaQuandria and Jalani?"

"Fine."

"Where are they?"

"Their dad's oldest sister has them now."

"How did she get them?"

"When Darius got shot last month, she asked if she could have them, so I let her. I figured they stood a better chance with her, but I support them and go see them as often as I can."

"Darius got shot? Is he okay?"

"Yeah, he got shot in the arm at a club."

"Girl, when are you going to give up the thug life?"

"And do what?"

"Help her, Lord." Nikki prayed so Rae could hear.

"Yes, Lord. Please help me. So you like it down there?" Rae asked in an effort to change the subject.

"I love it."

"Hey, that's my pager. I gotta go," Rae said.

Nikki hung up and sighed. She knew God had a plan for Rae.

Chapter Twenty-seven

While Nikki waited for her father to call, her mind wandered to her childhood. She had spent a lot of her time at her Aunt Tee's. Her aunt was always in bed. She suffered from deep depression. Nikki's mother had tried everything she knew to help her baby sister, but nothing worked. She eventually resolved to let Nikki go over there and be with Tee's children, since Nikki was older and very responsible. When they were little, Nikki loved playing in the backyard with her cousins. She recalled their games from long ago.

"You're it, Rae," said Leonard, who was two years younger than Nikki and two years older than Rae.

"No, she's not. You are because she tagged the base before you touched her," said Nikki, Rae's self-appointed defender.

"I did touch her shirt," Leonard said.

"That's not her. Now you're still it."

"You don't play fair," Leonard said.

"Just close your eyes and count," Nikki bullied.

"Come on, let's hide, Rae."

Rae followed Nikki, who told her exactly where to hide. "If he finds me first, I'll run him around while you go tag the base. If he comes toward you first, I'll make noise so he can come after me because I'll be closer. Then you tag up because he won't catch me and he'll be it again," Nikki instructed.

"Okay," Rae said, nodding. The plan always worked.

Leonard would count and try to find them. As promised, once Nikki saw that Rae was safe, she would slip past Leonard and tag the base before he could catch her.

"You're it again," Rae and Nikki would say in unison, and fall out laughing at a thoroughly frustrated Leonard.

"Cheaters! I quit," Leonard yelled every time.

She was smiling from the warm memories when the phone rang. It was her father.

"Hey, baby," Jim said.

"Hi, Daddy. What's up?"

"How are my grandbabies?"

"Doing good. We've met some really nice people. Taj couldn't be better. We have two big football players who happen to be college graduates, teachers, football coaches, and real good role models for him living right under us. I've also met a really good friend, Erica, from the church. She took us out, and we had a ball, so you can relax," Nikki said.

"Not until I see for myself. Did your mother tell you that we plan to come this weekend?"

"Yeah, she said you'd fill me in on the details. Can't wait to see you. What time will you get here?"

"We're leaving Friday morning. We're going to take our time, enjoy the scenery. Need anything?" Jim asked.

"Just some hugs," Nikki answered.

"Got plenty of them. We'll see you Friday around four, sweetheart."

"Okay, Daddy. Tell Ma I'll talk to her later."

"I will. Bye, baby."

"Bye, Daddy. Love you."

"Love you too, baby. See ya soon."

After breakfast on Friday, Nikki and the kids cleaned the apartment spick-and-span, then she called Erica.

"Hey, whatcha doin' this weekend?"

"Just running some errands. What's up?" Erica asked.

"I want you to meet my parents."

"I would love to meet them. Where are they?"

"They'll be here later today."

"Maybe I can stop by after work," Erica said.

"Do that. They'll probably just want to chill tonight after that long ride, so we'll be here. Just stop on by."

"Cool. How're the kids?"

"Blessed. We had the best time the other day. Thanks again for that."

"Girl, I bet I had more fun than anybody," Erica said.

"You were into it, girl, that's for sure."

"Running around with kids keeps me young," Erica said.

"I hear ya," Nikki said, laughing.

"Talk to you later."

"Bye."

Nikki looked through the peephole later that day and saw her father. She swung the door open. "Daddy!" she shouted, practically choking him as she hugged him tightly. The children came flying out of their rooms.

"Granddaddy! Grandma!" They jumped on Jim, almost knocking him down. He managed to make his way to the sofa and sit down while they hugged and kissed him all over. Nikki hugged her mother. When she finished, the kids grabbed Jean.

"My babies, my precious babies. Thank God you're all right," Jean cried.

"Oh, Ma. Of course they're all right," Nikki said.

When they all felt they had sufficiently hugged and kissed, Nikki said, "Sit down, relax, get comfortable. I'll go get your stuff out of the car."

"I'll have to help you with the suitcase, Nikki," Jim said. "It's pretty heavy." He got up, and together they went outside to the Caddy.

"Let me see if Kevin and Randy are home," Nikki said. "I want to introduce you to our neighbors."

When she knocked on the door, Randy opened it.

"Hey, I want you guys to meet my parents. They came down for a visit. Is Kevin here?"

"Yeah, I'll get him. We'll be right out," Randy said.

The two guys came over to the car while Nikki and her dad were getting the bags out.

"Daddy, this is Randy and this is Kevin. They are really good neighbors."

"You are some big guys," Jim said, sticking out his hand.

They smiled as they took turns shaking Jim's hand.

"Nice to meet you, sir. Let us get those bags for you," Kevin said.

"Thanks, man," Jim said.

Randy and Kevin followed Nikki and Jim up to the apartment with the suitcase and other bags.

"Just put them anywhere," Nikki instructed.

Nikki went on about the guys as if she was introducing the evening's speakers to an audience.

"They both graduated from Atlanta State University. They played on the championship football team together, and they are teachers at Riverdale High School. They aspire to be NFL coaches, and they are excellent role models for our children, especially our young black boys. I'm pretty lucky to have them for my neighbors and friends," Nikki praised.

Kevin and Randy were blushing and grinning from ear to ear. Neither one of them could say a word. Nikki wasn't just praising the guys to make them or her parents feel good. She really and truly believed what she said.

"Well, since my daughter speaks so highly of you, you must be all right," Jean said.

"Nice to meet you," Randy said.

"Nice to meet you, ma'am," Kevin said, looking shy again.

Nikki concluded that if Kevin didn't know a person, he went into some type of shell, but after he got to know people, he was quite talkative.

"Hope to see you again before you leave," Randy said as they walked toward the door.

"Thanks for the help," Jim said.

"Anytime," Kevin replied, and they were gone.

"They seem like nice young men," Jean said.

"The best," Nikki confirmed.

"Do you like them, Shay?" Jim asked.

"Yes. They're cool," she answered.

"They're real nice, Granddaddy," Mia said.

"They said I can go to football practice with them and

be on the field during games, Granddaddy," Taj exclaimed.

"All right, then," Jim said. Then leaning into Nikki's ear, he said, "You still watch them."

"Don't worry, Daddy. I watch as well as pray."

"That's my girl. Now, where's the bathroom?"

"I'll give you a tour, Granddaddy," Taj said.

As her parents made themselves at home, Nikki checked on dinner. She prayed that it tasted as good as it looked.

"Are you guys ready for something to eat? I cooked your favorite, Daddy, steak with grilled onions and mushroom gravy and roasted potatoes with a fresh spinach salad on the side."

"That sounds delicious, baby. Jean—"

"I'll fix your plate," his wife responded before he could ask.

"Not too much now, I'm cutting back," Jim said.

"I'm the only one who knows what cutting back means," Jean told Nikki.

"Okay, Ma. I'll fix the kids' plates," Nikki said, opting to serve from the stove.

While they were eating, there was a knock at the door. It was Erica. Nikki answered it and made the introductions.

"Get a plate," she instructed Erica.

"Okay," Erica said, and helped herself. "Your daughter sure can cook, Mrs. Harris. So can that adorable grandson of yours. I've tasted his baked chicken that he said you taught him to make, Mr. Harris. Simply delicious."

"That's my boy," Jim said proudly.

Everyone thoroughly enjoyed the meal. After dinner, the children crashed all over their granddaddy in front of the TV.

"I'm going to unpack some things, Nikki. Nice meeting you, Erica," Jean said, getting up to go into Taj's room. Taj had graciously given it up to his grandparents.

"Wonderful meeting you, Mrs. Harris, and you too, Mr. Harris," Erica said. "Will you be coming to church during your visit?"

"Don't know yet," Jim said, basking in the love that was being poured on him.

"Well, enjoy your visit. I'm going to go on home, Nikki. Got some work to do."

"Okay. I'll talk to you later, and thanks for coming by."

"Wouldn't have missed it," Erica said.

After Erica left, Nikki took fresh towels to her mother.

"These people sure do appear to be nice, but you keep your antennas up. Can't be too careful where my babies are concerned," Jean said.

"I know, Ma."

Chapter Twenty-eight

Everything appeared to be in place and everyone seemed to be satisfied after Nikki's parents had checked things out for themselves. After her parents left, Nikki decided to touch base with Erica.

"Way Maker Ministries. This is Tonya. How may I direct your call?"

"Sister Erica Scott, please?"

"Just one moment, please."

"Personnel, this is Sister Erica Scott, how may I help you?"

"Hi, sis. Are you busy?"

"Hey, girl. Always busy. How are Mom and Dad?"

"Gone. Left this morning. The older you get, the more you hate to leave home, I guess. They couldn't make it a week without thinking they were missing something back home, but we really enjoyed the time we did have with them."

"Did they make it to church?" Erica asked.

"No, and I didn't make them feel bad about it either."

"Good for you."

"I went to register for my classes."

"Good."

"While I was up there, I looked at the board and saw my job posted. What's the status?" Nikki asked.

"It won't close for another couple of weeks, then I'll give all the qualified applications to the controller. Once he decides who he wants to interview, we'll set it up and give you a call."

"Sounds great. I should be done with all my classes by then."

"It would be great if you could get them done that fast."

"Then it's done. I'll talk to you later."

"Bye."

Nikki pulled out several translations of the Bible, her notebook, audiotapes, Bible commentaries, and several other study guides and began to dig into the Word of God. She thoroughly enjoyed spending time with God in this manner as He revealed Himself to her and she became more and more intimate with Him. Just as she was getting deep into her study, the phone rang.

"You have a collect call from Rae. Press or say one to accept the charges," a recorded voice said.

"One," Nikki said.

The call was connected.

"Nikki, this is my one phone call."

"Your one phone call? What the heck does that mean?"

"It means I'm locked up."

"And you call me three states away?"

"I know. I couldn't think of anyone else to call."

"Where's Darius?"

"Girl, my babies' daddy is locked up himself."

"Dang. What did you do?"

"The crack house I was dealing in got raided, and I couldn't get out fast enough, trying to get all my stuff. Some of the people who were in there with me got away, but I was not leaving my stuff."

"Rae, you done lost your mind."

"I know, Nikki. I saw the light in that padded wagon. I said to myself, *Look what I'm doing.* I could have gotten away if I had left it, but I wasn't thinking. You know how I am about my stuff. It's my livelihood, but I thought about all of that on the ride down here. Everything you've said to me came to mind, and I know this isn't it. I'm for real, Nikki. You know I would not be calling all the way to Georgia and asking you to call Aunt Jean if I wasn't serious. I've been this route too many times, had too many close calls, and I see now that it's just not worth it. I'm ready for some help now."

"Fine time to see the light. You might be on your own. Ma wants nothing to do with the lifestyle you've chosen to live, so I know she's not coming to get you. Your father and his wife still won't have anything to do with you?"

"Not a thing. I terrorized them, remember?"

"How could I forget? You robbed the people blind after all they tried to do for you. Dang near drove the poor woman crazy. What about your kids' aunt? Do you want me to call her for you, since you've used your one phone call on me?"

"I'd hate to do that with all she's doing for my kids. No, I'll think of something else. I gotta go, cuz."

"All I know to do is pray," Nikki said, playing with her hair.

"I will definitely do that. Bye."

Once school started for the children, Nikki had more time on her hands to study. She got the most out of her new-members classes and looked forward to graduation.

Nikki's daily routine while she believed God for the accountant position included driving the children to the school bus stop in the mornings. She allowed them to walk home from the bus stop with the large group after school. After the children were off, Nikki spent her mornings at the church taking her new-members classes and was home waiting for them when they arrived back from school.

When the new members' final exam came, she passed and was ready to graduate. Kevin and Randy were invited to the event. The graduates had to be there early for more than three hundred of them to line up and get their instructions. Randy couldn't make it to the graduation, but Kevin came and brought the children with him so they wouldn't have to sit around waiting for so long. Nikki heard them clapping for her when her name was called to receive her certificate. It was a special moment in her life. After the ceremony, the graduates were instructed to go over to the fellowship hall. She met Kevin and the children outside.

"I have to go to the reception now. Do you want to come?" Nikki asked the kids.

"Not really," Taj said, speaking for himself and the girls, who were shaking their heads in agreement.

"I'll take the kids on home with me, then. Just stop by

when you finish up here," Kevin said. "And congratulations!"

Nikki gave him a big hug. "You're a sweetheart. Thanks," she said.

She hugged and kissed each child before telling them she would see them shortly. She went to the reception, where all the graduates gathered in order to be recruited by the different ministries. The hall was overwhelming. There were so many ministries to choose from, including Children's, Nursing Home, Parking, Athletic, Dance, Substance Abuse, Singles, and Marriage. There was something for everyone. She got some juice and cookies and wandered around in almost a daze. *This is an awesome church, and I'm a part of it. I don't know what to choose.*

The various ministry groups were literally calling out to her. They had candy, pens, and pads as incentives. There were flyers, banners, and all kinds of things to make their ministries look like the best one to join. Nikki couldn't think straight. All she could do was thank God that she was an official part of such a great work.

She gathered handouts from most of the ministries to read later. The entire graduation experience was almost as amazing as the first time she was in the sanctuary when she couldn't stop crying. She felt tears of joy welling up and decided to leave so that she could let them flow freely. She ran to the minivan and praised God all the way home.

Chapter Twenty-nine

Now that Nikki had graduated from new-members class and her paperwork was submitted for the only job she ever truly wanted, she had to find something productive to do. She couldn't decide which ministry to join . . . besides, she was too preoccupied with the accountant position. She decided to call Erica.

"Hey, Erica. Any word on my job?"

"I'm waiting on the controller to tell me who he wants to interview. I'll let you know once things are all set."

"Okay." Nikki sighed. "Talk to you later."

"Patience, sister," Erica said.

Nikki had been thriving on all the activity. Now that things were quieting down, she was going through thrill withdrawals. She looked at the list of ministries again.

Later that day, the phone rang.

"Hello," Nikki answered.

"This is Sister Erica Scott from Way Maker Ministries personnel department. May I please speak with Sister Nicole Riley?"

"Girl, what?" Niki responded, excited to hear the official tone in Erica's voice.

Erica laughed at Nikki's impatience.

"Can you come in for an interview Monday at ten?"

"Yes, I can. Are there any special instructions?" Nikki asked, sounding as professional as Erica.

"Yes. When you come into the lobby, go to the receptionist's desk and let her know that you're here to interview for the accounting position. She will instruct you from there."

"Do I need to bring anything?"

"You can bring a calculator because you will be given a test."

"What! You are the testingest people I have ever seen," Nikki said, all professionalism gone.

They both laughed.

"You'll be fine, girl," Erica said.

"What kind of test?" Nikki asked.

"An accounting test. The controller is a stickler for giving tests to prove one's competency. You can handle that, right?"

"I told you I got this."

"Handle your business, then. I'll talk to you later. Got to set up more interviews," Erica said.

"What does my competition look like?" she asked.

"Bye, Nikki."

"Just teasing. See, you're rubbing off on me already."

As soon as Nikki hung up with Erica, the phone rang again. It was Rae.

"Cuz, I got somebody to get me out."

"Who?" Nikki asked.

"One of my suppliers. He said I was a good customer

and it was the least he could do. He knew I was good for the money. I didn't want to go that route, but my choices were limited."

"Guess you had to do what you had to do."

"Yep. It doesn't look good, cuz. I met with a lawyer, who said he can probably get me eighteen months."

"Dang."

"That's what I say. You were right, cuz. Fine time to finally see the light."

"Well, keep hope alive and know that Jesus is with you, no matter what."

"I don't know why I keep calling you. That's all you ever say."

"Because you're beginning to believe it the more you hear me say it. Faith comes by hearing. Plus, you feel better after you hang up, that's why."

"I don't know why I feel better. You don't do anything but talk, but you're right. I do feel better after talking to you."

"Then let's keep talking. What do you want to talk about?"

"About my mom."

"Okay. My Aunt Tee. A raving beauty. Sweet as she could be. Called me Niecy. Made the best iced tea."

"You crazy, cuz," Rae said. "Why did she have to kill herself?"

"I think about that all the time, Rae. She was so beautiful, so smart, and at one time so full of life. She could have been anything she wanted to be. I think she might have lost hope of ever being able to fulfill her dreams. She had dreams too. I remember her talking about Africa. She had this bad dashiki and an Angela Davis

Afro. She really wanted to go there. I guess she couldn't figure out how to get to the Motherland. I don't know, cuz, but I wonder the same thing."

"She was gorgeous, wasn't she?"

"Stunning. No supermodel I've seen can hold a candle to her natural beauty. You got those genes, cuz. You can be doing so much more."

"It takes more then good looks to make it in this world. I might be a lot of things, but I ain't no prostitute. Unfortunately, all I know is what my brother taught me—how to hustle."

"I didn't teach you anything?"

"You preached school. I hated school. I couldn't hang your way."

"You still have a chance to find your way—not my way, not Leonard's way. Ask God to lead you into the way He has made just for you. When you find your way, everything else will fall into place if you stay on the straight and narrow. Pray and ask God to show you. I guarantee you He will."

"I believe you, cuz," Rae said.

"That's the first step, baby. Just believe."

Nikki was at the church at nine-thirty the day of her interview. She let the receptionist know that she was the accountant coming to claim her job. The receptionist was amused and smiled at Nikki as she instructed her to have a seat in the lobby. She called Vincent Coles to let him know that Nikki had arrived.

After ten minutes of waiting, a couple came in the door and went to the receptionist's desk. The receptionist called one of the counselors to let them know that the

Holomans were there for their appointment. The couple sat at opposite ends of the lobby seating area with Nikki in the middle. They never looked at each other.

They must be here for marriage counseling, Nikki thought.

A few minutes later, a woman came in and asked the receptionist who she could talk to about financial assistance. The receptionist had her take a seat. She sat beside Nikki.

"Hello," the woman greeted Nikki.

"Good morning," Nikki spoke as she smiled brightly.

"They're going to put my things out today if I don't pay my rent," the woman said.

"Believe and trust God, sis. He'll see you through," Nikki encouraged.

"Do you think they will give me money to pay my rent?" the woman asked.

"I don't know, but I do know that God can make a way out of no way. If they don't, let God know that you trust Him to provide."

"Okay," the woman said.

Just then a bearded man appearing to be in his late forties, early fifties, wearing a black suit and bow tie, came into the lobby.

"Nicole Riley?" he asked in a thick northern accent, looking at Nikki, the only obvious candidate among those seated.

She immediately stood, pulling down the knee-length skirt to her conservative navy suit. The thought that the distinguished-looking gentleman might prefer a less stylish candidate made Nikki wish she had worn a long black dress instead.

"Yes, I'm Nicole Riley."

"Brother Vincent Coles," he said, shaking her hand. "Please follow me. Did Sister Erica tell you about the test you will be taking?"

"Yes, she did," Nikki answered.

"We'll have you take the test first, then I'll meet with you for the interview. Please follow me."

He directed Nikki to a conference room. "You have forty-five minutes. Use that phone to dial extension thirty-seven if you finish sooner. Do you have a calculator?"

"Yes, I do."

"This is not the CPA exam, so feel free to use it. Here is scratch paper and plenty of pencils. Do you have any questions?" he asked, handing her the exam booklet.

"No."

"Then you may begin," Vincent said, and left.

Nikki read over the test. The questions took her back to college, Mr. Hutt's Principles of Accounting class. She completed it in twenty minutes, checked it twice, and dialed extension thirty-seven.

"Hello, this is Nicole Riley. I've finished the test."

"I'll be right there," Vincent said, sounding surprised that she had finished so early.

Vincent checked her answers right there, and Nikki had aced the test. He informed her that she had done well, and they proceeded with the interview.

"Why should we hire you?" he asked pointedly.

At that precise moment, an anointing came upon Nikki, and it was no longer her, but the greater One who lived on the inside of her who spoke.

Nikki yielded. "Because in my fifteen years of experience I have probably seen every type of accounting transaction. I've worked in auditing, internal controls, daily operations, and financial reporting. I have worked in both the public and private sectors. I volunteered at my church in Virginia. With my knowledge of accounting, experience, and the help of the Holy Ghost, nothing is going to happen in the accounting department that I won't be able to handle, Brother Coles."

He sat back in his seat visibly impressed.

"We are currently going through a reorganization," he said. "The task at hand is to establish a separate accounting department to deal with the financial resources and expenses that are generated outside of the local church. What would you say that main resource would be?"

"I've been a supportive partner with Way Maker's for years, so I would have to say partnership income."

"That's exactly right. And what would the largest expense be?"

"TV. I can't imagine anything more expensive than the television broadcast, especially with the millions of households it reaches all over the world," Nikki said without hesitation.

"Right again," Vincent said. "The position requires approximately twenty percent travel to oversee the finances at the national and international conventions."

"How long do these conventions last?"

"The team is normally gone for three days. Is that a problem?"

God will have to work out that part of the job, Nikki thought.

"Not a problem," she responded.

"Good. Are there any more questions?"

"None at this time."

"Well, it has certainly been a pleasure talking with you today," Vincent said, standing and extending his hand.

"The pleasure was all mine," Nikki said.

They shook hands, and she thanked him for the interview. She also let him know that she looked forward to hearing from him soon.

Vincent escorted her back to the lobby.

She went to the minivan and once again praised the Lord all the way home.

Chapter Thirty

There had been no word from Way Maker Ministries since her interview more than a week ago. Nikki was determined not to ask Erica about it when they talked. She figured Erica would let her know when there was something to know. In the meantime, Nikki decided she couldn't just sit around and not do anything. Besides, it was time to start bringing home the bacon. She called Accountants R Us, a temporary agency that only placed professional accountants, so the salaries were competitive. She was asked to come in and complete some paperwork. It felt good to dress up, corporate-style, again. Black or navy was safe, so she chose her black suit with pale gray pinstripes and knee-length skirt and black pumps.

Nikki was required to take several competency tests and then meet with two of the placement executives. They assured her that based on her qualifications she would have no problem landing a lucrative position in Atlanta. She asked them to hold off on aggressively trying to place her because she was working on something on her end, but by all means to keep her informed of opportunities.

The next day, Way Maker Ministries didn't call, but Accountants R Us did—with a thirty-dollar-per-hour indefinite temporary assignment.

"Where is it located?" Nikki asked.

"At a large company downtown. We cannot divulge the name unless you are interested in interviewing for the position," said Cindy, one of the placement executives Nikki had met the day before.

"That was really quick, Cindy," Nikki said, stalling.

"Actually, I was already recruiting for the position. I was just waiting for the right person. I told the client all about you, and he is very interested in talking with you."

Nikki was listening and praying at the same time. She heard from within, *This is not what I called you here to do.*

"I'm really not ready to go to work right this minute, since I just got here and I'm still learning my way around."

"I understand. It has to be tough getting settled in a strange new city. I'll keep you posted."

"Thanks for understanding, Cindy."

They hung up. "I bind you, Satan," Nikki said out loud. She began talking to God. "That was a trick of the enemy trying to get me to lose focus on what I came here to do. Thank You, Lord. Us Christians sure don't have the same problems the world has. If I told somebody of the world that the devil was trying to get me off track by offering my unemployed self thirty dollars per hour, they would look at me like I was crazy. I can imagine what Rae would say. 'Shoot, get *me* off track with a thirty-dollar-per-hour job.' Lord, I guess we are peculiar people."

Nikki and the children were believing God for the job. They sowed faith seeds and named the seeds by writing on the back of their envelopes "accountant position." Nikki had learned long ago to get her children involved in what she believed God for, because their faith and prayers were not hindered by some of the issues that might hinder adults.

A few days later, a different executive from Accountants R Us called Nikki, who was just about ready to give up, cave in, and quit waiting. He had a job for Nikki ten minutes away from where she lived with an annual starting salary of sixty thousand dollars.

"Can I call you right back?" Nikki asked before hanging up and calling Erica.

"Personnel," Erica answered.

"Erica, they are tempting me. I can't keep turning down these job offers when I don't know what you are going to do. I have to call this guy back today. If I'm not absolutely sure that I have the job at the church, then I'm accepting the offer."

"Let me call you back," Erica said.

"You got the job if you want it."

"Why would you say if I want it?" Nikki asked curiously. "Of course I want it."

"The offer is thirty thousand dollars a year."

Nikki was shocked. She had just been offered double for the other position.

"Can I counter that offer?"

"I'm afraid not," Erica said solemnly.

It only took Nikki a second to realize that she was no

longer working for money, but to fulfill God's purpose for her life. God, not a job, would take care of her and meet her needs.

"I accept," Nikki said. "Now I have to call Accountants R Us back and decline their offer."

Chapter Thirty-one

Nikki changed clothes three times, trying to find the perfect outfit to make a good impression on her first day. She wanted to be stylish yet conservative. She was the new accountant at Way Maker Ministries. Hallelujah! Her boss, Brother Vincent, seemed strait-laced and conservative, but he was cool in the interview, so she didn't know what would impress him.

"Whatever! I got the job," she said, giving up trying to impress. "I'll just be me."

Feeling eager and daring, she decided on her red suit.

Kevin had offered to take Mia to the bus stop the first couple of days so that Nikki could get the hang of her new routine. He had taken her and the children out for pizza to celebrate the new job. They made all of the arrangements then. He even offered to help out when she had to travel. Nikki was very grateful for her neighbor.

Erica parked right beside the minivan before Nikki could even get out. She had been caught checking her makeup. It was a gorgeous fall day, and Nikki's window was down.

"You look beautiful, sis. How do you feel?" Erica asked.

"Like a million bucks," Nikki said, gathering her purse and briefcase.

They walked to Erica's office so that Nikki could complete the required routine paperwork. Erica turned on her radio. Nikki could hear "Victory," one of her favorite songs.

She began to hum. The Spirit hit Nikki, and she jumped up and began to dance right there in Erica's office, the first day on her new miracle harvest job, all dressed up.

Erica just looked at her at first. Then she laughed, and before she knew it, she was up praising God herself. They danced until the song was over. Then, worn out, they fell into their seats and began to pull themselves back together.

"God is just so good to me," Nikki said.

"I feel you, sis. I feel you."

Nikki completed all of the paperwork. Erica gave her the grand tour and introduced her to the staff. They ended the tour in the accounting department.

"I will leave you in the capable hands of Brother Vincent," Erica said.

They hugged and she left.

"Welcome to Way Maker Ministries' accounting operations. Are you ready to get started?" Vincent asked.

"Thank you, and yes, I am," Nikki said.

"Well, as I told you before, we are making outreach and the local church separate companies in the accounting system. It is all one accounting operation right now. Each account has to be analyzed and applied to the appropriate company. You will head up the project of separating the outreach accounts. You will also be responsible for preparing a monthly report of all outreach accounting activity. You can be as creative as you'd like. This is a copy of the report the way it is prepared now," he said, handing her a file.

Nikki skimmed the report.

"Use it as a guide to create your own. As you get into the process, you might come up with other ways to present your information. Any questions?"

"No," Nikki said.

"Then I'll introduce you to the staff."

Vincent introduced Nikki to the two accounting clerks, who welcomed her to the department.

"We will meet this afternoon at three o'clock about your travel schedule," Vincent said.

"Should I come to your office at three?"

"Call me to make sure nothing has changed," Vincent instructed.

"I'll do that."

Nikki settled in and determined that she liked the sisters with whom she would be working. However, after the three o'clock meeting, she was beginning to have second thoughts about leaving the children to travel. That along with the low salary opened the door for doubts. The sixty-thousand-dollar offer from Accountants R Us had confirmed her worth. Now she had to struggle to consider her work efforts differently. *God is my source, my paycheck is my seed,* she kept telling herself.

Erica had assured Nikki that she would be available to

keep the children when she had to travel. Initially, she was comfortable with leaving the children in the care of Erica, Kevin, and Randy. The children were certainly thrilled with the idea when she pitched it to them. She would see how she felt when the time came to leave them for the first time in the hands of these virtual strangers. She had time to get used to the idea, since the next convention wasn't for two more months.

The first six weeks on the job went pretty well; however, Nikki was having a challenge getting to work on time. She came in at eight-fifteen one morning and got written up for being consistently late by five to fifteen minutes, which she thought was no big deal, since she usually stayed late every day. Kevin and Randy watched out for the children when she worked overtime.

Well, it appears that I have an issue that needs to be resolved. Just in case it can't be, I'll give Accountants R Us a call, she thought.

It was a school night, and Nikki made sure the children's homework was done and checked. The kitchen had been cleaned after dinner. All baths had been taken, and the children were asleep. Nikki was up praying and pacing. She wasn't sure if calling Accountants R Us was a lack of faith. She knew she had to do what she had to do for her and her family, but she also believed that she was called to the accountant position at the church.

She was lost in thought when there was a knock at the door.

"You're a sight for sore eyes, a friendly face," she said, opening the door to Kevin.

"What's wrong?" he asked.

"I don't know."

"How's work?"

"I don't know."

"Oh Lord, come talk to me."

He took her by the hand and led her to the living room. They sat down on opposite ends of the sofa.

"Now tell me what's going on," he said.

He was the best friend a girl could have: cool, rational, reasonable, and very mature. He was easy to talk to and an excellent listener. Nikki told him about her doubts about the job.

"Didn't you sow a big seed for that job?" he asked.

"Yes," she answered.

"And you're thinking about giving it up already? Come on. It can't be that bad."

"I may have made a mistake."

"No way. You are the sharpest sister I know. The way you handle your business, you do not make those kinds of mistakes. Give it some more time. Whatever it is, it'll work out. Just give it time," Kevin said, reaching over and patting her on the back of her hand.

"Okay. You're right," she said. "So how are you doing?"

"My students are a trip. There's so much going on in the homes that it filters over into the classroom, but I maintain control regardless. Can't let that slip."

"I can only imagine. You have a special gift to be able to deal with it all, that's for sure," Nikki said.

"You only have to really care about them to do a good job, and I really do. They know when you don't. It's too critical not to care in these classrooms."

"I can only imagine," was all Nikki could say again.

• • •

Taj was spending more and more time downstairs. He would go to a football game with the guys on Friday nights, and Nikki wouldn't see him any more until Sunday. She would call down on Sunday mornings for him to come get ready for church.

Kevin had joined Way Maker Ministries on his second visit after a few weeks of Nikki praising the church non-stop. He felt at home there just like Nikki said he would. He said Pastor Freeman broke down the Word in a way he had never heard it before. He was hooked. Randy liked it a lot too but was a member elsewhere. He was brought up to believe that you never left your home church, so he just visited Way Maker's.

Nikki had given them a key to keep in their apartment, since the children sometimes lost theirs or left it at home when they went to school. The guys' apartment was becoming an extension of their own. She could see Taj growing up, and she didn't want to let go. The guys had tactfully let Nikki know that boys will be boys and that she had to loosen up at some point. They assured her that she had put the best of everything in her children that they needed in order to live happy, productive lives. She felt good about her new brothers in Christ and thanked God for them, especially Kevin.

Chapter Thirty-two

The children went to Virginia to spend Christmas with Jim and Jean. They would also see their father, Sam, but would stay at their grandparents' house. It was the first Christmas ever that Nikki did not spend with her family. In fact, she spent it with Jesus, in front of a roaring fire, blankets all over the floor, watching old classic movies. She felt like she was in heaven and couldn't remember ever feeling this good: safe, secure, and at total peace. Jesus was with her, and she basked in His glory, thanking Him for all that was happening in her life, with her job, and with the wonderful people He had placed around her.

After she talked to her parents and children Christmas morning, she spent the rest of the day in the presence of God, praying and rejoicing. Later that evening, there was a knock at the door. Feeling interrupted, she got up and looked through the peephole. It was Kevin. With her hair sticking up all over her head and decked out in flannel pajamas, she opened the door slightly.

"How're you doing up here by yourself?" he asked.

"Just fine, and I am never alone. Jesus is all up in here with me," she said.

"Good. Just checking on you. Here's a card we got for you," he said, handing it to her through the partially opened door.

"Oh, that's so sweet. I got y'all something too," she said, taking the card and finally opening the door all the way so he could come in.

She went to her bedroom to get the small gift she had bought for her neighbors, and he entered the apartment. Nikki came back and handed him the package.

"This is just a little somethin', somethin' to let you know I really appreciate you guys."

Kevin took the gift and looked at Nikki without saying thank you.

"Well, I have to get back to Jesus now," she said, snapping him out of his trance.

"Oh, okay. Glad you're doing all right without the kids. Call us if you need anything," he said, blinking like he had just woken up.

The rest of the Christmas break without the children was good for Nikki. She was even getting to work on time. Erica took her to some different places around Atlanta. They saw a play, and she tried sushi. Since she vowed not to cook while the children were away, the guys checked on her every day to make sure she had eaten. Her friends took good care of her. She did miss her children, though.

The holidays were over, and things were getting back to normal. Work was good. Nikki hadn't been late at all while the children were gone. She concluded that it was taking them to the bus stop and waiting until the bus came that was the problem. But no way was she leaving her baby alone at the bus stop, especially since it was still dark. She didn't care how many other children were out there. She explained the situation to Vincent and asked that her hours be officially changed so that she could come in and leave a half hour later. Vincent agreed. The half hour made a big difference, resolving the issue of her punctuality.

A storm during the night had shut off the electricity while everyone was asleep. It eventually came back on, but the alarm clocks were no longer set. Nikki had time to take the children to school and still make it to work on time. In such a rush, she left her cell phone at home. After dropping them off at school, she took a back road to get to work on time and ended up behind a stopped school bus. Time was running out. Instead of waiting, she made a stupid decision. Impatiently, she backed up to make a U-turn on the narrow street but slipped into a ditch. She was stuck on a back road as she watched the school bus pull off. With no cell phone, she didn't know what to do. She definitely could not lift a minivan out of a ditch, so she sat there, closed her eyes, and prayed.

"Father, look what I've done. I'm so impatient. I need Your help, Lord. Please get me out of this ditch. In Jesus' name, amen."

The prayer took all of three seconds. When Nikki opened her eyes, she saw two black men wearing white uniforms and caps in a white truck walking toward her car. They walked to the back of Nikki's van and lifted it out of the ditch. They waved to her as they got back in the truck and pulled off. She waved and yelled thank you out of the window. It took all of thirty seconds. In less than a minute, God had answered her prayer.

As she praised the Lord on her way to work, she tried to remember what company the men worked for. She couldn't, for the life of her, picture the logo on their white uniforms. She tried to recall the sign on the truck and couldn't. All she could visualize was white. Nothing was on their caps. Just white. Then it hit her. Those weren't men; those were her angels manifested in the flesh to help and protect her. She had seen her angels. She was overwhelmed with God's love.

Nikki was still late by a few minutes, but she was so excited telling everyone about her angels that Brother Vincent didn't reprimand her; however, he did note her tardiness in her personnel file. She couldn't wait to get home to tell the children about her angels, and of course she had to tell the guys.

That same evening as she told Kevin, he looked at her funny.

"What's wrong? You don't believe me?" she asked him.

"Of course I believe you, Nikki," he said, looking at her strangely.

Nikki was so excited she barely gave his expression much thought.

Chapter Thirty-three

On a lazy, rainy Saturday afternoon, Nikki gave Taj the key so he could go get the mail. Among the bills and other junk mail was a letter from Rae. This was the first letter Nikki had received from her cousin since she had been incarcerated in Virginia. She was wondering why she hadn't heard from her. The letter explained why.

Dear Cuz,

How are you? I know blessed of the Lord. I have wanted to write you but thought that you would be so disappointed in me that you wouldn't want to hear from me. I know now that it was just a trick of the devil to keep us apart.

I love you, cuz, and appreciate all that you shared with me before I wound up in this place. This is not a good place, but because of what I know about Jesus and the Word of God, I am dealing with it. I got beat up by some inmates one day, and God was with me. I always remembered what you said about God taking what the devil meant for evil and turning it around for good. My friend Sharia and I went to the warden and asked if we could start a Bible study. I figured I could talk to these women like you talked to me, and, cuz, it's working. The girls who beat me started coming to Bible study to intimidate me, but I ignored them and kept talking. I even give an invitation for them to get saved at the end of each session, and guess what? The same girls who jumped me came up and got saved. For real. I thought they were just trying to mess with me, but they kept coming, started acting different, and got even more girls to come. There has been a big drop in the fighting, and the warden is aware that it has something to do with the Bible studies. God is ruling and reigning even up in here. All that stuff you shared with me was right. I just wanted you to know that and to thank you for continuing to talk to me no matter what I did. I understand now and appreciate you so much. Please write back soon.

Love,
Rae

Tears had met underneath Nikki's chin by the time she finished reading the letter. She loved her cousin so much. She immediately began writing Rae back, and soon they were writing each other at least weekly, sometimes more. Nikki sent poems, stories, and devotionals for inspiration to keep building her cousin's faith. Without the distractions of the outside world, Rae continued to grow in the things of God.

A few weeks after she started writing Rae, Nikki finally admitted to herself that Kevin had been looking strange lately. Nikki recognized the expression but didn't want to admit it. *Anything more than a friendship would just mess up everything. Besides, he's too young,* she thought. He never said anything to her, but she knew because a woman knows. It was a special vibe. Maybe it was women's intuition. Whatever it was, it was driving her crazy. She needed to talk to Erica.

When Nikki got to work, she called her friend before she even turned on her computer.

"Let's do lunch today. I have to talk to you about something," Nikki said.

"Okay," Erica agreed.

At noon, as they walked into the lobby together, a woman stood and greeted Erica. Erica introduced her to Nikki as Sister Jada, a volunteer.

"Sister Jada will be joining us for lunch," Erica said.

Nikki was furious. She wanted to discuss Kevin with Erica. Not with Erica and Jada. Who was Jada anyway?

Nikki didn't say two words during lunch. She let Erica and Jada talk. She hoped she wasn't pouting. If she was, she didn't care. She needed to talk about Kevin.

The next day, Erica had a luncheon meeting, so Nikki had lunch alone. Jada came into the restaurant and spotted Nikki. She came over to her table.

"Hello, Nikki. You come here often?"

"When I want to treat myself."

"I hear you. It's pretty upscale for around here."

"Would you like to join me?" Nikki asked, yielding to an urge to be nice.

"Sure," Jada said, taking a seat.

Once she was settled and lunch had been ordered, Nikki began her inquiry.

"So where are you from?"

"Boston. And you?"

"Richmond, Virginia."

"I lived in Richmond for five years."

"Really? What church did you go to?" Nikki asked, now interested.

"The Assemblies of God."

"I went to Richmond Baptist Church. I've been to plays at the Assemblies, though."

"I was in the Christmas and Easter productions."

"They were wonderful. The kids and I thoroughly enjoyed them."

"How many children do you have?" Jada asked.

"Three. Two girls and a boy. Do you have any?"

"I have twelve-year-old twin boys. Matthew and Mark."

"Wow. I bet you and your husband stay busy."

"I'm divorced. The boys are the best things that ever happened to me, though."

"I feel the same way about my children. I don't know what I would do without them sometimes."

"I am so proud of them. They both want to be lawyers like their mother."

"You're a lawyer?"

"Attorney Ross at your service. I've only been in Atlanta for a few months. I have to take the Georgia bar to be able to practice here," Jada said.

"My prayers are with you, sis."

"Thanks, I definitely need them."

Nikki began to like Jada more and more. By the time they were finished eating and interrogating each other, Nikki had forgiven Jada for interrupting her lunch with Erica the day before.

Chapter Thirty-four

Nikki was enjoying traveling with the Way Maker convention team. It was a new and exciting environment, one that in all of her years in accounting, she had never experienced.

After she returned from the New York convention, Nikki finally found some time to tell Erica about Kevin.

"You know, you're our guardian angel. I don't know what I would do without you, girl. Thanks for staying with the kids," Nikki said.

"The kids are great, Nikki. We have a ball together. It's a pleasure to stay with them."

"I'm so glad to hear you say that. Children are a huge responsibility, so I feel truly blessed. Girl, I have been trying to tell you something for a long time. We've been so busy, and then I had to travel."

"Tell me, girl," Erica said.

"It's about Kevin. Girl, he's changing. He's looking at me all funny."

"Well, what do you expect as nice as you've been to that boy?"

"He's the one who's been nice."

"What did he say?"

"He hasn't said anything to me, so maybe I'm just imagining things, right?" Nikki asked hopefully.

"Wrong. They don't have to say anything to us women. We just know. If you think he has developed a crush on you, then he probably has."

"So what am I supposed to do about it?"

"What do you want to do about it?"

"I have no idea."

"Well, you have to figure that out first," Erica advised.

"I guess you're right."

After Erica left, Nikki thought about it and couldn't imagine what she would say if Kevin approached her. *Maybe he won't,* she hoped.

With Jada volunteering and Nikki working in the same building at Way Maker, they became close. They decided their children should meet.

Jada stopped by with her boys to visit Nikki and her children. Introductions were made all around.

"Want to play some basketball?" Taj asked the twins, staring back and forth at them.

Matthew and Mark looked at their mother, who looked at Nikki.

"That's fine. Stop downstairs and see if Kevin will go with you," Nikki told Taj.

While the girls played in their room, Jada and Nikki sat and talked. Nikki was surprised and a little nervous when Kevin returned with the boys and asked her to call him later, no matter what time.

After Jada and the twins left and the children were all tucked in, Nikki called downstairs.

"Hello," Kevin answered.

"What's up?" she asked.

"Can I come up just for a minute?"

"Sure."

One minute later, he was in the apartment facing Nikki. After they settled on the sofa, he began, "I don't know when it happened, but I am in love with you. I'm sorry. I didn't mean for it to happen, but it did, and I can't keep it to myself any longer," Kevin said with a slightly desperate tone, yet his cool still reigned.

Nikki was in shock. She knew something was going on with Kevin, but to hear it forced her to have to deal with it.

"How old are you exactly?" she asked.

"Twenty-nine," Kevin answered.

"I'm thirty-nine. That's a whole decade."

"I can't tell," he quickly responded.

"It makes a difference."

"Not to me it doesn't. How I feel matters, and this feels right. How does it feel to you?" he asked, taking her hand.

She couldn't answer. Looking down at his hand holding hers, all she felt was his warmth and love, and it felt right, but she wasn't ready to admit it. Now that the words had been spoken, she was forced to explore her feelings.

"I need some time," she said finally.

"I understand. I'm sorry. I just had to let you know how I felt. Call me when you're ready to talk."

She nodded. He gently kissed the back of her hand, then got up to let himself out.

"Call me," he said as he closed the door behind him.

Nikki went in her room and prayed. *Lord, what in the world is going on? Are You setting me up? I don't know what to do.*

Pastor Freeman preached on peace at the early Sunday service. Nikki wrote down what he said about letting the Umpire of Peace, the Holy Spirit, make the call on the difficult decisions we have to make in our lives. She wrote: *Ask God what to do about Kevin, then wait for Him to respond. An uncomfortable feeling equals "no." A calm, peaceful feeling means "yes."*

Afterward, Nikki and Jada were in the lobby deciding on where to take the children out for breakfast when Erica walked up.

"What's up, ladies?" Erica asked.

"Hey, sis," Nikki said. "Trying to figure out where to go eat breakfast."

"You were going out to eat without me?" Erica asked, only slightly smiling.

"You are perfectly welcome to join us. Do you know of any good all-you-can-eat breakfast buffets that the children would enjoy?" Jada asked.

"Mamanems Restaurant has the best pancakes, omelets, and lots of other goodies the kids will love," Erica said.

"Yeah, I've been wanting to check out Mamanems," Nikki said.

"I've heard good things about it too. Let's go there," Jada decided.

"Well, we can all just meet over there. You know where it is, right?" Erica asked.

"I do," Nikki said.

"I do too," Jada said. "See you there in about fifteen minutes."

At Mamanems, all of the children sat together at a large table in the middle of the restaurant close to the buffet, and Nikki, Erica, and Jada got a quiet booth.

"How's the studying for the bar going, Jada?" Nikki asked.

"It's going, girl."

"How's Kevin's crush going, Nikki?" Erica asked.

"What!" Jada exclaimed.

"Yeah, girlfriend got youngblood's nose wide open," Erica offered with a hint of sarcasm.

"What? I thought he was just a good neighbor. Like State Farm," Jada said, chuckling.

"Tell her, Nikki. Tell your girl here about how you can drive a truck up his nose," Erica insisted.

"Actually, he told me that he was in love with me," Nikki said.

To their surprise, Erica stood. "Get out of here!" she said.

"Yep," Nikki said.

"What's he going to do with you and those kids as young as he is?" Erica asked, still standing, with her hands on her hips.

Both Nikki and Jada looked at Erica silently until she realized there would be no response until she sat down.

"He didn't propose, Erica. What's your problem?" Nikki asked.

"I'm just looking out for you is all," she answered, calming down.

Nikki nodded, doubting Erica's last words.

"So just how long has this been going on?" Jada asked.

"I've been feeling the vibe for a few months now, but last night was the first time he ever mentioned anything to me."

"It won't work," Erica said.

"Why not?" Nikki asked.

"He can't handle you," Erica said.

"I don't need to be 'handled,' as long as he can handle himself. Besides, he has goals, dreams, and vision," Nikki replied.

"Does he have any money, houses, and cars?" Erica asked.

"How materialistic is that?" Nikki asked. She was starting to get perturbed with Erica's line of questioning.

"You need a man to help you with those kids. He's a good friend and all, but your rich prince might be right around the corner," Erica said.

"That's you, Cinderella. I can take care of me and my babies, and I don't need a man for that."

"She's got a point, Erica. I lived in a mansion when I was married, and we slept in separate bedrooms, so I hear ya, Nikki. I feel the same way," Jada said.

"Thanks, Jada," Nikki said.

"So how do you feel about him?" Jada asked.

"I don't know," Nikki answered. The Umpire of Peace had yet to make the call.

"Well, just take your time and be honest and true to yourself," Jada said.

"Yeah, you do that and let us know what he's bringing to the table," Erica said. "If you think about it, probably not much, and you deserve more. We are virtuous women, and our price is far above rubies. Read Proverbs 31, girl."

"See, now, that's why you had to go to the hospital diving for that bouquet, like catching it was really going to get you a husband. I saw the video," Nikki said.

"Don't go there. My side still hurts," Erica said.

"The way that girl tackled you for that bouquet, you need to let me send that tape to *America's Funniest Home Videos*. When you win, then you'll have enough money so you can stop tripping and get a real man and not waste your time waiting for a rich fairy-tale prince," Nikki said.

"See, she went there, Jada."

"Yes, you did, Nikki, now apologize," Jada said.

"I apologize to the wide receiver. But on that wedding video, you went for that pass and that girl tackled your—"

"Nikki!" they yelled.

Chapter Thirty-five

Nikki and Kevin had not seen each other since Kevin's announcement. He made himself stay away until he heard from her. In the meantime, she had begun to entertain some thoughts about him.

What is the point in having a man, a boyfriend? What would we be able to do that we aren't doing now? Like Pastor asked the teens: "What do you mean you go together? What is the difference between being friends and going together to a Christian?" That's what I want to know too, Pastor. We can't sleep together like the world defines going together. If you are seriously striving to walk upright before the Lord, that can only happen in marriage. All the other benefits come under the umbrella of friendship. Everything is cool just the way it is.

Then she did something she had dared not do before. She entertained the thought of being married to Kevin. She couldn't be afraid to deal with her true feelings. What if he wanted to marry her?

No. It just will not work. Forget about it. He has grown

tremendously in the things of God since we first met. I trust him just as much as I trust anybody. He's ambitious, no-nonsense, and boy, can he sing. I like that, she thought. Then out loud she asked, "Is that You, God? Throwing in little extra special touches that You know I like in order to let me know that You approve? I wonder what ever happened to that girl I saw him with on that first day. I haven't seen her anymore and haven't had the nerve to ask him about her. Doesn't matter, since she appears to have fallen off the face of the earth. Then there's my number one priority, Lord, my kids. They adore Kevin and he adores them. I don't know what Taj would have done without him when we first got here. I respect teachers and coaches to the utmost. I can get up under a mission like that, which inspires and influences our young people to be all they can be. It's a part of the solution. And I'll admit it to You, Lord, because You already know. I do love him. But what kind of wife would I make with all my baggage? Umpire of Peace, you make the call."

Just then a calm peacefulness flooded Nikki's entire being. When she was done praying, she called Kevin.

"We need to talk."

"Be right up."

The children were outside playing with their friends. She and Kevin sat at the dining room table, Kevin at the head, Nikki across from him.

"So what do you have in mind?" Nikki asked.

"I have never felt the way you make me feel. You are smart, funny, open, honest, caring, and absolutely beautiful inside and out. You make me think and laugh. You inspire me and you understand me. I feel your love for me. That feeds my love for you, which feeds your love for me, and our love is just growing out of control, and now we have to do something about it."

"Something like what?" she asked.

"I know you came to Atlanta to begin a new life, and you have. I just know in my heart that we can have an even greater life together," he said, then paused for a reaction.

There was none. She was quietly still, listening to every word. He continued.

"The only thing I have that is worthy of you is all my love. Now, you haven't even shown that you are interested in that type of a relationship with anybody, and that may have something to do with the way I feel about you. But I know for a fact that in addition to everything else, I just want to hold you."

There. He said it. She exhaled. She had been subconsciously holding her breath. "Nikki, baby, you are a serious sister, and I want you to be my wife."

Even after all of her praying and preparation, Nikki was still amazed at all he had said.

A cool, confident, and patient Kevin waited silently for a response. Everything she had been thinking about, analyzing, and figuring out made sense and felt right. She had gone on with her life, and Kevin was the only person she could imagine being with as she moved forward. She decided his response to her next question would be the determining factor.

"How will we overcome the obvious challenges that we will face from every direction?" she asked.

"By the Spirit of God that lives inside the both of us. We will overcome them together and as one," was his eloquent response.

"Then the answer is yes."

• • •

The first challenge was to inform the children. Kevin and Nikki gathered them on the sofa. Holding Nikki's hand, which did not go unnoticed by any of the children, Kevin began.

"Your mother and I are best friends. I first realized that I loved her a while back. Now we both realize that we love each other and—"

Mia jumped up, cutting him off. "They're getting married! I'm moving back to Richmond with my daddy!" she yelled.

Nikki thought, *This is not going to be easy*, but she let Kevin handle it just to see him operate under pressure.

"I understand how you feel, Mia," he said in a calm, soothing voice. "And I will never try to replace your daddy. I love you guys. Your mother and I want to spend the rest of our lives together. We can hang out like we always do. I'm here for you, and I want to make your mother happy. She believes I can make her happy. She deserves to be happy, don't you think?"

"Yeah, okay," Mia said, and she went into her room to watch TV.

"Here, Taj," Shay said, handing him a dollar.

"Thank you very much," he said, smiling as he took his winnings.

"What's that for?" Nikki asked.

"Taj bet me a dollar that you two were going to get married. I said you seemed to like things just the way they are, so I bet you wouldn't. Thanks a lot, Mommy," Shay said.

"Well, what if I give you your dollar back?" Nikki asked.

"That'll work," Shay said.

"Are we all still cool?" Kevin asked.

"I'm cool," Taj said, stuffing his dollar bill into his pocket.

"Yes, you are, sweetheart," Nikki said. "What about my girls?"

"I'm fine, Mommy, and I know that little drama queen is too," Shay said.

"Are we still going to Six Flags tomorrow?" Taj asked.

"Just like we planned," Kevin said.

"You coming, Mommy?" Shay asked.

"No, baby. I have some business to take care of."

"I got the kids. You handle your business, baby," Kevin said.

She planned to do just that. Nikki went to her bedroom to make a couple of calls. First she called Jada.

"Jada, we have to have a meeting after service tomorrow. Let's get together for brunch."

"All right. Should we meet in the usual spot?"

"Exactly."

Next she called Erica. "What's going on after church?"

"Nothing, why?" Erica asked.

"We're meeting for brunch."

"Cool."

"Meet Jada and me at the usual spot after service."

"Yes, ma'am."

After church service, they all walked to Nikki's van.

"Where're the kids, Nikki?" Erica asked.

"Kevin is taking them to the amusement park after late service," she responded.

"He's really pouring it on, isn't he?" Erica said.

"He's doing what he's always done since I met him."

Nikki had decided to do something different and take her friends to an upscale restaurant in another part of town. The beautiful buffet was supplied with a delectable-looking array of foods from which to choose, including all types of breakfast dishes, fruit and vegetable salads, seafood, and an assortment of roasted and smoked meats. Nikki checked out Erica's plate and shook her head.

"You can take the girl out of the country, but you can't take the country out of the girl. Is there anything you don't eat grits with, Erica? Smoked salmon, mussels, oysters, poached eggs, steamed shrimp, and a bowl of grits."

"I can't help it," Erica said, putting a spoonful in her mouth. "Hmmm, they're good too. What is this meeting about?"

"Why didn't you send an interoffice memo so that we could be prepared?" Jada asked.

Erica and Jada laughed. Nikki was serious.

"Ladies, I have an announcement to make. Kevin and I are getting married."

Jada gave Erica a quick glance.

"Congratulations, sis," Jada said. "You're an intelligent, spiritual woman who knows what she's doing. I'm happy for you."

"If you're sure, then congrats," Erica said, feigning a smile after getting over the shock.

"Well, thank you both. And I am sure," she said. She was pretty sure about Jada's sincerity, but doubted Erica's.

"Wow, we have a wedding to plan," Jada said.

"No hoopla. Only our immediate family and close circle of friends will be there. That's you guys, the kids, and my parents, of course. Kevin's parents died when he was young. His grandmother raised him and his sister, but the grandmother is in a nursing home with Alzheimer's. So that leaves Randy; Kevin's sister, Chanel; and her son, Rashad. That's it. We don't need any negative spirits I'm not sure about lingering around. Know what I mean?" Nikki asked, glancing at Erica, who was preoccupied with her grits.

"Yeah, girl. I know exactly what you mean," Jada said.

Chapter Thirty-six

The children were spending their summer vacation in Virginia with their grandparents. Nikki and Kevin had plenty of time alone together to get to know each other better and to complete their marriage counseling.

Work had been going well, and Nikki had not pursued a higher-paying job because she liked working near Erica; however, since her marriage announcement, her favor at work seemed to have left. One day Vincent called her into his office.

"Nikki, your children are away for the summer, correct?"

"Correct."

"Then you should be able to come in at eight with the rest of the staff."

"If you don't mind, I have gotten used to this schedule and would like to keep it."

"Personnel orders are that since you no longer require the flexible schedule, you begin at eight o'clock with the rest of the staff. Sorry."

"No problem."

"That's it. Thank you."

Personnel orders, Nikki thought as she decided to pray about reopening her employment options.

That night, she and Kevin discussed their careers.

"My job is not fun anymore," she told him.

"Well, then we have to make it fun," Kevin said, and began tickling her.

She laughed hysterically.

"No, silly," she said, trying to get away.

"No what?" he asked as he stopped tickling and just held her.

Lying relaxed in his arms, she began to explain.

"Being employed at the church is a lot of work, and it used to be fun and rewarding. If I could have afforded to do it for free, I would have. But lately, I don't think they can pay me enough to stay there."

"Why, baby?"

"Well, Erica was a big part of my wanting to be there. She's my very first friend in Georgia, but she hasn't seemed like my friend lately."

"How so?"

"She's been distant. She doesn't call anymore, and when I call, she's always busy."

"Maybe she is."

"Well, she wasn't that busy before we got engaged."

"You think that has something to do with it?"

"Yeah, I do."

"You talk to her about it?"

"She's been avoiding me."

"Well, if it's bothering you, talk to her. Lay it all out

on the table and deal with it is my motto. That's how I got you, baby," he said, and started tickling her again.

The next day, Nikki went to Erica's office to invite her to lunch.

"Sorry, I'm busy," Erica said.

"You have been quite busy lately, girlfriend," Nikki said.

"I'm sure you have been too."

"Kind of," Nikki said. "I also wanted to ask you about me continuing to come in at eight-thirty."

"No more exceptions to the rules. With your new husband, you should be able to figure out how to get the kids to school and yourself to work on time. It can't be that difficult."

"I'm sure we can. Now, what's your problem?" Nikki asked, closing the door.

"What?"

"You have been acting weird since I announced my engagement."

"You are imagining things, darling."

"No, really, Erica. You're my girl, and things have not been the same."

"I'm just giving you your space, Nikki. We're still cool. Now, if you will excuse me, I really am busy," Erica said.

"Fine," Nikki said as she opened the door and left.

Nikki couldn't figure out what Erica's problem could be. They had been too close and had too much fun together for her to not be concerned about her friend. She needed some advice. She called her friend Zakia from back home.

"I need you, girl," Nikki said when Zakia answered the phone.

"You got me, sis. What's up?" Zakia asked.

"My best friend down here has been tripping on me lately. And I honestly don't know what I have done to her," Nikki said.

"You can't remember doing anything? People are so funny, there's no telling what you may have done. Think," Zakia advised her friend.

Nikki remembered the glance Jada gave Erica at the restaurant when she first told them about her engagement. "I know who might know something," she said.

"Go for it," Zakia said.

"I'm going to do just that. Thanks," Nikki said.

She decided to pay Jada a visit.

"Okay, come clean. I know you know something. What is wrong with our girl Erica?" Nikki asked.

"What do you mean?"

"Oh, come on, Jada. I know you, attorney-at-law, have noticed a difference. Tell me, what did I do?"

Jada paused, then relented, not out of betrayal, but out of the same concern Nikki had for Erica.

"You got engaged, Nikki. What Erica wants more than anything in the world is to find Prince Charming, but she'll settle for a good man who loves her and wants to marry her."

"And avoiding me is going to help her reach that goal?"

"Give her some time. That's been her constant prayer, and you could have cared less if you never got married again. It seems like you stole her blessing."

"Give me a break."

"Understand, Nikki, it's not intentional. Spending so much time with the kids while you travel, she was really feeling the family thing. Now with Kevin, you have the whole package she's been praying for, while she goes home alone."

"Again, is that my fault? Why take it out on me?"

"You are living her dream. It's tough to watch somebody get everything you have been fervently praying for. So try to understand her. She'll get over it."

"Dang. But it makes sense. How did I get so blessed?"

"God knows what He's doing, girl, and Erica is going to just have to trust that."

"So what do I do?"

"Nothing. Keep loving her and being her friend, and she'll come around."

"So no need to mention this to her?"

"No need whatsoever."

"Okay. Wow! Revelation is an awesome thing."

"Yes, it is."

Nikki and Kevin decided to get married when Jean and Jim brought the children back from their summer vacation. Erica had come down with a virus and couldn't attend the wedding. Jada stood up for Nikki, and Randy was Kevin's best man.

They had decided to have an intimate wedding ceremony and an elegant steak and lobster dinner reception, all at a swank hotel. Their marriage counselor, Minister Slater, married them. The beautiful bride and handsome groom stood before each other and exchanged the vows they had written, both pledging to keep God at the center of their union. They both were dressed in soft cream.

Nikki's short pearled gown complemented Kevin's tux perfectly. The glory of God filled the room, and nothing other than the groom or his bride could ever break the bond that was formed that day.

Jim and Jean stayed in Georgia with the children while Nikki and Kevin went on a Caribbean honeymoon cruise.

On the ship, Kevin scooped Nikki up and carried her across the threshold of their cabin. He set her on his lap and looked at her. She gazed at him, smiling. All the love they had been carrying for each other was about to be unleashed.

Chapter Thirty-seven

When Nikki and Kevin returned from their honeymoon, Jim and Jean were packed and ready to go.

"What is it that you guys think you're missing in Richmond?" Nikki asked.

"Atlanta is nice, and we love staying with our babies, but your dad has begun all of these projects—the pool, the barbecue, shelving the garage walls, the yard—and none of that is being taken care of while we're here relaxing," Jean explained.

"That's right. Put it all on me," Jim said.

Before they got in the Caddy, Jim took Nikki aside and looked deep into her eyes as if he was searching for something.

"I have never seen you this satisfied before. And for that reason, I can leave in peace. Kevin's a good man, but if anything changes . . . well, you know what to do," Jim instructed his daughter.

"I know, Daddy. I love you," she said, hugging and squeezing him as tight as she could. "I am very happy and satisfied."

• • •

Nikki went to the store to get milk. On her way back, she stopped to get the mail and noticed a letter from Rae. She had sent her cousin a postcard during her honeymoon to let Rae know about her marriage and was anxious to read her cousin's response. She opened the letter right there, standing outside beside the mailboxes.

Dear Nikki,

You go, girl! I'm so happy for you, cuz. I'm doing as well as can be expected up in here. The Bible study group is the best thing that has ever happened to me. I am respected, not for being tough, but because of what the others see God doing through me. Inmates and guards come to me for advice. And I put the Word on them, just like you do me. My time could even get reduced for good behavior. Thanks for not giving up on me.

Love,
Rae

P.S. And tell your new husband he better treat you right.

Nikki smiled as a calm peacefulness came over her. She knew that Rae was going to be all right.

A month into her new marriage, it was time to move forward. Nikki wanted to know where things stood with her girlfriends, so she called Jada.

"What's the deal, sis?" she asked when Jada answered the phone.

"Hey, newlywed. How was the cruise?"

"Short. We learned a lot about each other. We both have a desire to visit Africa, so we're planning to go there next summer," Nikki said.

"That's great," Jada said.

"How's Erica?" Nikki asked.

"In denial."

"I'm going to talk to her," Nikki said.

"It's sensitive right now. Be with your husband. She'll get over it. You take care of your family," Jada advised.

"All right, but Kevin and I decided on the cruise that I would accept one of those offers that Accountants R Us has been throwing my way. I mean, working at the church doesn't feel right anymore."

"Hey, all good things come to an end. New marriage, why not a new job? New beginnings are great. Go for it. Warren and I have been having some serious talks too." Jada had met Warren Alexander, who was also studying for the bar, and things had been going so well between them that shortly after they passed the exam, they decided to start a practice together.

"All right, now! I wish you nothing but the best, sis."

"Same to you, sis. Now, go see if that husband of yours needs anything."

Nikki called Accountants R Us and was sent on an interview that called for her corporate best. She wore her navy brass: her special navy knee-length skirt, brass-buttoned jacket with matching jewelry, nude shimmering hose, and navy pumps. She had studied the company's financials and was ready to dazzle them. The interview team of the Fortune 500 company was indeed impressed with her and her credentials, assuring Nikki that she would be hearing from them. A few days later, they made her an offer she couldn't refuse. The seventy-five-thousand-dollar salary was far above her expectations.

Nikki went in to give Vincent her two weeks' notice. She had briefly thought of telling Erica but dismissed the thought. Vincent reluctantly accepted Nikki's resignation.

"Why are you leaving us?" he asked after reading the letter.

"It's just timing. I have grown so much here, have learned to trust and believe God in every area of my life, and the time has come to move on."

"You have done a wonderful job here. I'm sorry to see you go, but I wish you much success in your future endeavors," Vincent said.

"Thank you. It has truly been an honor and a pleasure to serve this ministry. I'll look for you at church."

Chapter Thirty-eight

Following service a few days after Nikki resigned, the children went home with Kevin, and Nikki rode with Jada to brunch. She was surprised to learn Erica was joining them.

"So what was her one-eighty about?" Nikki asked Jada.

"Let her tell you, but I have some news of my own to share."

"What?"

"Oh, here she comes now," Jada said.

"Hello, sisters," Erica said as she sat down. "I'm famished."

"Me too," Jada said as they all looked at their menus.

Nikki hadn't spoken, still curious about this change of attitude, but glad to see the old Erica back.

Once their orders were taken, Erica took both of Nikki's hands into hers and looked deep into her eyes.

"The Word was so on time today. I had been hiding behind issues that I didn't even know I had, Nikki. Since I got a revelation about my denial, breakthroughs have been coming forth left and right. I had my own issues I needed to deal with, and I took my unhappiness and frustrations out on you rather than being happy for you. I knew I had gone too far when you didn't even tell me you were leaving the job. I'm sorry you didn't feel you could come to me. I want you to know I'm changing. God is really speaking to my heart."

"I'm happy to hear that, Erica," Nikki said.

"I'm so sorry I took my unhappiness out on you," Erica apologized.

"Girl, give me a hug," Nikki said, and they both embraced and fought back tears.

Enough was said.

"Great! Now I have some news," Jada said.

All eyes were on Jada as they watched her remove a small jewelry box from her purse. She slipped on the ring and held out her hand for them to see.

"Warren asked me to marry him last night."

"What did you say, girl?" Nikki asked, grabbing Jada's hand to get a closer look.

"What does it look like she said? She's wearing this rock, isn't she?" Erica said, taking Jada's hand from Nikki for a better view.

"She had it in the box, girl. What's up with that, Jada?" Nikki asked.

"Nothing. I just didn't want to distract Erica from doing what she came here to do, but I couldn't resist that bald head, so I said yes!" Jada exclaimed.

"Well, congratulations, girlfriend. I am truly, truly happy for you," Erica said.

"And you're next, Erica," Nikki prophesied.

A distinguished gentleman at the next table was eating

alone. He had witnessed the entire scene. He got up and came over to congratulate Jada.

"Hello, my name is Cal Carrington, and I could not help but overhear your conversation. It seems that congratulations are in order," he said, looking at Jada.

He was quite impressive, immaculately dressed in a chocolate tailored suit and spit-shined shoes. He was tall and slender with a caramel-colored bald head.

"Thank you," Jada said.

He nodded to Jada, then turned all of his attention to Erica.

"Actually, I was waiting for an opportunity to come over and meet you, lovely sister," he said, looking deep into Erica's eyes until she blinked.

"I'm Erica Scott. Nice to meet you, Mr. Carrington," she said, offering him her hand to shake.

He gently held her hand in both of his instead.

"I was wondering if you would be available for dinner sometime," he asked, holding her hand like he never wanted to let it go.

"I think that can be arranged," Erica replied.

Jada leaned over and whispered into Nikki's ear. "Knowing Erica, they'll be married before you get back from Africa."

"I wouldn't doubt it one bit, not one little bit," Nikki said.

PART THREE

Out of the Mouths of Saved Babes

Richmond, Virginia
Several Months Later

Through wisdom is an house builded; and by understanding it is established: And by knowledge shall the chambers be filled with all precious and pleasant riches.

PROVERBS 24:3–4

Chapter Thirty-nine

Stop jumpin' on those bunk beds before I come up there and slap you to sleep!" Grace Mitchell shouted to her grandchildren.

Grace was from a time when corporal punishment was in full force. In the sixties, she and her friends Alexis Wilkes, Jean Harris, and Bea Pierce played cards, partied, and traveled from state to state attending concerts and vacationing. Through the decades, they had remained close, starting their own families, surviving tragedies, and getting through this latest epidemic, crack cocaine. After her husband, Herman, died, Grace raised her two daughters, Sharia and Karen, the best way she knew how. She could not understand how her children had gotten caught up in the drug culture, while her friends' children had turned out so well.

She had custody of her grandchildren while their mother, Sharia, her older daughter, served time at the Women's Correctional Facility in Goochland, for a drug possession conviction. She had not seen her younger daughter, Karen, in more than a year. Word was that she was strung out, living from crack house to crack house. Grace, in all her sixty-plus years, had never seen the kind of devastation that crack was imposing on her children's generation. In an effort to save her grandchildren, she became their legal guardian.

"Girl, I'm too old for this," Grace said on the phone to her friend Jean. "Damon and LaKisha have seen too much. What do I look like trying to raise a seven-year-old think-he's-grown boy? Not to mention a too-hot-to-trot fourteen-year-old hoochie mama?"

"You have it under control, Grace. I've seen you with those kids. I'll be calling you for advice when Nikki brings the kids here for the summer. Jim won't be any help. He believes that it's our duty, honor, and privilege to spoil them rotten," Jean said.

"Oh, that's right. You're going to have all three of your grands this summer. Is the pool ready?" Grace asked.

"Yes, finally. Jim has been out there working from morning till night. Virginia Beach has nothing on my backyard," Jean said, laughing about how obsessed her husband was with his grandchildren. "Now who are you threatening?"

"Alexis's grandson, Ahmad, is spending the night with Damon," Grace said.

"Oh, that's nice. Where's LaKisha?" Jean asked.

"Walking around here rolling her eyes and sucking her teeth because she wants to use the phone, which I ain't paying that mess no mind."

"Teenagers. Guess I have that to look forward to when Shay gets here. I'd better set some ground rules about long-distance phone calls."

"Lay down the rules up front, girl. I pay this phone bill, so I better not see her rolling her eyes and sucking her teeth anymore, or she'll be missing some," Grace threatened.

"Girl, you put the fear of God in those kids, but somehow they know you love them," Jean said.

"I loved my girls too, so why they turned out like they did is a mystery to me. I ask God every day, what in the world did I do wrong?"

"Stop blaming yourself. Children have minds of their own and are going to do what they want to do no matter what. We pulled out all the stops trying to convince Nikki not to uproot those kids and move to Atlanta. She went anyway, and it's probably the best decision she ever made. In the end, they're going to be all right if we keep the faith. Look at Alexis's son, Zachary. Boy made the cover of *Black Enterprise* and never went to college, as much as Alexis pushed higher education on him," Jean said.

"You're right about what you say. I'm keeping the faith and know that it ain't over till it's over. I got a letter from Sharia from jail saying that she and your niece Rae were holding Bible study for the inmates twice a week. Now, I know that was a sign from God that everything was going to be all right," Grace said, feeling better that her faith was being restored.

"Yes, it is. Nikki told me that Rae had written her all about the positive effect those Bible studies is having on the inmates. She said there is a noticeable decrease in the violence, and they attribute it to more and more of the women joining the Bible studies and learning alternatives to fighting. God is good, works in mysterious ways, His wonders to perform," Jean preached.

"That's right. Sharia said instead of cussing somebody out, she goes off on them in tongues, confusing the heck out of them. She told me about when she found Rae in the showers one day after she had been attacked and Rae was speaking in tongues. She said Rae blew her mind with the way she handled the incident, and that's when she joined her in getting the Bible studies started. So He's a miracle-working God for sure."

"Who hasn't brought you this far to leave you."

"You got that right," Grace agreed. "Shut that noise up, up there! Girl, let me go find my belt. I'll talk to you tomorrow."

"Okay, Grace, but don't hurt nobody," Jean said, laughing.

When Grace got to Damon's room, the light was out and the boys were snoring, pretending to be asleep.

"Ummmm-huh, you better be asleep," she threatened as she softly closed the door, smiling to herself.

Chapter Forty

In Atlanta, Nikki and her husband, Kevin, had been planning and packing for their African tour for weeks. She was at a point in her life, being blessed with the right partner, to satisfy her fascination with the Motherland. Taj, Shay, and Mia could not wait to get to Richmond and break in their grandparents' new swimming pool while their mother and stepfather traveled abroad. Finally, Nikki had a date for her parents to expect them.

"Hello."

"Hi, Daddy!" Nikki exclaimed.

"Hey, baby. When are you bringing my grandkids to me? The pool is ready and waiting," Jim said.

"That's what I called to tell you. We're coming a few days early. I want to spend some time with Pam before we leave for Africa. I called her after Miss Bea's heart attack. I haven't seen my girl in years."

"Oh, that's nice. Pam didn't come home much after she went off to college. Bea and Jean think she let the fact that Micah had that baby by that girl keep her away, so we were glad that she moved back to take care of Bea," Jim explained.

"Yeah, she was pretty upset about that. Pam called me and vented about it. Then Zakia came back from college pregnant. Boy, I'm glad I had my daddy in the house with me," Nikki said.

"That happens to girls who have their daddies in the house with them too."

"That's right. Plus, both my girls achieved great success in spite of it. I'm so proud of them."

"Well, both of those babies are all grown up. Micah's son, Jaron, is in some seriously deep trouble right now. He was arrested for killing somebody."

"Ma told me. Now, that's tough. I have so much to talk to Pam about when I get there. We were on the phone for hours the other night. I can't wait to see her. Imagine, a big-city district attorney putting criminals away."

"Yeah, most of you kids did all right for yourselves," Jim said.

"To God be the glory."

"Well, attorney or not, it's good for Bea that Pam is with her. Between Grace, Alexis, and your mother, she is well taken care of, but it's better for her to have Pam around. She's all the family Bea has. I know if anything were to happen, Taj would take care of me," Jim said confidently.

"Yes, he would Daddy, and so would I. But nothing is going to happen to you, so quit talking like that," Nikki said.

"Okay, baby. So when can we expect you?"

"Tomorrow afternoon sometime. You know the kids are little fish, and since school let out, they've been just itching to get to that pool."

"All right, then. Y'all drive safe and get here in one piece."

"Okay, Daddy. See you tomorrow."

Jean came into the room with two cups of herbal tea as Jim was hanging up.

"Who was that?" she asked as she handed her husband a cup.

"Nikki. They'll be here tomorrow. She wants to spend some time with Pam before they go to Africa," Jim said.

"Good. They were close growing up. They pretended to be sisters, both being the only child. I'm sure Pam's daughter, Taylor, will hit it off with Mia just like their mothers did," Jean said.

"I'm sure they will. Taylor is just like Pam, and Mia . . . well, Mia is in a class by herself," Jim said, smiling with adoration.

"With all the grandkids between us, they should have a ball this summer," Jean said.

Zachary Wilkes was the most eligible bachelor in the entire state of Virginia. He had made his fortune by putting his hand in diverse businesses, from publishing and distribution to computers and e-commerce to real estate. His mansion was located on the outskirts of Richmond, where he was relaxing in his den when he decided to check on his friend Micah, who answered the phone on the first ring.

"How's everything going, man?" Zach asked.

Micah had been a little jumpy lately but was keeping the faith.

"The trial date is approaching fast. All I can do is lean on God's everlasting arms," he said.

"You have the best attorneys out there. And now with Pam home, single and free, maybe that's a sign from God that He's got your back. Besides, you need something or someone to divert your attention. Stress kills. There is nothing else you can do, man. You have stuck by Jaron all the way through this thing. He's innocent, and my attorneys will prove it. Zakia and Eboni have a serious prayer line going, so no need to stress out," Zach said.

"I don't know how I will ever repay you, man," Micah said.

"Man, please. Jaron is my son too. He is the first of the second generation of Execs. The boy is innocent. He just happened to be in the wrong place at the wrong time with the wrong people and got caught up. He'll be exonerated."

"I am truly blessed to have friends like you. I really appreciate you being there for Jaron and me."

"We're all family, and Zakia lets me know that my finances aren't for me, but so that all families of the earth can be blessed or something like that. So whatever you or Jaron need, don't ever hesitate to let me know."

"Brothers to the end, man. Thanks for everything," Micah said.

"Anytime, bro. Anything, anytime."

Chapter Forty-one

The minivan was packed with suitcases, toys, book bags, and Nikki's family. Only half an hour behind schedule, Kevin was pulling onto Interstate 85 north.

"I forgot my bikini," Nikki's nine-year-old daughter, Mia, said.

"Granddaddy will buy you another one. I need him to buy me a sarong to go with mine to cover my hips," said Shay, Nikki's twelve-year-old girl.

"You wish you had some hips," said Taj, now a teenager.

"Shut up!" Shay yelled.

"Chill out. We have a long ride ahead of us, and it will be a peaceful one, understand?" Nikki threatened.

"Yes, ma'am," all the children said.

"Good."

Eight hours later, they pulled into the driveway of Jim and Jean's spacious home boasting a beautifully manicured lawn. Jim was in the yard keeping himself busy. Jean had been looking out the window every ten minutes for the last hour. When she saw the minivan pull up, she ran outside to greet them.

"You made it!" Jean shouted.

"Granddaddy! Grandma!" Shay yelled.

She ran to greet her grandparents and gave them the biggest hug she could muster.

Mia ran toward Jim and leaped off the ground. Jim caught her in midair and spun her around while she planted kisses all over his face.

Taj, growing bigger and cooler by the day, hugged his grandmother, who kissed and squeezed him back. When Jim finally put Mia down, she hugged her grandmother too, while Jim paused and looked at Taj.

"You're getting big, man," he said, hugging his grandson.

"Save some for me," Nikki said, climbing out of the minivan and stretching her legs.

Nikki hugged and kissed her mother and father, then made her way to the bathroom. Outside, Kevin hugged Jean and shook Jim's hand once they were finally free from their grandchildren's embraces.

"Are you hungry? Dinner is ready," Jean announced once the children staked their claims to their rooms.

"Yes, Grandma! Can we eat outside on the patio?" Mia asked.

"That's a good idea, sweetheart," Jean responded.

During dinner, the children brought their grandparents up-to-date on all the Atlanta news, including their friends and activities. Afterward as the family relaxed in the den, each child laid out honor roll report cards, which brought tears to Jean's eyes. Jim nearly ripped his pocket off pulling out money to reward his scholars.

"I'm going to make some calls, baby," Nikki told Kevin, then kissed him and handed him the remote control.

Nikki called Zakia who was excited to hear her girl's voice. They talked about their lives, marriages, children, jobs, and the goodness of the Lord.

They decided to plan brunch with Pam and Eboni. Since Nikki was going to call Pam next, she would invite her. Zakia was sure Eboni would be thrilled to join them as well.

Brunch at the Raven Restaurant turned into a prayer meeting revival reunion. Nikki, Zakia, Pam, and Eboni shared testimonies, laughed, cried, inspired, encouraged, and just had a ball in the Lord.

"Girl, how does it feel to get your groove back with that young man?" Eboni asked Nikki. "Eli be acting like he is as old as your daddy."

"It must feel good because she doesn't look a day over thirty herself," Zakia said.

"Thanks, girl. None of us look like we're right at forty. And the marriage is just groovy."

They all laughed, including Pam, who had never married but had a nine-year-old daughter, Taylor, from a relationship she had with an opposing defense attorney. Lately, she had been too busy reestablishing herself in her hometown and taking care of her mother to even think about a relationship, let alone marriage.

"Are you coming back to get the kids after Africa, or are your parents bringing them to you?" Zakia asked Nikki.

"They're going to bring them to me, but we definitely

have to get together like this again when I do come back. This is so much fun. I'm having a ball."

"It's great seeing everybody. I really missed you guys," Pam said.

"Wow, y'all are going to make me cry again," Eboni managed to sniff out before the tears began to flow.

They all laughed and cried with her.

When Nikki arrived back at her parents' home, Grace was there with her grandchildren. Damon was already smitten with Mia, who could not have cared less. Shay was curious about LaKisha's nails and weave.

"Who did your nails?" Shay asked LaKisha.

"I did," LaKisha responded.

"Could you do mine?"

"Have you ever had tips before?"

"Nope. My mom doesn't even get tips. We give each other manicures when we do our mother-daughter thing."

"Is she going to let you get tips?" LaKisha asked.

"Maybe press-ons. Let's go ask her now," Shay exclaimed, getting up to go find her mother.

Nikki was out on the patio having a nice conversation with Grace about Sharia and Rae conducting Bible study in prison.

"Mommy, can LaKisha do my nails? Pleeeaaase?"

Nikki looked at LaKisha's nails.

"Did you do yours, LaKisha?" she asked.

"Yep," LaKisha answered.

"Yes, ma'am," Grace corrected.

"Yes, ma'am," LaKisha responded.

"Do you have tips?" Nikki asked.

"Yep . . . I mean, yes, ma'am."

"Can you do those designs without the tips?"

"Let me see your nails," LaKisha said, grabbing Shay's hands.

Examining Shay's nails, LaKisha informed Nikki that there wasn't enough natural nail on which to put any kind of noticeable design. Nikki gave permission to work with the natural nail as best she could, without the tips. After a little more begging, Shay gave up and settled for whatever LaKisha could do with her own nail. Shay would get her granddaddy to take her over to LaKisha's for her manicure later that week.

Chapter Forty-two

Nikki and Kevin were up early to get the minivan ready to head back south. Jean had prepared a hearty breakfast of western omelets, hash browns, country ham, bacon, chicken strips because of Jim's blood pressure— not that he wouldn't sneak a piece of bacon—homemade biscuits, and an assortment of fresh fruit and juice. The morning was clear, fresh, and warm so they ate outside on the patio. After breakfast, Nikki called her friends to say good-bye.

"We're about to leave, Z. I wanted to say good-bye before we got on the road, then on to another continent," Nikki said.

"Aw girl, you leaving so soon?" Zakia asked.

"I'm sorry I didn't get a chance to see Jay and the boys."

"Next time for sure when you can stay for longer than two minutes. I had an absolute ball at brunch. It thrills me to see the Lord ruling and reigning in the lives of my girls," Zakia said.

"I hear you, sis. I did want to see Zach before I left so

I could give him a hug and let him know how proud I am of him. Girl, I showed his picture on the cover of *Black Enterprise* to everybody in Atlanta," Nikki said.

"He never ceases to amaze. He already had it going on, but after he finally wised up and got saved, it's like he has the Midas touch. And I have never been prouder watching him stick by Micah while they prepare for Jaron's trial."

"Girl, God has got that situation under control. But thanks for reminding me. I'm going to give Micah a call before I leave and build him up in the Lord."

"Good idea. He can use all the edification we can give him," Zakia said, looking out of the window. "Hey, Zach is pulling up. Want to speak to him?"

"Of course," Nikki replied excitedly.

"Okay, hold on," Zakia said as she opened the door and handed him the phone. "Nikki's on the phone. She's leaving today and is disappointed that she didn't get to see you."

"Nikki's here from Atlanta?" Zach asked, taking the phone. "Nikki, baby!"

"Zachary Wilkes, Mr. Black Enterprise. Man, you just don't know how proud I am of you. I wish I could give you this big hug I've been saving since I saw your picture on the cover."

"You ain't said nothing but a word. Are you at your parents' house? 'Cause I can be there."

"Oh, please come. I would love to see you."

"You got it. I just came to pick up JJ. That's my little partner."

"Bring him. Oh, I can't wait to see you."

"On my way, baby."

• • •

Kevin didn't think twice about the affectionate hug that Zach gave his wife . . . the genuine brother-sister love between them was all too apparent. He knew all about Zach because Nikki had talked about him nonstop when the magazine came out. Kevin felt honored being introduced to such a brother. Nikki called Taj, who came and took JJ, who was a year younger than Taj, out back by the pool.

"Do you like to swim?" Taj asked JJ.

"Sure."

Shay came out to join them.

"Mommy said we had company. Hey JJ," she said. They had not seen each other since Christmas.

"Hey Shay." JJ said thinking how beautiful she looked.

"What are you staring at JJ?" Taj asked, observing how he was looking at Shay.

JJ looked at Taj with a quick don't-front-me-while-your-sister-is-standing-right-here look that Taj immediately discerned. In the next split second, as if on cue, they both laughed.

Zach and Nikki came outside.

"We're about to leave, man," Zach told JJ.

"Can Taj come with us?" JJ asked.

"His mom is about to leave on a trip, and I'm sure he wants to spend as much time with her as possible before she does. Am I right, Taj?" Zach asked.

"Right, sir," Taj answered, admiring Zach from his mother's stories about him.

"Well, can he come to work with us sometime?" JJ asked.

"Now, that sounds very doable. What do you say, Taj?" Zach asked.

"I say that sounds great," Taj responded.

"JJ comes to work with me during the summer," Zach explained to Nikki.

"Oh, you have him in Exec training already?"

"It's all his idea, believe me."

"I think it will be good for Taj. Help to balance him out. He's surrounded by athletes. He loves football. Exec training would be great for him."

"Yes!" JJ said, giving Taj a high five.

"Let's go tell Mom and Dad," Nikki said.

Kevin and his in-laws were in the kitchen, where everybody still congregated to talk.

"Mom, Dad, Zach and JJ wanted to run something by you," Nikki said.

"What is it?" Jim asked.

"Propose your plan, partner," Zach instructed JJ.

JJ looked each person directly in the eye as he addressed them.

"Ladies and gentlemen, I go to work with my Uncle Zach during the summer, where I learn things to help me when I go back to school and earn money to finance my dreams. We would like Taj to come too, when he can. It's really fun."

"Wow, Zach. Man, what are we going to do with you? That is the sharpest Junior Executive I have ever seen. I don't think you were that sharp at that age," Nikki said.

"Not even close," Zach agreed.

"Maybe once or twice a week, because Jim has plans," Jean said. "You can share him a little bit, right, sweetheart? After all, it will be beneficial to his development and overall well-being."

"Yeah, Daddy, it's a great opportunity," Nikki added.

To help with Jim's reassurance that no one was trying to impose on his time with his grandson, Zach jumped in. "Yeah, Mr. Jim, he'll only be gone for a few hours on the days he comes to the office. You won't even miss him."

Taj went over and rubbed his granddaddy's shoulder and said, "You come first, Granddaddy. I'll only go when you don't have anything else for me to do, okay?"

Taj's words seemed to be the only ones that soothed Jim.

"Okay," Jim said as he got up and left the room.

"I'll see you tomorrow, JJ," Taj said as he gave his new partner five, then followed his grandfather into another room.

"He'll be all right," Jean said. "All he wants is what's best for these kids. I think it's great what you do for our boys, Zach."

"Zakia tells me that it's my calling."

"Well, I'm glad you answered it," Nikki said.

Zach wished Nikki and Kevin well on their trips back to Atlanta and to the Motherland and let Jean know that he would be picking Taj up at eight o'clock sharp.

Chapter Forty-three

When the alarm clock went off at six-forty-five, Taj got up and dressed before he went to the kitchen for breakfast. He was waiting in the kitchen with Jim and Jean when JJ rang the doorbell promptly at eight. Taj answered, looking dapper in his navy-blue suit, white shirt, and burgundy paisley tie. Jim had helped him shine his black shoes the night before.

"Good morning, partner," Taj said.

"Good morning," JJ responded. "Are you ready?"

"Yes, I am. Grandma, Granddaddy, I'm leaving."

"Wait a minute," Jean yelled as she and Jim came hurriedly out of the kitchen. "Well, don't you look nice, JJ? Where's your Uncle Zach?"

"He's in the car on the phone, ma'am."

Jean went out on the porch as Zach finished his call, while Jim sized up the two little executives before him. *Well, at least the boy will be well balanced*, he thought as Taj hugged him before heading to the car.

"Zach, don't you want to come in for some breakfast, a cup of coffee, or something?"

"No thank you, Ms. Jean," Zach said as he got out of the car and approached her. "I'll have Taj call you from the office. He'll be home by lunchtime. Don't want to keep him all day the first day. Not that Taj can't handle it. It's Mr. Jim that I'm concerned about," Zach said, smiling.

"Thanks for understanding, baby," Jean said.

Jim watched in silence as Taj and JJ slid into the backseat of Zach's Benz.

"He'll be fine. Did Nikki and Kevin get off okay?" Zach asked.

"Yes, they did. Made good time too. They called to let us know they made it back safely," Jean said.

"That's great. Well, we'll see you this afternoon," Zach said as the boys waved good-bye.

Jean threw them a kiss, and Jim went back into the house to wake up his granddaughters.

At the office, JJ introduced Taj around. Taj was intrigued with the graphic art displayed in the advertising department. However, he opted to work in the legal department with JJ. Zach had mentioned that he could never have too many attorneys. So Taj, along with JJ, decided to do their part in providing Zach with what he needed: young, brilliant legal minds.

As promised, Zach and JJ dropped Taj off at Jean and Jim's at lunchtime but planned for him to stay a full day the next time he came into the office. Taj went to get a reading on his grandfather so that he could figure out exactly when that would be. A huge grin appeared on Jim's face when he saw Taj come out onto the patio.

"What are we going to do now, Granddaddy?"

"First you are going to get out of that monkey suit."

They both laughed as Taj went to change clothes.

"Now that the prodigal grandson has returned, I'm going over to Bea's to see how she's doing," Jean told her husband. "I'm taking Mia with me to visit with Taylor. Shay has LaKisha, and Taj has JJ to play with."

"Mia has me," Jim said.

"Of course she does, darling. They all do. But now that Pam and Taylor have moved back, Mia has someone her age to play with. We'll see you later. Shay is in her room. Take her with you if you and Taj head out somewhere, or drop her off at Bea's. I would take her now, but she didn't feel like going anywhere."

"Then we'll be here until you get back," Jim said.

Jean and Mia stopped at the grocery store to get some fresh fruit and juice on their way to Bea's house. When they arrived, Pam opened the door.

"Hello, Ms. Jean," Pam said. "Come on in. Hi, sweetie. Aren't you a doll?"

"Thank you," Mia said, blushing.

Jean gave Pam a big hug.

"How's your mom doing today?" Jean asked.

"Very well. She's in the kitchen. Go on in. I'll get Taylor," Pam said.

"That's why I brought Mia. I know they're going to hit it off. My other grandkids have their friends, and Jim is jealous already."

"Mr. Jim is so sweet," Pam said, laughing. "Come on, let's go get Taylor, Mia."

Taylor was in her room reading.

"Taylor, this is Mia. Mia, this is Taylor. Your grandmothers have been very dear friends most of their lives, and Mia's mother, Nikki, and I have been friends since we were little girls. Mia is here visiting her grandparents for the summer. We were thinking you girls could probably have some fun together while she's here," Pam said.

"Hello," Taylor said, closing her book.

"Hi. What are you reading?" Mia asked as Pam slipped out the door.

"*The Royal Diaries of Cleopatra*," Taylor said, handing Mia the book.

"Is it good?" Mia asked, flipping through the pages. "I had to do a report on Egypt and learned about Cleopatra, but not the stuff that would be in her diaries."

"It's interesting. Do you like to read?" Taylor asked.

"I love reading novels. I'm going to be an actress. What are you going to be?"

"An attorney, like my mom."

"Cool."

A little while later, Jean and Bea came into Taylor's room.

Mia jumped up, ran over, and gave Bea a hug. Her grandmother had told her that she hadn't been feeling well.

"Hi, Ms. Bea, I hope you are having a good day today," Mia said, gently squeezing her.

"Aw, I am now, darling. How sweet."

"Gives Jim cavities," Jean said, and they both laughed, knowing that Mia had her granddaddy wrapped around her pinkie. "How're you, Taylor?"

"Fine, Ms. Jean, and you?"

"Wonderful, baby. There's some fruit and juice downstairs if you girls get hungry."

"Okay, Grandma," Mia said.

• • •

As Jean and Bea sat and sipped tea, they decided to have Jean and Jim's first pool party the following weekend. The children were hitting it off wonderfully, yet they were all scattered from house to house, office to office. The ladies thought it would be great to have all three generations together. Bea and Jean had been friends since they were young, their children had been friends since childhood, and now the grandchildren were establishing their own friendships.

They called Grace Mitchell to come over to help with the planning. Their friend Alexis Wilkes still worked during the day, by choice. Her son, Zach, wanted her to stop working and spend her days doing what she wanted, but Alexis was used to working. Grace's husband had left her in decent financial condition. That, in addition to her small pension from the school system and the supplement for her grandchildren, was sufficient. She came right over and joined in the planning.

"This pool party is going to be such a blessing," Grace said. "I'm thankful to God for the opportunity to have Damon and LaKisha around some positive youth, considering the neighborhood they were brought up in before I got custody. The influences from their old neighborhood took their toll on them as well as their mother."

"They're sweet kids, and this party will be great for them all to get better acquainted with each other and maybe get something as wonderful as we have established," Bea said.

"Then Saturday it is. We'll call and make sure everyone is available," Jean said.

"Sounds absolutely wonderful," Grace agreed.

Chapter Forty-four

Professional party planners would envy the grand-mothers' organization of the pool party cookout. The middle-generation men had three grills smoking, but Jim had the huge open-pit barbecue with marinated ribs and T-bone steaks sizzling. Zakia's husband, Jay Carter, worked the seafood grill with fish, jumbo shrimp, and scallops. Eli had chicken on his grill, while Zach had burgers and hot dogs with the little lines grilled to perfection.

There were two picnic tables filled to capacity with food, one with bowls of beans, pastas, and salads, the other with bread, chips, cakes, cookies, and pies. Coolers were all over the yard and were filled with juice, bottled water, soft drinks, and flavored iced tea.

Micah was standing beside Zach at his grill discussing Jaron's trial when Pam appeared. It was the first time he had seen her since she left Richmond after high school graduation. She was stunning, and he was speechless. To her, Micah looked mature, not old, still handsome, although burdened. Micah suddenly had an unfamiliar feeling in his stomach. Seeing Pam seemed to alleviate a bit of the burden. Or was that feeling the added burden of regret? He couldn't tell as he watched her approach.

"Micah, long time no see," she said as she embraced him with all the compassion and empathy of a true and dear friend. She had only been back a couple of months, but was up-to-date on Jaron's case thanks to the grandma grapevine. She had been a tough prosecutor, yet she hadn't felt led to contact Micah or Zach about the case.

"Pam—you—you—how are you?" Micah stuttered.

"Steady, man," Zach whispered in his ear.

"I'm fine, thanks. Hey, Zack," Pam said, smiling as she kissed Zach's cheek.

"Hey, Ms. DA," Zach said, turning his other cheek for her to kiss as well.

"You look great," Micah finally managed.

"Thanks. So do you. Look, if there is anything I can do," Pam began.

"Thanks, Pam," Micah said, cutting her off, feeling somewhat uncomfortable talking to her about the son that broke them up. "Zach here has furnished me with the best team of attorneys on the East Coast."

"Well, I would expect nothing less from Mr. Black Enterprise."

"As long as we aren't facing you, my dear, we'll be okay," Zach said.

"I'm always on your side," she said before turning to Micah. "Don't hesitate to call me, even if you just want to talk. What's done is done. We're still all family and will always be there for one another. I mean, the way Mamalexis, Ms. Jean, and Ms. Grace pitched in and took care of my mother after her heart attack until I could close up shop and get back to take care of her myself—well, they just taught us so well how to be there," Pam said.

"You said it," Zach agreed.

"I appreciate that, Pam," Micah said, finally feeling forgiven.

The youngest generation was told stories of yesteryear. Zakia, Eboni, and Pam even did some of their old high school cheers while LaKisha, Shay, Mia, and Taylor tried to copy their moves. As the Execs told stories of their childhood business club, one could see the wheels turning in JJ's and Taj's heads. They soaked up every word and were nonverbally communicating with each other. The only type of club seven-year-old Damon knew of was the street gangs from his old neighborhood. He didn't really understand all of what was being said, but he felt he wanted to be a part of a club too. He watched JJ and Taj go off together and followed them.

"What are you talking about?" Damon asked.

"Business. We are going to form our own club, the Junior Executives," JJ answered. "Why don't you go play with Ahmad?"

"Can I join your club?" Damon asked.

JJ looked at Taj. They both looked Damon up and down and burst into laughter.

"Like I said, go play with Ahmad," JJ said as he turned to Taj and they went on like Damon had already walked away.

Offended, Damon stormed off. He thought the look they had given him meant he wasn't good enough. He had received it numerous times when he transferred to the new school in Grace's neighborhood. He felt rejected. He sat by himself brooding until Ahmad found him and snapped him out of it.

"Come on, let's have a diving contest," Ahmad said.

Damon had a better idea.

"Let's start our own club," he said.

"Okay," Ahmad said, and ran and jumped in the pool.

Damon was deep in thought. He spotted Mia, and his heart skipped a beat. He had been influenced by the guys he had seen around his mother. He even remembered his sister laughing and enjoying her old boyfriend grabbing her and putting his hands all over her. He went over to where Mia was standing talking to Taylor and patted her on the behind. She jerked around and slapped him as hard as she could. Instinctively, he punched her back, and they started fighting. Zukia's oldest son, Zeke, who witnessed the whole scene, ran over and snatched up Damon. Eli and Eboni's daughter, Essence, who had been deep in conversation with Zeke at the time, ran over and grabbed Mia, who was almost hysterical. JJ and Taj looked up to see what the commotion was about. They really didn't want to be disturbed, so they decided that the grown-ups could handle whatever was going on and went back to their strategy.

By the time the grandmothers were made aware of what had happened, everybody had been calmed down and the situation was under control. Jim could barely hear what was going on above the music and the sizzling of the steaks. Jean rushed over to him to make sure he didn't find out what had happened, since he was so overprotective of his grandchildren. She would tell him later, but definitely not while Damon was still there.

Due to the resiliency of children, everything was back

to normal, except Mia now despised Damon and rolled her eyes at him when she caught him looking at her from across the yard. Zeke had instructed Damon to stay away from her for the time being. Grace was embarrassed to tears by her grandson's behavior. It took all the grand-mothers to restrain her from tearing her grandson's behind completely off his body.

"Man! Has the whole world gone mad?" Zeke asked Essence as they resumed their conversation.

"I'm telling you, man. Look at that frisky LaKisha parading her fast behind in front of you. Keep ignoring her. Maybe she'll sit her ghetto self down," Essence said to Zeke, not at all trying to hide the fact that she did not like LaKisha.

"Aw, give her a break or I'll call you Essie," Zeke said, laughing.

Essence playfully hit him in the chest. "You better not call me no Essie! Besides, this is our time. With me away at college, we only have the summer to catch up and hang out like we used to. Now with Jaron's situation, it's just us, so we have to stick together. And ain't no hoochie mama going to distract us," she informed him.

Essence had just completed her freshman year at Manna State University, where she was a cheerleader. She laughed at her mom and her friends when they did their old-school cheers. Nowadays, cheerleaders were more like gymnasts with all the running, jumping, flip-ping, mounting, and throwing that had replaced the old-fashioned stomping and yelling. To Essence, the hoochie mamas at her school with their distinct style had no class. With their loose morals and values, they made it hard to gain respect for the women who displayed class, sophistication, and home training. Even though just as many of the classy women were loose too, they didn't flaunt it. Essence, being heavily influenced by her mother and her Auntie Zakia, was focused and truly strove to maintain her morals and values. It was a challenge, and she often talked to Zakia's sister, Raquie, who came to MSU to recruit for her New York entertainment firm. Raquie was a big help to Essence, and she could talk to her about things she couldn't talk to her mother and Zakia about. One powerful thing about the villagers, these generations of neighbors, was that they stuck together and were there for each other no matter how many miles separated them.

Dusk turned to dark, and the mosquitoes began to bite. That was the signal for cleanup to begin. The adults pitched in while the youngest boys and girls played and watched videos. Zeke and Essence supervised, keeping Mia and Damon far apart. After the cleanup, everyone left within minutes of one another and arrived home safely. Damon wished they had had an accident on the way to Grace's house to avoid his punishment.

Chapter Forty-five

The morning after the party, Shay overheard her grandparents talking about what happened between Damon and Mia. Jean assured Jim that the boy was appropriately punished, and after much soothing, she was finally able to calm him. However, Shay was worried about Damon; Jean had made it sound like he would surely end up in the hospital. Shay called LaKisha to find out.

"Hello, LaKisha. This is Shay. How is Damon?"

"Girl, Gramma tore his butt up. When he tried to run, I caught him for her this time. That was the worst beating he ever got. It was great."

"Oh wow. Taj got one of those kinds of beatings before. One was all it took."

"But, girl, I dreamed about Zeke all night. He is so fine and so built," LaKisha said.

"You dreamed about Zeke? He's nice. Fine and built are okay, but nice is important. You see how he handled your little brother? He sounded like a preacher or something."

"Oh girl, I know. The way he came in and broke up that mess and calmed my brother down . . . I just fell in love with him then because nobody but Gramma can calm that little monster down, but Zeke did it."

"Yes, he did."

"But, girl, that skank Essence ain't trying to let him nowhere near me. She acts like he's her man. I always heard they were tight like family calling themselves cousins. Why is she all up on him and rolling her eyes at me? Is she doing him or what?"

"Doing what to him?" Shay asked.

"You know," LaKisha said.

"No. I don't. What?"

"Sexing him."

"Oh no. They aren't married."

"What?"

"They aren't married," Shay repeated.

"So?" LaKisha responded.

"So they can't be doing that."

"Are you for real?" LaKisha asked.

"Yeah, why?"

"You're serious?

"About what?"

"Girl, you done lost me. Look, help me figure out how we are going to get Zeke away from Essence. We don't have long because he's going away to college at the end of the summer. And I want to get with him before he leaves, put something on him so that he will come looking for me when he comes back next summer," LaKisha said.

"Something like what?"

"Shay, girl, what is it that I'm saying that you don't understand?"

"None of it."

"What do you think I just said?"

"That you like Zeke, you don't like Essence, and we have to figure out how to make Zeke like you before he leaves for college. But I think he already likes you. He is so nice he seems to like everybody."

"*Aaaaaggghhh!* Not that kind of like, girl. I want to get with him."

"Now, that's the part you lost me on."

"Sex him. Now do you understand."

"Nooooo! You can't do that."

"Why not?"

"You're not married."

"Here we go again," LaKisha said, frustrated. "Obviously, you're still a virgin. But hasn't your mother had boyfriends?"

"Nope, just two husbands."

"Well, they had to be her boyfriend before they were her husband."

"I guess."

"And don't you think she sexed them before they became her husband?"

"No."

"Then how did she know she wanted to marry them? I mean, who wants to marry somebody who doesn't know how to sex? So if you do it before you get married and find out they can't do it good, you can dump them before you get married."

"Is that all marriage is about?"

"Pretty much. So just do it and avoid all the marriage-divorce drama."

"I really don't think that's how it's supposed to work."

"Well, none of it works, if you ask me."

"Why do you say that?"

"Well, look at my mama. Plenty of boyfriends, some got high with her, some beat her butt, none of them married her or took care of her, so she did what she had to do. She sold drugs, got caught, and is now locked up."

"I'm sorry, I didn't know that."

"Why else would I be living with my grandmother?"

"I don't know. I guess I thought maybe she died or something."

"Almost, a few times. But I have a praying grandmother."

"And prayer works, LaKisha. You have to believe that. My mom prayed us out of Richmond all the way to Atlanta. God took care of us all the way. My mom left my dad because of drugs, but I think her prayers kept my dad's drug use from doing to her what your mother's boyfriends' drug use did to her. It seems to me that prayer made the difference. God even gave her a new drug-free husband, and she didn't even pray for him, so she got more than what she prayed for."

"Do you like your mother's husband?"

"He's cool."

"He mess with you?"

"Huh?"

"He touch you like he touch your mom?"

"Are you crazy? Of course not! My granddaddy would kill him dead. What kind of man would do that?"

"One of my mother's boyfriends."

"Dang, I'm sorry, LaKisha. Did you tell anybody?"

"Who would believe me? Besides, right after that, Mama got locked up, and we were with Gramma, and I don't have to ever worry about that happening with Gramma."

"That's good. Keep that thought. But I think you should tell your grandma. I'm sure she would believe you. I know mine would. Tell your mom too, so that she can pick her friends better."

"I might. When she gets out, she does need to do things differently."

"If she hangs around nicer people, she'll do nicer things, and those bad things won't happen to you anymore. Let's change the subject, though. This is getting depressing," Shay said.

"Back to Zeke," LaKisha said.

"No, not him either, because that's going to lead to you dogging out Essence, who I think is cool being a college cheerleader and all. Let's talk about when you're going to do my hair. I just love what you did to my nails."

"Okay, party pooper, how do you want your hair?"

"Okay, let's see."

Micah decided to give Pam a call, maybe invite her to dinner. Something definitely sparked at the pool party, but he had to be sure that his heart and mind were clear, with all the drama going on in his life. He was glad that Pam was home and was sure that from now on, they would always be friends. Zakia and Eboni had been like mothers to Jaron since his biological mother, Simone, moved to Las Vegas. They hardly ever heard from her, but she was informed that Jaron had gotten into trouble. She said she would trust Micah to handle it and to let her know if they needed anything. Jaron had long since stopped needing her for anything, and Micah never did. He was doing fine being a single dad.

Pam agreed to have dinner with him. He said he would pick her up at six-thirty, which gave him several hours to attempt to shift his world back into some sort of normal condition so that his conversation wouldn't reflect the chaos.

Chapter Forty-six

Bea was happy that Pam was going out. Her doctors were amazed with Bea's rapid recovery, which she attributed to Pam's care. Her daughter and granddaughter had brought new life into her home. Now that Pam was settled, she needed to relax and have fun. Micah rang the doorbell promptly at six-thirty, and Taylor answered it.

"Hello, Mr. Micah," she said, remembering him from their pool party introduction.

"Hello, Taylor."

"Come in and have a seat. Mommy will be right down."

"Hello, Ms. Bea," Micah said when he entered the house and saw Bea sitting on the sofa in front of the TV.

"Hello, honey. You're looking mighty fine this evening."

"Thank you, ma'am. So are you. How are you feeling?" he asked as he kissed her on the forehead and sat down beside her with his arm across the back of the sofa behind her.

"I'm feeling a lot better these days."

Micah had considered bringing all three ladies flowers but decided to get a temperature reading first. He didn't want anyone to make assumptions about his intentions. With all that was going on in his life, he would take Zakia's advice and let the Spirit lead. Although his instincts told him to take flowers, he didn't feel led, so he didn't.

"Hello, Micah. Don't you look dashing?" Pam complimented him as she entered the room.

He stood as she approached him.

"Thank you. And you are as radiant as ever."

"Still charming, I see."

"Are you hungry?" he asked, blushing.

"A little."

"Great. That sounds like nothing heavy. I know just the place."

"Good. I'm ready," Pam said.

"Then let's make like a banana and—"

"Don't. No corn," she said, laughing, putting a stop to his worn-out punch line.

Micah laughed.

"Night, Ma. Ten-thirty, Taylor, lights out," she said as she blew both of them a kiss.

"Good night, ladies," Micah said, still laughing because Pam never, even when they were kids, let him finish a silly joke. She couldn't deal with a corny boyfriend, she would say, but he knew she secretly loved it. *Not much has changed at all,* he thought.

They went to the very popular Raven Restaurant. It was upscale with a swanky atmosphere, where businesspeople took clients and men took first dates to make a good impression.

Since at the pool party they had caught each other up

on their lives, and since Pam was an attorney, it was inevitable that they discussed Jaron's situation over dinner. They both tried to think of something else to talk about, but the fact of the matter was that there was nothing else to discuss. Pam had personal and professional thoughts on the issue, but she would not push, recognizing Micah's discomfort with laying his burdens on her. She did want him to truly believe that all was forgiven for his infidelity with Simone that resulted in Jaron's birth, which caused Pam to run away from him twenty-one years before. Discerning that this might be the cause of Micah's hesitancy to discuss his son, she silently reached across the table and placed a reassuring hand on his that broke the ice for Micah.

"I really don't know what I would do without Zach. That brother has stuck by me like Jaron is *his* son."

Pam saw an opportunity to further break the ice.

"Are you sure he's not? Kidding. I'm just kidding. If a knockout like Sheba Spencer couldn't keep Zach's attention back in high school, surely Simone couldn't even get it. I'm sorry. That is your baby's mama. Please forgive me." Pam laughed.

Her plan worked. Micah was shocked, to say the least, but relieved that Pam was still a down-home girl with a wild sense of humor who said what she felt and didn't sugarcoat it. The flame was being fanned. With the ice broken, they talked about the case in depth. He told her how he had convinced Jaron to at least go to a junior college, since he insisted that he wanted to get straight to work after high school and own his own business like Zach.

"Zach has always been a strong influence ever since we were kids. Thank God he's a positive one," Pam said.

"That he is. So much so that he gave Jaron and a couple

of his classmates some old computers that his company no longer used to start a little rebuilt-computer business," Micah explained.

"That's our Zach," she said.

"Absolutely. Always there, always on time, always making a difference," he responded. "He beat the odds, single mom household, no college, just a will and the drive to make it happen."

"Sometimes that's all you need," Pam said.

"And a faith-filled prayer warrior for a twin sister doesn't hurt," Micah said.

"Can only enhance and facilitate whatever he has going on."

"Well, that's exactly how they work it," Micah said.

"Then with that twin team on your side, working it like that, I've got a feeling everything is going to be all right," Pam said. "You want to tell me what happened?"

Micah, feeling comfortable, safe, and secure with his friend, began to share the whole ordeal.

"Jaron and his partners were delivering some computers in a rough neighborhood. His partner, Justin, had a gun. He said it was in case somebody tried to jack them. He never expected to have to use it. Jaron even told Justin to leave the gun behind, that they would be okay without it, but he watched Justin put the gun in the small of his back anyway and pull his shirt over it.

"They met these guys on campus who wanted to buy some computers they were working on for the business they started. Jaron said later that the guys looked out of place on campus, but Jaron and Justin were concentrating on making the sale, so they accepted a down payment that included an extra charge for delivery. So in their naiveté they went to deliver the computers to the address they were given. They were initially hesitant once they learned the delivery point, but the agreement and down payment made them overcome their apprehension. They agreed to deliver the computers that night.

"As soon as they saw the four guys approach them after they got out of the van, they knew the deal wouldn't close. They recognized a Latin-looking guy as the one who gave them the money to deliver the computers, but the other ones were strangers—and mean-looking. They surrounded the boys and ordered them to put the computers in the back of a van. Jaron and Justin were standing back-to-back looking at the guys. Then Jaron said he remembered that Justin had his gun. Maintaining hope that the situation wasn't as bad as it seemed, Jaron told the guy he had dealt with earlier that they could have all six computers for six hundred dollars instead of the original twelve hundred.

"Instead of being shown the money, though, Jaron and Justin were shown the barrel of a nine-millimeter. Jaron described the gunman as a big, fat, bodyguard type who asked for their wallets. Jaron and Justin were still standing back-to-back when Jaron heard the gun click. He said he instinctively reached under Justin's shirt, snatched the gun, and cocked it as Justin turned around, hitting his arm. The gun went off, shooting the bodyguard in the head. I bet the last thing he expected was Jaron's reaction. The other guys ran, and so did Jaron and Justin. Jaron went to Zeke's and called the police from there. Jaron didn't know if the guy was going to shoot them or not. All he knew is that he had a gun in his face in a neighborhood where people died from bullet wounds on a regular basis. He was trying to survive."

And that should be his defense, Pam thought.

Chapter Forty-seven

Grace heard the mail truck pull off as she was coming down the stairs. She went to retrieve the mail from the box. Among the junk were three letters from the Women's Correctional Facility. She gave her grandchildren their letters from their mother, and she read hers.

"Ma said now she is helping Rae teach Bible study and that we should be reading our Bibles," LaKisha said.

"That's what she said in my letter too," Damon said, excited about his mail. "Gramma, can you buy me a Bible? An easy one, with pictures?"

Damon loved his mother and was excited about any good news concerning her. He wanted to please her even while she was in jail; therefore, anything that she asked him to do he had every intention of doing. He tried to please her in the past, but she was often otherwise occupied and didn't notice. So Damon would act out. School and medical professionals labeled him as hyperactive, when all he wanted was his mother's attention.

"Of course, darling, first chance I get. What about you, LaKisha? They have Bibles specifically for teenagers."

LaKisha nodded enthusiastically; she wanted her own Bible too. Grace knew if she had just up and bought her grandchildren Bibles and insisted that they read them, they never would, so in her wisdom, she waited on the Lord to get them to ask her for Bibles. Now she would make probably the most important investment in the lives of her grandchildren.

The next day Zeke, Ahmad and Essence came to pick up Damon to take him to get a haircut. Essence rushed into the bathroom as soon as they entered the house. LaKisha broke out of her room when she heard Zeke's voice. She was barefoot and dressed in very tight, very short shorts with a tank top that exposed her pierced belly button.

"Hello, Zeke," she sang, having just finished doing her hair and thanking God for perfect timing.

"Hey, LaKisha. Your hair looks nice," he complimented her.

"Thank you," she said, feigning a blush as she moved closer to him, sticking out her chest and behind.

"Don't encourage her," Essence said, coming out of the bathroom and startling LaKisha.

LaKisha jerked around and went up in Essence's face.

"Why you all up in my business, huh? You doing him?" she asked in her toughest voice while rolling her neck. She was boiling mad.

"Little girl, you need to respect your elders," Essence said as she walked around LaKisha toward Zeke and the door. Right before LaKisha could lunge at her, she heard

Essence tell Zeke, "See, what did I tell you? No-class hoochie. I'll wait in the car."

LaKisha had learned enough from staying with Grace to know never to prove your enemy right, so she quickly composed herself. She decided to overshadow her ghetto outburst with a victim act.

"Why doesn't she like me, Zeke? What did I do to her? She's going to make you hate me too," she cried, and moved closer to lay her head on his chest.

The girls loved Zeke. He was handsome, polite, athletic, and spiritual. The combination was irresistible. He was not naive when it came to females. Hip to the games girls play, he anticipated her reaction once Essence was out of sight.

"Nobody can make me hate anyone else, LaKisha," he said, grabbing her shoulders and forcing her to stand straight.

As he disappeared into the kitchen to see what was keeping the boys, she heard him say, "Your hair really does look nice."

She ran to her room and cried from a combination of anger and happiness. Once they left, she called Shay and informed her they had to do something about Essence.

Pam decided that it was time for a little-girls' night out. As she often did to cultivate her daughter's cultural experiences, she decided to take Taylor and Mia to dinner and to the theater. At the restaurant, just as they were seated, Zach walked in with JJ and Taj, who spotted Mia and came over to the table.

"Hey, Mia," Taj greeted her, excited about his ever-increasing summer adventures.

"Taj! What are you doing here?" Mia asked, shocked but happy to see her brother.

"Uncle Zach brought us here for dinner after work. Hi, Miss Pam. Hi, Taylor," he said.

"Hello," Taylor responded simply. She was mature and wise beyond her years.

"Hello, Taj," Pam said as Zach and JJ approached the table.

"Great minds think alike, I see," Zach said, kissing Pam on the cheek.

"The kissing part is not required to be a successful businessman," JJ whispered to Taj.

"Cool," Taj said as he exhaled, wanting to do everything he saw Zach do.

"Won't you join us? I'm sure the waiter can find us a bigger table," Pam suggested.

"If the girls don't mind. We don't want to intrude," Zach said.

"Girls?" Pam inquired, allowing them to decide.

Taylor and Mia looked at each other, then shrugged, indicating that it didn't matter to them. They were moved to a larger table in the middle of the restaurant.

"Do you ladies have big plans for tonight?" Zach asked.

"Yes, sir. We're having dinner, then we're going to the theater," Mia answered.

Taylor and Taj were eyeballing each other in a staring contest. There was some kind of competition developing between them.

"That's wonderful. I do hope that you enjoy the play," Zach said. "And may I suggest that you guys save room for dessert? The dinner would not be complete without the Raven's light and creamy tiramisu," he said, aware of the staring contest.

"Sounds good," Taylor responded without blinking, determined not to break her concentration.

"Sounds delicious," Taj said, demonstrating that he could talk and stare too.

Zach received their menus from the waiter and handed them to both Taylor and Taj simultaneously in an effort to end the staring contest. He succeeded when they both blinked. The rest of the evening was pleasant. For Mia, it was glorious.

Chapter Forty-eight

Damon was playing with Ahmad in Ahmad and JJ's room. A courtroom drama was on TV while they searched the toy chest for a video game. Ahmad stopped searching and stared at the screen instead.

"That man on TV said the same thing that Jaron told Zeke the night he shot that guy. Then the lady told the judge he was not guilty," Ahmad said.

"So?" Damon responded.

"Then Jaron is not guilty because he didn't mean to hurt anybody either, just like the man on TV," Ahmad said.

Just then JJ came into the room with Taj.

"Why don't you guys go outside and play?" JJ ordered.

"We were here first," Ahmad said.

"Here's a dollar each, now beat it," JJ said.

Ahmad and Damon snatched the dollars.

"And Jaron is not guilty," Ahmad said as they left the room.

"Wait a minute," JJ said as he stood in the doorway. "How do you know Jaron is not guilty?"

"I just know."

"Can you prove it?"

"Yep. I heard him talking to Zeke. He didn't mean to do it. Just like the man on TV."

Taj stood beside JJ listening. The Junior Execs were both very interested in this piece of information and looked at each other, thinking the same thing. Wouldn't Uncle Zach be impressed if they could prove that Jaron was innocent? Their plans suddenly changed from creating the national Junior Execs to figuring out a way to show that Jaron was not guilty.

JJ and Taj strategized, remembering all of the adults' conversations they had overheard. They came up with the idea to have a mock trial. They knew enough of the details of Jaron's case to be able to build a defense, but who would prosecute? They were partners and didn't want to work against each other.

"I got it. Taylor's mom is a prosecutor. Taylor could be like her mom," Taj said.

"Oh yeah. Then you and I could stay on the same side and Mia can be on Taylor's side."

"That's it, then. Damon will act like he's Jaron, and we will be his lawyers. Taylor and Mia will be the prosecutors. Ahmad will be our surprise witness."

"We're gonna win," JJ said, giving Taj a high five.

Taj explained the whole deal to Mia. It appealed to her, especially the fact that she would get to act in a courtroom drama and play the part of a big-time prosecutor. Taj gave her all the details to pass on to Taylor. Mia was mesmerized and got caught up in the drama and excitement of the case. As soon as Taj was finished explaining everything to her, Mia called Taylor and repeated what Taj had said. Taylor was excited about the idea of competing against Taj and was determined to win, but who would be the judge? It didn't matter. They would win regardless. She was the daughter of Pamela Pierce, Esq. She had the advantage.

Chapter Forty-nine

The new Bibles were on the coffee table. Damon was washing his hands after using the bathroom for the third time in an hour. LaKisha was checking her hair one last time.

"Let's go," Grace called out to her grandchildren.

LaKisha came down first and decided to take Shay's advice and tell her grandmother about what had happened to her.

"Gramma, Mama's boyfriend, Buster, tried to have sex with me."

"Oh my God, baby. When? What did you do?"

"Right before Mama got locked up, he told me how pretty I was, and when I said thank you, he touched my breast. When I tried to back up, he grabbed me and started kissing on me and putting his hand down my pants. I kneed him in his privates and told him I was going to tell Mama, then I ran outside."

"Where was your mother?"

"Buster had given her some money to take Damon to get some new sneakers."

"Were you hurt? Did you tell your mother?"

"No, ma'am. I wasn't hurt, and I didn't have a chance to tell Mama. She got locked up right after that. Since I came to live with you and probably would never see him again, I just didn't say anything. Not until I told Shay and she said I should tell you and Mama."

"Shay was right, darling. You shouldn't carry that kind of burden around. Always tell me, your teacher, or school counselor or call 911 anytime something bad happens to you. We have to protect you children from perverts like that. But you're right about never seeing him again. You won't be going back to that neighborhood, so I won't press charges, since he didn't hurt you."

"Should we tell Mama?"

"Your mother is doing good. Knowing and facing the truth about the danger she put you in with her lifestyle and choice of boyfriends might be just what she needs to help her keep it together when she gets out. Yes, you should tell her just what you told me."

It had been a while since Grace and the children's last visit to the prison. While they waited in the visiting room for their mother, Damon thought he was going to wet himself from excitement. He couldn't hold it. When he was in the restroom, Sharia entered the visiting room. She hugged her mother and daughter, tears trickling down her cheeks. When Damon came back and saw his mother, he screamed, "Maaammaaa!" running full speed ahead, and jumped into her arms as she stood to catch him. The dam of tears broke loose in full force, and she squeezed him as tight as she could. He felt no pain because he was squeezing just as hard.

"I love you, baby, I love you so much. Mama misses you too. I'm so sorry, baby. Please forgive me. I'm so sorry. I'm going to make it all up to you. I promise. I promise. God is going to see me through. He's going to put us back together. He is. He is. I believe that. You believe it too, okay?" Sharia cried to her son as she hugged and kissed him.

LaKisha, too, was moved by the hope her mother had just imparted and began to cry.

"You look beautiful, baby," Sharia told her daughter.

"Thanks, Mama," LaKisha said. She sensed something different about her mother. She was missing her edge. Sharia was looking her directly in the eye with love and compassion that was softening something hard deep inside of LaKisha.

"Mama, the kids look great. They look healthy and happy, and I just want to thank you and say that I'm sorry for everything. When I get out of here, I'm going to make it up to you, Mama. Please believe it," Sharia promised.

"That is my daily prayer, baby, that you get it together and keep it together for these children. We can't do anything without God," Grace said, thinking that must have been where she went wrong with her daughters. If she was going to be completely honest with herself, she had to admit that she also ran in the streets in her day when her girls were young. Maybe by the time she saw the light, it was too late. *Well, too late to speculate about how we got to this point,* she thought. *We can't change the past. But we can start right now and shape the future. First things first. My daughter and granddaughter need some time alone together.*

"Come on, Damon. Let's go get some goodies from

the vending machine," Grace said as she nodded at LaKisha to take this opportunity to open up to her mother.

As Grace and Damon went to get treats, Sharia gave her daughter a great big hug.

"What's up, baby? Mama never leaves us alone like this. We always stay together the entire visit as a family. Is everything all right?" Sharia asked, concerned.

"No, Mama. I was just talking to my friend Shay, and I was telling her how Buster tried to have sex with me," LaKisha confessed.

"What!" Sharia shouted. LaKisha dropped her head in shame, wishing she hadn't said anything. Sharia grabbed her and squeezed her tightly.

"I am so sorry, baby. Did he hurt you?" Sharia asked soothingly as she held her daughter close.

"No. I kneed him in his privates and ran."

"Why didn't you tell me, baby?"

"Because you got arrested and we went to live with Gramma."

"Oh, baby. I am so sorry. I promise you that will never happen to you again. I promise, baby. I'll make it up to you."

LaKisha dropped her head again.

"What is it, baby? Tell me. Tell Mama. I know I can't do much in this place, but I'm here for you. I can pray to God, and He will answer my prayers. Please talk to me," Sharia begged.

"I had a boyfriend in the old neighborhood."

"And?"

"And he touched me and it felt good."

"Did you . . ."

"Yes."

"Did you use a condom?"

"Yes."

"Good. But condom or no condom, sex outside of marriage is wrong, baby. Wrong, wrong, wrong. I know I haven't been a good example to you in the past, but when I get out of here, things will be a lot better. I have learned so much about parenting and the Bible. I am always in some class. It's going to be different, baby. Please understand, you should not be having sex. I shouldn't have been having sex because I wasn't married. I was wrong, baby. Don't make the same mistakes I did. Please," Sharia said, hugging her daughter.

"I won't, Mama. I understand."

"Okay, baby. Just pray to God. Pray all the time."

"I will, Mama."

Grace and Damon came back to join Sharia and LaKisha.

"Mama, you remember Rae? She's over there visiting with her children. Their aunt brought them to see her," Sharia explained. "Hey, Rae!"

Rae looked up. Sharia waved and pointed to her mother and children. Rae waved, and they all waved back.

"Did you get my letters about the Bible studies I'm teaching?" Sharia asked her children.

"Yes, Mama. Gramma bought me this teen study Bible," LaKisha said, handing it to her mother.

"Gramma bought me this Bible with pictures in it, and I can read the words too," Damon said, giving his to Sharia also.

"These are wonderful," Sharia said, flipping through the pages. "Thanks, Ma. I really appreciate this."

"You're welcome, baby," Grace said.

"Rae is the one I was talking about who got me into studying the Bible. It has really made a difference in my life."

"I can see it, Mama. You look happy, even in this place," LaKisha said.

"I have prayed to God to get me out of here, and I believe He will the next time around. I want you all to be in agreement with me on that."

"I want to pray with you for that, Mama," Damon said.

"Of course, baby," Sharia said.

They all joined hands right there, and Sharia prayed.

"Father, thank You for my wonderful family. Thank You for my beautiful, healthy, obedient children. Thank You that my sister, Karen, is alive, and I pray that she comes to know You as I have. And thank You for my loving, supportive mother. Give her daily provision, health, wisdom, and strength, dear Lord, to take care of Damon and LaKisha until You release me from this place, which will be very soon. Keep me safe from temptation and make me into the mother, daughter, and woman of God that You will have me to be. In Jesus' name, amen!" she prayed.

"Jesus, please bring my mommy home. Amen," Damon added.

Two weeks after their family visit, Sharia was up for parole. Just as she had instructed her children to do, Damon and LaKisha would come together daily in agreement and pray for their mother's release. They often read their Bibles together. They also followed their mother's instructions and read the same scripture every day until they had it memorized, then moved on to another. She wanted her children to get the understanding she was getting while they were young. Understanding would make their prayers more powerful and effective. Eventually, the children had John 8:36 memorized.

"So if the Son sets you free, you will indeed be free," Damon said proudly during a Bible study one evening. "Lord, please set our mama free. Then she can come home. Amen."

"Amen," LaKisha agreed.

Chapter Fifty

Mia was spending the night with Taylor. They had a lot of work to do to prepare for the trial.

"Mommy, can you help us with our opening statement?" Taylor asked Pam.

"That wouldn't be fair, honey. You have all the information you need to prepare an opening statement and build a case on your own. Then, after all of the evidence has been presented, you'll sum up only the parts that add up to a guilty verdict, and present your closing argument accordingly. You girls can do this, can't you?" Pam asked. She truly wanted to see what the girls would come up with by themselves.

"Of course we can. Come on, Taylor, we can do it."

Mia would do most of the talking, with Taylor's coaching, of course. They decided to capitalize on each other's assets. Being exposed to her mother's approach to preparing for a case, Taylor's strongest point was finding the evidence to present. Mia's power was in her presentation. She couldn't resist an opportunity to perform.

With Mia's outgoing personality and Taylor's studiousness, they were an awesome team.

Over at Jay and Zakia's house, Taj was spending the night working on the case with JJ, prepping their surprise witness, five-year-old Ahmad. They didn't need Damon. He was the defendant. All he had to do was sit at the table, be quiet, and look innocent.

Over at Jim and Jean's house, Shay was cuddled up in her granddaddy's arms on the sofa watching her favorite Disney movie, *The Lion King,* eating popcorn, thankful to have him all to herself. He didn't even feel neglected by Taj and Mia with all the love Shay showered upon him. He absolutely adored this very special grandchild. The next day, the trial would begin in Zach's huge basement.

"Here comes the judge. Here comes the judge," courtroom spectators and witnesses Zeke and Essence chanted.

The grandparents were the jury along with Eli, Micah, and Pam. Ahmad stayed upstairs in the kitchen with Zakia and Eboni and helped them prepare lunch. LaKisha and Shay didn't care in the least about the trial. They were doing hair and nails in Zach's gigantic guest suite. Taj served as both JJ's assistant and bailiff.

"All rise," Taj instructed as the Honorable Judge Zachary entered his home-theater-turned-courtroom.

Zeke and Essence burst into laughter because he actually had on a robe. His bathrobe. The other adults snickered, but the young attorneys did not crack a smile. They were intensely serious, and both sides were ready to present their cases and win.

"You may be seated," Taj directed like a seasoned

bailiff after Zach took his seat at his desk before giving instructions.

"After the opening statements, the prosecution will call its witness for direct examination. Then the defense has the option to cross-examine the witness. Afterward, the prosecution will have an opportunity to redirect or rest. Do you understand these instructions?" Zach asked looking at the prosecution table.

"Yes, Your Honor," Mia and Taylor answered in unison.

"Good," Zach said. Then he turned his attention to the defense table.

"Next the defense will call its witness for direct examination. Then the prosecution will have the option to cross-examine the witness. Afterward, the defense will have an opportunity to redirect or rest. Do you understand these instructions?" Zach asked JJ.

"Yes, Your Honor," JJ said.

"Good. The prosecution may begin with its opening statement," Zach said.

Mia took center stage.

"Ladies and gentlemen of the jury," Mia said. She took a long pause to ensure that she had their undivided attention before continuing. "The evidence will prove to you today beyond a shadow of a doubt that the defendant is guilty of murder."

With those words, things instantly got serious, especially for Micah. Pam put her hand on his knee, sensing his tension. Being on this side of the fence for the first time, she felt what those she had prosecuted felt. She was grateful for this dry run for Micah before the real trial began.

"We will prove that he"—Mia walked over and pointed directly at Damon—"deliberately took a gun to use on anybody who tried to take his computers from him." She paused for effect. "He went looking for trouble . . . and he found it. Thank you very much," she said as she bowed deep.

Jim stood up and started clapping.

"Order in the court," Zach yelled as he banged his wooden spoon gavel on the desk. Damon was glad that this was for play because Mia definitely made him feel guilty. He would do what JJ and Taj told him to do: just ignore everything and play with his handheld video game. As long as he couldn't get into any real trouble no matter what they said about him, he was fine. Plus, he had all the snacks he could eat. He didn't mind this at all. It was like watching Court TV with his grandmother, except it was live.

Since the defense opted to make its opening statement before the prosecution called its witness, JJ took the floor.

"Ladies and gentlemen of the jury, our client is not guilty, and we will prove it. As you all know, people take umbrellas with them when they leave home just because it looks like rain. It may or may not rain, but as we've been taught, better safe than sorry. In other words, be prepared. We will prove that our client was prepared to feel and be safe. Thank you," JJ stated, and sat down.

Zach was grateful that he had the foresight to set up the video camera to tape the mock trial. He knew these children were smart, but he had underestimated just how brilliant they were.

"Is the prosecution ready to call its witness?" Zach asked.

"Yes, Your Honor. I would like to call Essence White to the stand," Mia said.

"Place your left hand on the Bible and raise your right hand," Taj instructed, and Essence obliged.

"Do you promise to tell the truth, the whole truth, and nothing but the truth so help you God?"

"I do," Essence said.

"State your name."

"Essence White."

"You may be seated."

"Essence, do you know the defendant?" Mia asked.

"Yes."

"For how long?"

"All our lives."

"So you know him pretty well?"

"Yes."

"Has he ever been in a fight?"

"Yes," Essence answered.

"Did he start it?"

"Objection! Relevance!" JJ shouted.

"Overruled," Zach stated, wanting to see where the prosecution was going. JJ grimaced.

"Let's just hear her out," Zach said softly to soothe JJ. "The witness will answer the question."

Mia was elated.

"So did the defendant start any fights?" Mia asked again, smirking at JJ.

"I doubt it," Essence said.

"Did he win?"

"Every one I witnessed."

"Did he try to walk away from a fight?"

"Not that I remember."

"So to your knowledge, when the defendant found himself in a fight situation, his choice was always to fight, never to walk away?"

"Sometimes he didn't have a choice."

"Thank you. No more questions," Mia said gleefully as she pranced back to her seat, full of confidence. JJ got up to cross-examine the witness.

"So you know the defendant well, you say?" JJ asked as they looked over at Damon, who was totally tuned out, concentrating on his video game and blowing bubbles with a big wad of grape bubble gum.

"Yes, very well," the witness answered.

"Is he an instigator?"

"No."

"A bully?"

"No."

"A troublemaker?"

"No."

"A man who isn't afraid to defend himself?"

"Yes."

"No more questions," JJ said.

"Mia?" Zach inquired.

Mia and Taylor had their heads together.

"The prosecution rests," Mia answered.

"You may step down," Zach said to Essence. "The defense may call its witness."

As Essence left the witness chair, JJ got back up.

"I would like to call Ezekiel Carter," JJ stated.

Zeke went through Taj's swearing-in process and took the seat Essence had vacated.

"How long have you known the defendant?" JJ asked his brother, turning toward the defense table to see and hear Damon loudly slurping the remains of a juice box, still oblivious to the attention.

"Since I was a baby."

"Would you say you are good friends?"

"More than that."

"Would you lie for him?"

"No."

"Did he tell you what happened that night?"

"Yes."

"What did he tell you?"

Taylor poked Mia in the side as she wrote something on a piece of paper.

"Objection!" Mia yelled, reading the paper and jumping to her feet. "Hearsay!"

"Because of the unusual nature of this case, I'll allow it. Objection denied," Zach said calmly. Zach had planned to overrule every objection because he wanted to hear everything the children had to say. Mia was livid.

"Denied?" she asked, pouting.

"Denied, sweetie," Zach said lovingly. "The witness will answer."

"He said that he went to sell some computers and it was a setup. The guys who had given them a down payment to make the delivery just to get them off campus had no intention of buying the computers. They had planned to rob them all along. It wasn't his idea to take a gun, but he remembered they had it, and he just got to it real fast thinking that he was going to die. He didn't want to die. He said he didn't want anybody else to die either; he just wanted to sell his computers, but it was a setup that backfired, and fortunately, he didn't get hurt. Unfortunately, the robber did," Zeke testified.

"Your witness," JJ said, looking at Mia with a deal-with-that expression.

Taylor whispered something to Mia. Nodding, Mia got up to cross-examine.

"So the defendant had a kill-or-be-killed attitude?" Mia asked the witness.

"No. He had a let's-close-this-deal attitude that turned into an I-will-not-die-tonight attitude when a gun was put in his face. It's called self-preservation."

"What about the preservation of someone else's life?"

"With a gun in your face, the only life you are thinking of preserving is your own."

"But do you have to kill to live? Can't we all just try to get along?"

"Objection, Your Honor. Calls for conclusion," JJ stated.

"Denied. Please answer," Zach said.

"I suppose under different circumstances," Zeke responded.

"No more questions," Mia stated smugly, confident she had proven her case.

Chapter Fifty-one

The defense would like to call a surprise witness," JJ stated.

"Objection!" shouted Mia. "Sidebar, Your Honor?"

Taylor had instructed her to call for a sidebar in case there were any surprises.

"Counsel may approach the bench," Zach said.

Mia voiced her displeasure at JJ calling a surprise witness without giving her a chance to prepare for a cross-examination. JJ was able to convince the judge that this witness was crucial to the case, as his testimony would bear out. Zach warned JJ against any theatrics. This was solely for Mia's benefit. Then he allowed the testimony. Mia was incensed as she took her seat.

"You may proceed," Zach stated, bubbling over with pride.

"The defense calls Ahmad."

Taj had slipped out earlier to get Ahmad, who was, at this point, sitting beside Damon smacking on his own wad of bubble gum.

"Ahmad, sit right here," Taj instructed, pointing to the witness chair.

Ahmad did as he was told and completed Taj's swearing-in process.

"Did you overhear Jaron tell Zeke what happened that night he went to sell his computers?" JJ asked, keeping the names real so as not to confuse his young witness.

"Yep," Ahmad stated, smacking loudly on his gum.

"Did he say that he had shot somebody?"

"Yep," he answered, trying to blow a bubble.

"What did he say about why he shot that guy, and how did he say it?"

"Objection, Your Honor! Hearsay and leading!" Mia insisted.

"Again, because of the unusual nature of this case and the litigants involved, I'll allow it. You may answer the question, Ahmad, but first, please remove your gum until after you finish speaking," Zach instructed.

Ahmad took his wad out of his mouth and held it between his thumb and forefinger, with every intention of putting it back in after he completed his testimony. He proceeded.

"Jaron was scared, and he was crying. He kept saying, 'I didn't mean to do it, I didn't mean to do it. I have to go to the police because I came over here thinking somebody had a gun and was gonna shoot me in that neighborhood. I was praying that he didn't die. I just didn't want to die.' Jaron really didn't want the guy to die. He said he maybe could have tried to take the gun, but the guy was bigger than him and would have beat and killed him. He didn't know what else to do to make sure the guy didn't shoot him," Ahmad testified.

"Your witness," JJ said, sitting down, leaning back, and crossing his legs at the knee.

Mia looked at Taylor, who shook her head. She had nothing else for Mia.

"No questions," Mia said.

The defense rested.

Zach adjourned for lunch. It was a pretty intense morning. Zakia and Eboni had prepared a wonderful meal of pastas, salads, deli meats, fresh-baked bread, gourmet soup, fresh fruit, and juice. All of the adults were impressed with the children's efforts. Having been instructed by Zach not to discuss the case, they limited their conversation during lunch. The attorneys were famished, having worked up hearty appetites. Damon and Ahmad hardly touched their food, full after all the snacks. Ahmad still had gum in his mouth. LaKisha and Shay were allowed to take their food back to the guest suite. They wanted to continue their girl talk in private.

After lunch, closing arguments began with the prosecution.

Mia was back in the spotlight.

"Ladies and gentlemen of the jury, everybody feels threatened from time to time. Everybody feels scared sometimes. If we tried to hurt or kill whatever or whoever threatened or scared us every time we felt threatened or scared, where would we be? The defendant should have taken time to think of a better way out of the situation instead of just killing a man. There had to be a better way," Mia said, ending her closing argument the same way she ended her opening statement, with a graceful bow.

Jim stood and clapped again.

Zach banged his wooden spoon and laughingly admonished Jim. "Another outburst like that, and I'll have you removed from this courtroom."

"That's my baby," Jim said as he obediently took his seat, grinning from ear to ear.

JJ took the floor, for the last time.

"Ladies and gentlemen of the jury, the defendant did think. He thought the man was too big for him to beat and take his gun. He thought he was going to die if he didn't do something. The Bible says that as a man thinketh, so is he. Therefore, according to the Bible, my client would be dead if he hadn't done what he did. Thank you."

Zach thanked and dismissed the jurors, who went up to the kitchen to deliberate. They were back in a matter of minutes and took their seats.

"Has the jury reached a verdict?" Zach asked.

Eli, the least partial juror, stood. "Yes, Your Honor," he said.

"Please state your verdict."

"We find the defendant not guilty!"

The defense table jumped up and cheered, startling Damon, who was deep into his video game and still blowing bubbles.

Mia burst into tears and ran to her granddaddy. He had no trouble assuring her that she had been absolutely brilliant and that the verdict had nothing to do with her performance. He made her feel better by telling her that it would be a bigger crime if an innocent man had gone to jail just because of her terrific talent. She could live with that.

Pam congratulated Taylor on a solid case, and she

didn't feel bad about losing to Taj. As a matter of fact, the whole house was more confident than ever. Their faith that Jaron would be acquitted had been elevated because of what had come out of the mouths of these saved babes.

Zach banged his wooden spoon for the last time and got everyone's attention.

"Guess what we're going to do now that the trial is over, Counselors," he said.

"What?" Mia, Taylor, JJ, and Taj asked in unison.

"We're going to Disney World!"

The entire courtroom erupted into a shouting, praising celebration.

Chapter Fifty-two

The faith of the villagers was contagious. The atmosphere was filled with happiness, joy, and peace. Everyone was extremely hopeful since the mock trial. Tensions were eased, and people were smiling and laughing more. Pam and Micah accompanied Zach as he fulfilled his promise and took the trial participants to Disney World for the weekend. Mia didn't know life could be so wonderful. She, Taylor, and Pam relaxed on the balcony of their hotel room after a day at the theme park. They had a good view of the fireworks as they enjoyed the sweet summer night's breeze.

JJ and Taj were up most of the night explaining their concept for the national Junior Execs to Zach in their hotel room. Micah tried to watch a little TV after Damon and Ahmad passed out as soon as they hit the beds. They had worn themselves out running, riding, and eating all day at the park. Micah was soon snoring right along with them.

Even though they were not trial participants, LaKisha

and Shay were invited to go with them. LaKisha thought she was too old to go on a trip with her little brother. Since Shay had been to Disney World, she opted to stay home with her grandparents.

When she sensed her granddaddy feeling neglected by Taj and Mia as they prepared for the trial, Shay poured on the love and got him through it. When the trial was over, her siblings were back and all over him. Taj and Mia, feeling quite accomplished, tried to make up for lost time spent away from him. Shay didn't mind. All she wanted was for her granddaddy to be happy. Because they had done such an outstanding job, Jim had absolutely no problem with Taj and Mia going away for just one weekend. He wanted Shay to go too and offered to pay her expenses, but she insisted on staying with her grandparents, especially since LaKisha wasn't going.

Shay asked Jim to drop her off at Grace's house.

"You look nice," LaKisha told Shay, checking out her hair with the front twisted and the back flat-ironed. "Can you do my hair?"

"You have weave in it," Shay said.

"I can take it out. Let's see how I look with just my natural hair done."

As Shay worked on LaKisha's hair, they had one of their serious talks.

"I saw your cousin Rae and her kids when I went to see my mom. Gramma told me she was your cousin," LaKisha told Shay.

"Really! I haven't seen her in so long. How does she look?"

"She looked good. Her kids looked happy too. My

mom looked nice and happy too. She was all excited about coming home soon," LaKisha said.

"Really? Your mom is coming home soon?" Shay asked.

"Well, we prayed, and she said she was believing God to deliver her."

"Oh well, she's coming home, then," Shay confirmed. "How do you know?"

"If she's anything like my mom, God gives her anything she wants, especially if she is happy and believing that He will do what she prayed about. Oh, He'll do it. He's done it too many times for my mom. And if He'll do it for my mom, He'll do it for yours. My mom always talked about going to Africa and she's there now."

"I wish God would get rid of Essence and make Zeke like me."

"I really don't think Essence is the problem."

"What do you mean? You see how she turns him against me."

Shay was finishing up LaKisha's hair. "Okay, now look at your hair. Doesn't that look nice?"

"Hey, I like that," LaKisha said, looking in the mirror. Shay had twisted her front and combed the back into a cute bob that hung just below her neckline.

"I'm going to show you how to get Essence and Zeke to like you."

"How?"

"You have nice hair and don't need that weave. You don't need so many flowers all over those long nails and you only need to wear one pair of earrings at a time, two at the most."

"What's wrong with my flowers and earrings?"

"Too much. And they don't go with your new hair-style. Trust me."

"Okay, I'll trust you. Nothing I do on my own seems to work for me anyway."

"Good. Let's find something longer and looser for you to wear," Shay said as she combed LaKisha's closet until she found an adorable outfit. It was a pair of solid purple capris with a matching striped multicolored T-shirt. It had always looked plain to LaKisha, which was why she never wore it. Grace bought it for her, and that didn't help her estimation of the outfit either. Shay thought it was perfect.

"Now, this is cute," Shay said, holding it up.

"Girl, that tired-looking thing?"

"I bet Zeke will like how this looks on you," Shay said.

Suddenly convinced, LaKisha tried on the outfit. Zeke was coming over later to look at Grace's VCR, which had a tape stuck in it. LaKisha would find out then if Shay was right about her new look.

To her surprise, LaKisha was pleased with her appearance. Now the girls concentrated on LaKisha's nails. She took the flowers off and painted them a very subtle pale purple to match her outfit.

"Too much?" she asked Shay, holding out her hands, shaking them dry.

"Just right," Shay answered.

When Zeke arrived, Essence was with him.

"Dang! Why she always got to be all up under him?" LaKisha said, deeply irritated as she heard them speaking to Grace.

"Don't worry about it. Let's go let him see you," Shay encouraged her friend.

Zeke was already working on the VCR when they entered the room. He did a double take at LaKisha and gave a huge, approving smile that caused goose bumps to break out all over her body.

"Well, don't you look lovely?" Essence complimented her. "Now, that's what I'm talking 'bout. I knew there was a pretty young lady in there somewhere."

LaKisha didn't know what to say. She was caught completely off guard. All hatred for Essence and attitude instantly gone, she just blushed, unable to verbalize a response.

"Doesn't that outfit look nice on her?" Shay chimed in, since her friend was obviously at a loss for words.

"It sure does," Zeke said.

LaKisha still couldn't manage to utter as much as a thank-you. Joy was overtaking her. Shay was to the rescue again.

"I love it so much I think I'm going to ask my granddaddy to buy me one, in a different color, of course. Where did you get it, LaKisha?" Shay asked.

"At the mall," she said, thankful to Shay for buying her time to find her voice.

"Hey, maybe I can pick you girls up later and we can go to the mall to find that outfit. What do you say, La-Kisha?" Essence asked.

LaKisha lost her voice again and just nodded vigorously, tears of joy filling her eyes.

Zeke finally got the tape unstuck. Before they left, Essence promised the girls she would be back to get them around six.

"You were right! You were right!" LaKisha shouted as she and Shay jumped up and down, screamed, hugged, and gave each other five.

"What's all the fuss about?" Grace asked, coming out of the kitchen.

"Essence is taking Shay and me to the mall. She likes me and so does Zeke. Yiippeeeeee!" LaKisha shouted, twirling around.

"Well, I have some more good news: Your mother's parole hearing was today. I just got off the phone with her attorney. He said get ready because she's coming home!"

Chapter Fifty-three

Jaron's defense team was overwhelmed when Zach showed them the video. They convinced him they had to have Ahmad to seal the case. Convincing Zakia would take divine intervention. Zach picked up Micah, and they went to see his twin.

"You have to, sis," Zach pleaded.

"Look, a mock trial is one thing, but a real-life courtroom and a real-life murder trial is an entirely different story. I can't believe you want to subject my baby to that," Zakia said to Zach and Micah.

"Jay, you see our point, don't you? What could happen? Ahmad might be young, but that's when they should be exposed, while we're around to protect them and explain things, before they grow up and it's too late. Besides, he's the sharpest of the sharp," Zach pleaded.

"I'm cool with it," Jay said. "It's up to Zakia."

"Sis, you know I would never expose my nephews to anything detrimental," Zach said, knowing how tough of a nut his sister was to crack, especially about her boys.

"All that money you're paying those lawyers, can't they do their job without my baby?"

"I'm sure they'll do a brilliant job, but Ahmad is the clincher, the slam-dunk at the final buzzer. You should have seen the defense team watching the video," Zach explained.

Zakia looked at Micah, who was there for one reason only, if they needed to play the sympathy card. It was being played. Micah was not saying a word. Just his presence would break Zakia down quicker than anything Zach could say.

"Dang, Micah. You know I love you and Jaron. Let me ask Ahmad," she relented.

They called Ahmad into the room. Zach asked him if he could do exactly what he had done at his house in a real courtroom.

"Better!" he said, thinking that would be the coolest thing.

"Oh, all right," Zakia said.

Zach and Micah kissed Zakia and left in a hurry to go tell the defense team to get ready for their surprise witness.

Sharia was about to leave her friend in jail. They cried and promised to keep each other lifted up in prayer. She assured Rae that if God got her released early, He could do the same thing for her. Besides, Rae was the one who really introduced her to God, and for that she would be forever grateful.

"I'll write to you every week. You keep teaching and preaching that Word, girl," Sharia said.

"I will. Oh, please tell Shay I got a postcard from Nikki from Africa," Rae said.

"Definitely," Sharia assured her.

"So what are you going to do after you get settled?" Rae asked.

"I want to find my sister, Karen. We haven't heard from her in so long."

In all the time Rae had spent with her, Sharia had never mentioned having a sister. All she talked about was her mother and children.

"I know a Karen Mitchell," Rae said. "We used to get high together, sold drugs together, did a lot of wrong things together."

"Short, light-skinned, whiny voice?" Sharia inquired.

"Skinny, big dark brown eyes?" Rae added.

"Girl, you know my sister."

"Well, dang. And I know where she used to hang out too. Go right to Creighton Court and ask anybody about her. They will know that whiny voice. They used to give her drugs just to shut her up. But please, please, be careful. I will definitely be praying for you to find her all right and get her off the streets."

They hugged, squeezing each other so tight it hurt.

"You saved my life, and now you are saving my sister's life. God has to get you out of here," Sharia said.

"You were here when I got here," Rae told Sharia. "You did your time in this place, and I did the crime, so I have to do my time. Besides, I'm making a difference in here. As much as I miss my kids, they are doing okay, and I know when the time is right, God will put us back together."

"I'm going to miss you, Rae. I love you, girl. Thanks for everything."

•••

Sharia moved into LaKisha's room so that they could bond. Grace and her daughter and grandchildren spent all their time together as a family, and Shay would sometimes join them because she and LaKisha really felt like sisters. Sharia liked LaKisha's look and had the girls help her to develop a fresh new style of her own. She started her job, which was set up for her by Zach, and attended women's fellowship with Zakia and Eboni regularly. Everyone treated her like she was a person, and she knew she would never go back to her old lifestyle, especially with the Lord keeping her in all of her ways. One night she went to a deep level of intercession for her sister, Karen. She understood that there was a time for everything. It was time for her to try to find her sister.

Sharia told Zakia and Eboni what she planned to do. They insisted that she not go alone.

"I have nobody to go with me," Sharia said.

"We can get the guys to go, right?" Eboni asked Zakia.

"Sure we can," Zakia answered confidently.

Jay, Zakia, and Eboni rode in the back of Eli's SUV as Sharia gave directions through Creighton Court. It was broad daylight when they parked by a convenience store. Jay and Zakia got out with Sharia and went into the store. They began to ask people if they knew Karen Mitchell. Nobody knew her. Sharia thought that Karen might go by a nickname, so she asked Jay and Zakia to describe her. When Jay offered one guy a five-dollar bill, he informed him that he had just left Shorty Girl at a crack house around the corner, so that's where they went. Jay told Zakia to stay in the SUV, and he went in with Sharia.

They entered the dilapidated bungalow and walked in and out of rooms looking for Karen. The people who were there, all high, totally ignored them. Prosperous-looking people came in and out to score and kept their heads down, trying not to draw attention. Jay and Sharia finally entered a room where they found Karen sitting on the floor. Sharia recognized her sister, even though she was dirty and raggedy. She knelt down and shook her, attempting to clear her mind, while Jay stood guard.

"Karen! Karen! It's me, Sharia."

"Sis, I thought you was locked up," Karen said, recognizing her sister, to Sharia's amazement.

"Karen, I'm out, baby, and the Lord sent me to get you."

"Who sent you to get me?"

"Jesus."

"Jesus?"

"Yes. Look at me. Look what He did for me. He wants to do the same for you."

"Ha ha ha! Yeah, right."

"Please come home with me, Karen. Then all of Mama's prayers will have been answered."

"No can do, baby, but you can give me a few dollars," Karen said, holding out her hand.

"You need more than a few dollars, sis. Please come with me."

Karen jerked away and spewed at her sister. "Look at me. I can't go to Mama's house like this. Now, give me some money and leave me alone."

Sharia felt in her spirit that their initial meeting was over. She didn't push it. She had planted the first seed. She knew where her sister was, and she would be back. Sharia left without giving her sister any money.

Chapter Fifty-four

Jaron's trial lasted three days. After much expert testimony and a five-year-old surprise witness, the jurors came back in less than an hour with an involuntary manslaughter conviction and a sentence limited to time served. Jaron was a free man. The local news highlighted the testimony of the "intuitive child wonder," as the media referred to Ahmad. Everyone met at Zach's to celebrate. Business associates, coworkers, friends from church, and villagers stopped by to offer their congratulations to Jaron and Micah. Ahmad knew that all the people around him were happy that Jaron was home, but he was enjoying all the hugs, kisses, and money that he was being given as well.

Now that Sharia knew where her sister was, she couldn't give up trying every chance she got to get her off the streets. She could tell from their conversations that she was wearing Karen down. Sharia had not mentioned to her mother that she had found Karen, since her sister kept insisting that she didn't want her mother to see her in her condition. Sharia shared with Zakia how she felt she was getting through to Karen and if she could get her cleaned up and feeling better about herself, that might help the situation.

Zakia talked to Jay, and they agreed to let Karen get herself cleaned up at their house if she agreed to let Sharia take her home to her mother. Finally, Karen agreed.

Zakia's ability to motivate and inspire was a blessing to Sharia and her sister. Karen was open to receive words of wisdom from her because Zakia made her understand, and she could also make her laugh. She told her about how God put her life back together several times when it had come apart. All she had to do was love, obey, and trust Him. She told her how God had given her good friend Nikki a brand-new life and a new man in a new city and He would bless her too, beyond anything she could imagine, if she let Him. When Zakia showed Karen the postcard she had received from Africa from Nikki with a big *X* drawn by the pyramid to indicate the exact location where she had gotten her groove back in the Motherland, Karen fell on the floor laughing.

Chapter Fifty-five

It was the end of a very eventful summer. There was much for the village to be thankful for. There was also much to reflect upon, much to look forward to, and much to celebrate. The plans had been laid for a big Thank God celebration. Jim and Jean's house and property were decorated with balloons, streamers, and banners. There was double the amount of food compared to the first pool party of the summer. There were four tables instead of two, and they were filled with everything to satisfy all types of tastes.

The same grills were smoking, except Micah and a free Jaron had a new one with marinated pork chops. The younger generation was earning its grill wings. Taj was right beside his granddaddy flipping ribs and sizzling steaks. Eli and Damon were working the chicken. JJ and Ahmad were at the seafood grill with Jay. Zeke was with Zach still strategically rolling the hot dogs over to ensure perfect little lines. Grilling was serious business to these men.

The old-school cheerleaders were being brought up-to-date by the new-school cheerleaders. Essence had taught Mia, Taylor, Shay, and LaKisha some new-school moves. The old-school cheerleaders—Zakia, Eboni, and Pam—watched in amazement, insisting, "That ain't no cheering!" They were impressed with the mounts, though.

Zeke made Jaron promise to look out for Damon when he left for Manna State University. To Essence's overwhelming delight, Zeke had decided to stay with the MSU family tradition. Jaron vowed to always be there for Damon and his hero, Ahmad.

The grandmothers were sitting around a table sipping iced tea and praising God for their health, strength, and children. Bea's heart felt better than ever. Her doctors attributed her speedy recovery to the love and care of her family and friends. Grace was praising God for her daughter being home when she looked over and saw Sharia walk out onto the patio with Karen.

"Oh glory hallelujah!" she shouted as she jumped up and ran over to her prodigal daughter. Karen was clean and fresh, stylishly dressed in an outfit that looked vaguely familiar to Grace. Then she remembered it was one she had bought LaKisha. Sharia had borrowed it for her sister, since she was the same size as her daughter. Shay had done Karen's hair during a pampering makeover session at Zakia's house. They hugged forever, crying a river of tears.

"My baby, my baby. You look wonderful, darling. Thank You, Jesus," Grace cried, squeezing and rocking Karen.

"I'm home, Mama. I'm gonna stay clean and make you proud of me. Everybody said they would help me. Please forgive me, Mama," Karen cried in her mother's ear.

"All is forgiven, and all is well now, baby. All is well," Grace said, holding her daughter like she was never going to let her go.

There wasn't a dry eye at the grandmothers' table.

Micah relinquished the pork chop grill to Jaron and went over to Pam.

"Everyone, may I have your attention, please?" he said.

Grace finally loosed her hold on Karen and along with everyone else turned her attention to Micah, who was getting down on one knee in front of Pam. The tears started up all over again, but at the old-school cheerleaders' table this time.

"Pam, I have loved you since high school. I never stopped. Now that the past is behind me, I want to go forward into the future with you as my wife. Will you marry me?" Micah eloquently proposed.

Tears had already met underneath Pam's chin. She was nodding vigorously.

"Yes, Micah. I never stopped loving you either. Yes, I will marry you."

Rejoicing went on all over the yard. Everyone was cheering and yelling, screaming and shouting, hugging and crying, until Damon stood on the table and yelled, "I wanna pray!"

Calming down and composing themselves, the villagers held hands as they gathered in a circle for Damon to lead them in prayer.

"Jesus, thank You for making everybody so happy. Thank You that I was not really in trouble when Mia was saying all that stuff about me at the trial, and thank You that whatever we did helped Jaron come home.

Thank You that Taylor is gonna have a daddy. Thank You for making Essence and LaKisha like each other. Thank You for my best friend, Ahmad. Thank You for bringing my auntie and mommy home to help Gramma. Thank You for all this good food. And thank You for all our neighbors and friends who are here to have fun with us. In Jesus' name, amen!"

"Amen!" the family cried in unison. All their prayers were answered.

As the villagers, neighbors, and friends rejoiced with the family, there was a loud noise, then total darkness. As light was restored, those who remained saw not a soul in the prayer circle, just empty clothes. They saw empty clothes all over the property. Those who were left knew what had happened, for they had heard it time and time again from the family—Jesus was coming soon— and began to cry out, "Oh God! No! Help us! Please, Jesus! Please, Jesus!"

In a number of cells at the Women's Correctional Facility, there were empty clothes on the beds. In one of these cells, there was a heart drawn on the wall. Inside it was written "Rae loves Jesus."

For the Lord himself shall descend from heaven with a shout, with the voice of the archangel, and with the trump of God: and the dead in Christ shall rise first: Then we which are alive and remain shall be caught up together with them in the clouds, to meet the Lord in the air: and so shall we ever be with the Lord. Wherefore comfort one another with these words.

1 THESSALONIANS 4:16–18

Reading Group Guide

PART ONE / Saved Babies' Daddies

In Part One Jay and Zakia seem to have it all—a nice home, a great portfolio, corporate jobs, and two good sons. They go to church, vacation together, and even have favor on their jobs. Yet even in the midst of all these worldly acquisitions, Zakia feels a deep void in her life.

1. Zakia tries to fill this void by coming up with new things to do, such as driving across country or redecorating the house. Is there any area in your life where you feel a void? Do you know what types of things you are using in an attempt to help you feel more fulfilled?

Read: JOHN 4:1–15

2. Jay and Zakia attend Jay's home church. How can it be that they attend church but still have no personal relationship with the true and living God? Do you know people like this?

Read: JOHN 4:22–24, JAMES 1:22–26

3. Zakia begins to attend another church and even joins without consulting her husband. She takes her children and gets more involved with the "things" of God, such as the choir, altar guild, usher board, et cetera. Have you ever been more involved with the "things" of God than the Word of God? What was the result of Zakia's behavior?

Read: MARK 3:25, PROVERBS 14:1

4. Zakia alienates her husband, family, and friends with her newfound zeal for God. What does the Bible have to say about our Christian lifestyle and walk? According to the Word of God, what should Zakia have done to win over her husband?

Read: I PETER 3:1–4

5. Sometimes one of the most important things we can do to solve our problems is to recognize our own part in creating them. Can you identify a problem in your life that is partly your creation? If so, what is your responsibility in owning up to and fixing it?

Read: I JOHN 1:9

PART TWO / Real Saved Folk

In Part Two, Nikki, a divorced mother, starts over when she moves herself and her three children from Richmond to Atlanta. While she is sad to leave her extended family, she is at the same time excited and hopeful for a bright future.

6. Has God ever asked you to begin "a new thing" in your life? Describe the emotional pulls you felt to stay where you were comfortable versus going into the unknown. Were you tempted stay? Did you do it on your own or did you need support?

Read: GENESIS 12:1–5

7. We all have things in our pasts that are more difficult than others to get away from. What keeps *you* looking back in one particular area instead of moving forward?

Read: GENESIS 19:12–17, 26

Children can often adapt to whatever situation in which they are placed. Nikki's twelve-year-old son, Taj, has already learned to study and imitate his mother.

8. The Bible tells us that children are a heritage of the Lord. The Word clearly tells us to bring them up in the love and admonition of the Lord. Even with the societal problems of today, how can we bring children up

according to this scripture? How did Nikki demonstrate her personal relationship with God in front of her children?

Read: PSALM 127: 3, LUKE 1:80, LUKE 2: 46–47, 51–52

9. Children often learn to develop their own relationship with Christ from the examples they see from their parents. How can we emulate the love of God to children around us? Whose responsibility is it to train children?

Read: DEUTERONOMY 6:1–9, DEUTERONOMY 11:18–21

PART THREE / Out of the Mouths of Saved Babes

In the beginning of Part Three we learn that Grace, Alexis, Jean, and Bea partied and traveled throughout the1960s. We also hear Grace and Jean discuss possible reasons why Grace's children and grandchildren have turned out the way they have *despite* the fact that she loves the Lord.

10. What do you think contributed to the choices that Sharia and Karen made in their lives? Which choices may have stemmed from the behavior of their mother? Sharia was promiscuous and did drugs, and Karen was a crack addict. Too often we label people by their degree of dirt. How does God label?

Read: ROMANS 3:23, ROMANS 6:23, MATTHEW 7:1–5

11. Even though we may do things "out of sight" of the children or while they are asleep, the Word says that God is not mocked: whatsoever a man sows that shall he also reap. How does this apply to rearing children?

Read: EPHESIANS 5:1–10, GALATIANS 6:7–8, JAMES 1:22–25

12. LaKisha believes that her body is the way to get attention. She has been molested by one of her mother's boyfriends and is already sexually active. We are often alarmed by young peoples' seemingly inappropriate behavior but excuse our own immoral behavior with the rationalization "I am grown!" When parents fail to recognize dangerous behavior in themselves, the children are often the ones who reap the pain. What types of adult behavior that parents think are not normally harmful can actually be destructive to an impressionable child?

Read: II TIMOTHY 2:19–22, GALATIANS 5, ROMANS 8, MATTHEW 18:6

Zachary, Micah, and Eli have grown up together and they supported each other throughout their lives. When they were younger they formed "The Executives," a brotherhood, which helped to keep them out of trouble and focused on their goals.

13. What does the Word say about friends? In time of crisis, how important is it to have support from loved

ones? How important is it for us to have Godly counsel?

Read: PROVERBS 17:17, PROVERBS 18:24,
PROVERBS 11:14, PROVERBS 15:22, PROVERBS 24:6,
PROVERBS 20:18

OTHER TRADE PAPERBACK FICTION AVAILABLE FROM WALK WORTHY PRESS

Soul Matters, by Yolonda Tonette Sanders

Infidelity and deceit threaten a Christian family when they are forced to face the secrets and lies that are creating mistrust, disorder, and tension in their lives.

What a Sista Should Do, by Tiffany Warren

A spiritually satisfying novel about three courageous women who must confront the harsh realities of their lives through faith and prayer.

All Things Hidden, by Judy Candis

A top female homicide detective confronts issues of racism, single motherhood, and the challenges of faith in this spectacular edge-of-your-scat thriller.

Heaven Sent, by Montré Bible

A compelling debut novel that details a young Christian man's discovery of the previously hidden truth of his heritage—and his decision to use his life for good.

Good to Me, by LaTonya Mason

This debut novel from a fresh new voice—full of unforgettable and imperfect characters who overcome personal challenges, hoping against all hope for perfect lives—addresses such diverse issues as romance with prison inmates, single parenthood, and domestic abuse.

Reading Groups for African American
Christian Women Who Love God and Like to Read.

BE A PART OF
GLORY GIRLS READING GROUPS!

THESE EXCITING BI-MONTHLY READING GROUPS ARE FOR THOSE SEEKING FELLOWSHIP WITH OTHER WOMEN WHO ALSO LOVE GOD AND ENJOY READING.

For more information about GLORY GIRLS, to connect with an established group in your area, or to become a group facilitator, go to our Web site at **www.glorygirlsread.net** or click on the Praising Sisters logo at **www.walkworthypress.net**.

WHO WE ARE

GLORY GIRLS is a national organization made up of primarily African American Christian women, yet it welcomes the participation of anyone who loves the God of the Bible and likes to read.

OUR PURPOSE IS SIMPLE

- To honor the Lord with <u>what we read</u>—and have a good time doing it!

- To provide an atmosphere where readers can seek fellowship with other book lovers while encouraging them in the choices they make in Godly reading materials.

- To offer readers fresh, contemporary, and entertaining yet scripturally sound fiction and nonfiction by talented Christian authors.

- To assist believers and nonbelievers in discovering the relevancy of the Bible in our contemporary, everyday lives.